The Palazzo

Also by Mary Chamberlin

Dear Friends and Darling Romans

Mary Chamberlin

The Palazzo

IDKPress
www.idkpress.com

Second edition

Printed in the United States of America

Library of Congress Catalog Card Number: 78-134930

Other books published by IDKPress:
Escape from Paradise by John & May Chu Harding
(www.escapefromparadise.com)
Dear Friends and Darling Romans by Mary Chamberlin

For Peggy

The Palazzo

The four-hundred-and-twenty-ninth annual assault of the spring rains on the Palazzo Salvini only appeared to be succeeding, even though the five-week bombardment had done an infuriating amount of damage. Water had invaded the superstructure, which had been designed in imitation of a "penthouse *americana*" and erected on the roof in 1957, when the Marchesa Luisa Salvini had divided the palace into separate apartments to let out. A glass veranda, added to modernize an apartment on the floor below the penthouse, had been shattered by a falling bay tree when the rain formed a nocturnal alliance with a strong gale which swept the potted plants on the veranda's terrace into a tangle of foliage and broken terra cotta and glass.

During the third week of the deluge, the damp attacked the always delicate wiring system, which hissed and puffed a tiny defense and then smoked out. The antiquated elevator was making one of its infinite upward journeys at the time, but fortunately it was unoccupied. As the *palazzo* offered no interior accommodations for such mechanisms, a system had been devised to attach the ornate box with its grilled door, mirrored fittings and upholstered bench to an exterior wall of the *cortile*. It was suspended between the ground floor and the *piano nobile* for two days before Gino, the *portiere,* coaxed the reluctant current back into the fragile wires.

Before another twenty-four hours passed, the aged furnace emitted a series of noxious belches and went into a coma. All attempts at revival failed. There was clearly nothing to do but install a new furnace, an impossible project for that time of year. Consequently, the humidity within the palace rose to a degree just slightly lower than that without. Moisture oozed behind satin-brocaded walls, mold built furry nests in cupboard corners, the table linens and sheets became clammy to the touch, the veneer on the furniture buckled, and gilt cornices, bronze statuary and silver candelabras gave off acrid fumes of tarnish. By the fifth week it could almost be said that no spot was to be found in the whole palazzo that wasn't dank or musty or dripping, but a water main had burst, so the faucets and water heaters were bone dry.

In the early weeks of the siege, Gino had delivered accounts of major and minor calamities to the Marchesa's quarters on the piano nobile along with the morning mail. These were received by Mario, Luisa Salvini's manservant, passed on to his wife, Bruna, the cook, who relayed them to Carmela, the housemaid, to present to the Marchesa with her breakfast tray. As the toll mounted, the Marchesa's brain had refused to assimilate any more facts pertaining to the catastrophes and had detoured them to her liver, where she could feel them lying in hard, painful lumps. She had simply to press below her right ribs. She took to her bed to pursue this occupation and her tenants gave up complaining. Everyone knew there was nothing to be done anyway, except to hope that the sun restored Rome's golden glow before the palazzo disintegrated completely.

This threat existed solely in the imaginations of the rain-weary, wet-witted occupants. Actually the Palazzo Salvini, itself, was quite unharmed. It was centuries removed from sharing a common fate with any twentieth-century installations intended to make modern life convenient. The exposed networks of vulnerable tubing and wiring which clung to the surfaces of the ancient walls were forever excluded by the impenetrable stone. The penthouse *americana* perched atop the roof was no more a part of the edifice than the nests the pigeons built in the eaves. A revisionist of Nagel's *Rome* would have as easy going as ever reaching the paragraph devoted to the palazzo's description. If there were larger and more imposing palaces in the city, there was still "no finer example of pure Renaissance style than the well-preserved Palazzo Salvini, which dates back to 1540 and was built for Cardinal Raffaello Salvini from designs by Vignola."

A guidebook, of course, is not expected to comment on the lives of the present inhabitants of historical buildings.

La Mattina

The clock in the tower of Santa Maria del Portico, opposite the Palazzo Salvini in the Via della Scimmia, tolled the hour. Anna raised her head from the pillow and held still to count the strokes. Only two. She lifted the black mass of her hair away from her neck and shoulders and it spread above her head like a fan as she lay back.

On the other side of the curtain that separated her part of the room from that of her parents, she heard the familiar protest from the four corners of the old oak bed as her father shifted sides. The soft gargling which characterized her mother's sleeping stopped, and the bed whined again as her mother turned in it. The door to the kitchen, the only other room in the portiere's quarters, was closed, muffling the symphony of sirens and whistles Zia Ida, her father's maiden sister, played as she slept. Above the door the dusty glow of a tiny electric bulb revealed the image of a ceramic Madonna. No light came from the window. The apartment was on ground level and the window had been cut so high in the thick stone wall that most of the room lay in shadow even on the brightest day.

The rain droned steadily on. Out in the street a man called "*Ciao,*" and another answered "*Buona notte.*" Footsteps sounded on the wet cobblestones. A car door opened and slammed shut. The automobile was sluggish in starting, and the battery seemed on the point of giving out when the engine finally turned over. Anna listened to the whir of wet tires on wet stone grow fainter and fainter until it couldn't be heard at all.

Just seconds later the rain changed rhythm and the even tempo gave way to a violent pounding. Anna placed the palms of her hands together and fixed her eyes on the ceramic Virgin. Her lips moved silently as she apologetically called the Holy Mother's attention to the hour and the immediate condition of the weather. Her faith that the rain would stop in time for her wedding that morning was steadfast as ever, but if it weren't too much trouble perhaps the Madonna might see to it that the skies cleared by daybreak. That way the early May sun would be strong by seven, and by ten it would have dried the surface of the street so she could cross to the church on the arm of her father without even having to lift the long skirt of her dress. Almost at once, a perceptible diminution in the drive of the rain assured Anna that the Madonna had heard her prayer and was giving it consideration. Anna smiled and crossed herself.

She closed her eyes and rehearsed her wedding drama once more as she had night and day for months and months. It began when she washed herself behind the screen in the kitchen which hid the basin and the portable bidet. Her cousin, Ersilia, who shampooed hair at Signor Michele's fashionable shop in the Via Frattina, would arrive at seven to arrange her hair in imitation of the high coiffure Signor Michele had created for the daughter of the French ambassador, and to manicure her nails. Everything she was to wear was new. She reached to the chair beside her bed, where she had laid out her underclothes, and her hand smoothed the rayon satin slip and the coarse lace that trimmed it. The stuff of her dress was a synthetic brocade, and Zia Ida had cursed the material's resistance to a needle all the while she was making it, but it had finally been shaped so it would cling to her narrow waist and flow down over her full hips and seem the purest silk when she knelt at the altar. Every detail of the ceremony was as clear as if it were already happening. The intonation of the Mass echoed in whispers in the high vaults of the ceiling. The smoke from the incense floated in pale, thin rings around the chalice. Her left hand, rough and red from three years of service in the household of Signora La Rosa, trembled as she held it out for the ring. Then came the moment when she turned toward Riccardo and, as always, the delicate framework of her fantasy collapsed, for she couldn't see his face. She tried to construct it feature by feature. People said they looked alike, and she knew this was mostly because of his eyes. Riccardo's nose was straight, too, but less broad than hers. Her lips were full and soft. Riccardo's were finer, smooth around his white teeth when he smiled as the lips on a statue. She dwelt on the smiling mouth of Riccardo, hoping to bring his other features into focus, but it was useless. Away from him, she could never see his face as a whole. It was one of the mysteries of her love.

There was a second mystery. She pressed her face against her bare shoulder and breathed deeply. After dinner that evening, she had sat on listening to her father and Riccardo talk while her mother and Zia Ida had cleared the table. She had sat in silence, Riccardo's arm about her, feeling the dampness from its pit warm her shoulder. Now her nostrils widened as she drew in his essence until she felt the swift sweet stab open the flow in the softness between her thighs. Riccardo's body pressed hard against hers. His open hand tightened around her breast and dug deeper and deeper into the firm flesh as she sank into a darkness where nothing existed but pain and desire. She moaned and his hand moved down to soothe the spasms that flamed between her legs. "*Amore mio*," he whispered, and guided her hand to where he, too, throbbed for release.

Anna's fingers tore at the mattress, her open mouth dry, the tears seeping from under her closed eyelids as the sensation of Riccardo's nearness left her. She threw back the bedclothes and reached out again to touch the rayon satin slip and reassure herself that this was the last of her nights of longing. Tomorrow they would be together in the wide matrimonial bed that had been set up in the tiny room that would be theirs in the apartment where Riccardo's parents lived above their wine shop. She had gone that afternoon to make up the bed with the sheets and pillow cases on which she had embroidered the chains of rose wreaths held by clasped hands. Riccardo's mother had stood in the doorway watching while she had encased the pink ticking of the new mattress in smooth, snowy white. Riccardo's mother had been tight-skinned and reticent as always, but her eyes had that peculiar eloquence by which Anna had learned to read her thoughts. Anna knew from her own mother that there was a time in this woman's memory when it had been traditional in her native Sicily for the stained nuptial sheets to be hung proudly from the windows as an evidence of the bride's virginity. Anna already loved Riccardo's mother, but she understood her love could not be returned until her own embroidered linen proclaimed her premarital innocence. Not until the morning following her wedding night when she stripped her bed and set the sheets to soak in the kitchen tub would she truly belong to Riccardo. There would be no words, but she would read the message of acceptance in the eloquent eyes. When she was turned away, an exchange of glances between Riccardo's parents and a nod from her father would confirm her worthiness to carry the family name. Sinking into sleep, Anna only half heard her father grumble into consciousness at the thud against the other side of the wall that was common to their own apartment and the one next to it.

"Only the American boys, Gino," her mother sighed.

"*Imbecilli*," Gino growled, and the bed winced as he resettled himself in it.

Randy Palmer was just sober enough to realize that Charlie West was even drunker than he was.

"Jesus, Charlie, knock it off." Randy staggered across his bed-sitting room and picked up the *fiasco* which had bounced from the wall. The broken glass rattled inside the raffia casing as he tossed it on top of a trash-filled cardboard carton that served as a wastebasket alongside a wooden plank supported by two columns of cement building blocks that served as a desk.

Charlie West gave no sign of having heard. He lay rather than sat in a seedy, sagging upholstered chair, his legs apart and extended, his lower lip slack, his bleary gaze blinking on a closed door across the room. He looked both older and younger than his twenty-two years. He was a bit under average height and extremely thin, but his tight jeans and the rolled sleeves of his shirt revealed a surprising muscularity. His head was strangely unrelated to his body, too large for it, disproportionately broad across the brow like the infantile and aged head of a fetus, and his fine, white-blond hair was several months away from its last trimming.

"Jesus," Randy repeated, suddenly feeling sober. He remembered there was an unopened fiasco, and he felt himself walking straight, hardly drunk at all, along the narrow passage that led to the kitchen to get it.

Charlie opened his mouth wider, having it dimly in mind to address the closed door, but he forgot why he wanted to before he could find his voice. He wet his lips and frowned, trying to remember. Beyond the door a chain rattled and a toilet flushed. Reminded now, Charlie threw back his head and bellowed the name "Lisa," just as Randy came back into the room.

"Cool it, West. You know goddam well Gino's bedroom is just on the other side of that wall . . ." Randy slumped to a sitting position on the floor and held the fiasco between his legs while he screwed the opener down into the cork. "So, cut it out! And turn down that music. Would you please turn it down? It's still too goddam high."

Charlie reached out and fumbled at the knob on the record player, and the volume of the Beatles' wail diminished. A few seconds later the disc spun to a finish and the machine sighed and clicked about its business of replacing it with another.

Randy filled his glass from the new fiasco. There was a bronchial sound in the amplifiers and then the sound of a guitar, soft but clear.

The closed door flew open, and a slim Negro girl stood framed against a background of rusty plumbing and peeling plaster. She threw the palms of her long hands toward the ceiling and her hips rolled with the melody:

> "Tall and tan and young and lovely,
> The girl from Ipanema goes walking—"

"Swing it," Charlie commanded.

> "And when she passes
> Each one she passes goes 'ahhhh.' "

"*Dai!*" Charlie smacked his hands together in rhythm.

Still singing, Lisa came into the room, kicking the bathroom door shut behind her on the beat. She wore a tight, shimmering silver sheath. Her eyes were heavily made up and her hair, which hung straight to her shoulders, was the color of a new red brick. Her voice was husky and insinuating.

"How about that, Ran?" Charlie asked. "How 'bout that? What'd I tell you, Ran? Am I right? Am I right, Ran?"

Randy had drained off half his wine glass in one gulp and things were beginning to blur again. He watched the swaying hips a bit and then nodded.

"Right! Was I kidding? Was I?" Charlie persisted. "Was I right, Ran, or wasn't I?"

Randy nodded again.

"You're damn right I was right. Damn right I was. Swing it, baby." Charlie flicked the volume knob on the record player, and the music exploded into the room.

"Jesus," Randy shouted, getting to his feet. He lurched across to the record player and switched it off. "*Basta,* Charlie. *Basta. Basta. Basta!*"

"What's wrong with a little music? You're just sore because

Maria Pia stood you up tonight. So be sore. Take it out on everybody else." Charlie smiled affably.

Giggling, Lisa swayed over to Charlie and lay face down upon him, her head against his, her legs together in the space between his outstretched legs. "Randy called you a bastard," she giggled into his ear. "You gonna fight him? You hear him call you a bastard?"

Charlie rolled his head to the side and looked into Lisa's face. "Christ, what a dumb broad."

"But he did call you a bastard," Lisa giggled and buried her face in Charlie's shoulder. "Yes, he did."

"A moron. You are a bloody moron. *Basta.* Ran said '*Basta.*' Bast*ah*. Not bast*ard*. Get it? *Basta* means enough . . . in wop. *Basta*. B, A, S, T, A," Charlie spelled.

"So, how should I know? I've only been here a month and you've been here two years. How should I know?" Lisa rolled on her side and yawned and traced Charlie's profile with her long forefinger.

"A moron," mused Charlie. "One of the dumbest broads I've ever known. Almost as dumb as The Bitch."

"Who's the bitch?" Lisa's forefinger moved slowly down the curve of Charlie's neck.

Charlie regarded the toe of his right moccasin with a dull smile.

"I asked you who is this bitch," Lisa said.

Charlie flung his head against the back of the chair and studied the ceiling with the same dull smile. "The Bitch is a beautiful blond bitch who lives in Paris. The Bitch is forty-three years old. The Bitch looks lots younger because The Bitch keeps on a steady diet of men," he singsonged in the manner of an adult telling a child a bedtime story.

"What's that supposed to mean? That she plays around?"

"Plays around! Plays? The Bitch doesn't play around. The Bitch doesn't kid, baby. It's hard work eating up men as fast as The Bitch. Specially when they're lots younger than she is. Right now she's working on a ski instructor she met this winter in Davos." Charlie brought his head up abruptly and addressed Randy, who had gone to sit on a wooden chair beside the plank table. "Hey, Ran, why don't we get with this ski-instructor racket? Dames really go for ski instructors. Ever realize that?"

Randy scowled down at the floor, his mood visibly black.

"Just who is this person you're talking about? Would you mind tellin' me?" Lisa asked. "Who is this woman?"

"What woman?" Charlie looked at Lisa and was a while recognizing her.

"The woman you call The Bitch."

"Oh, that woman." Charlie said. "That woman. Well, that particular bitch is my mother."

"Oh," Lisa squealed. "So, you are a bastard. So, Randy was right."

"I am not a bastard. A bastard is the son of a bitch. I am the son of The Bitch. There's a big difference. The Bitch has a lot of style. So, me, the son of The Bitch, I've got a lot of style, too." Charlie's head fell against the back of the chair and he closed his eyes. "I need another drink. Get me another drink, Lisa." He pushed her, his eyes still closed.

Lisa got to her feet, swayed over to Randy and took the fiasco from his hand. She filled Charlie's glass and her own. "What about you, Randy?" she asked.

Randy stared into his empty glass, not answering.

"Oh, snap out of it, Randy." Lisa swayed back to his side and gave his shoulder a gentle jab. "Maria Pia said she'd explain everything tomorrow. Why the big tragedy?"

At the mention of her name the sound of Maria Pia's voice came back to Randy with chilling clarity. "*Tesoro, quanto mi dispiace . . . ma non posso vederti stasera.*" Breathless, hurried. And then when he'd asked why they couldn't meet she had said she would explain tomorrow. The fast purring of a cat. But no regret in her voice. None. He could envision her stepping through the little door of the telephone booth from which she had said she was calling, veiling her great, gray eyes with their thick black lashes and smiling up at some man who waited outside. He remembered the smile from the first time she had broken a date with him and he had gone to the bar at the Club 84 and seen her at a table across the room with the gross, middle-aged film producer.

"Forget Maria Pia," Randy said. "Who needs her?"

"What'd I say?" Lisa curled an arm round Randy's shoulder and lifted his chin with her free hand. "Who needs her? Hi, beautiful. Hi, tall-dark-and . . . What about him, Charlie? What about Randy for the part of the clean-cut, white Protestant American boy in any movie you wanna name?"

"Forgot Anglo-Saxon," Charlie mumbled.

"Oh, yeah. Anglo-Saxon."

"Oh, lay off." Randy wrenched his head away from Lisa's palm and stood up. The room wavered and narrowed. "What the hell time is it?"

"Who the hell cares?" Charlie groaned.

Lisa swayed to Charlie's side and peered down at his left wrist. "Gee, with those old-fashioned numbers I can't hardly make it out. It's . . . it's ten past three. It's such a skinny watch. It's kinda cute." She leaned closer to read the make. "Cartier. Well, how 'bout that? Was it expensive?"

"How do I know? The Bitch gave it to me."

Lisa giggled and fell into Charlie's lap. "The Bitch. Breaks me up how you say it. The Bitch. Like that. Like it's an okay thing to call your old lady. It's not like she gave you a cheap watch or something. And the Porsche. Didn't she give you the Porsche?"

"Sure she gave me the Porsche," Charlie drawled, all good nature and nodding his head up and down.

"So, she must love you."

"Very much. The Bitch is crazy about me." Charlie nodded on, his eyelids nearly closed. "Crazy about me. You crazy about me?" He ran his hand under her dress and massaged her bare thigh.

"Nuts about you," Lisa giggled.

"Then get me a drink. Okay? Hey, Ran, want another drink?"

Charlie made an effort to locate Randy's position in the room, but his neck muscles weren't up to it. "Ran, where the hell are you?"

"He's there. On the bed. I think he's passed out." Lisa got up and swayed to the corner where Randy sprawled, face down, on a composition of steel-legged springs, a lumpy mattress, grimy sheets and army blankets. She lifted his arm and it thudded down lifelessly when she let it go. "Yeah. Man, is he ever. Stoned."

Lisa sank down on the unoccupied side of the bed, lay back and held her arms out toward Charlie. "Hey, you," she whispered. "Come on. Come to Mamma."

A night lamp on Luisa Salvini's bedside commode hooded a wee bulb which cast a faint light on a small, crystal water pitcher and matching tumbler, a silver bowl that held an assortment of hair pins, bobby pins, safety pins, rubber bands and a thermometer, a strand of rosary beads, a tube of petroleum jelly and another of zinc ointment, a jar of cold cream, a folded copy of the previous morning's *Il Tempo*, two bottles of pills wearing the label of a pharmacy belonging to A. Moriconi e Figli, a vial of Pyramidon, a saucered cup which bore the dried residue of camomile tea, an invitation to a concert at the Oratorio del Gonfalone, a printed plea signed by the parish priest for a donation toward refurbishing the altar of Santa Maria del Portico, a bottle of Roger and Gallet toilet water, calling cards of the Principessa Francesca di Bicci, Avvocato Raimondo Gatti and the first secretary of the United States Embassy, John Lewis Fuller, a box of Perugina chocolates and a two-molar removable bridge.

The bulb's tiny aura ended at the commode's edge. Semi-darkness robbed the vast room of Luisa's favorite purple and lavender, shades of which colored the rugs, draperies and upholstery by day. Carmela had brought in the pitcher, camomile and hot-water bottle at ten-thirty and, at Luisa's bidding, turned out the center chandelier before saying good night. Her shoulders propped by a brace of large pillows and her head by a satin cushion, Luisa's small pink-brown eyes had roved her chamber identifying shapes that were only momentarily unfamiliar. What appeared to be a camel on haunches against the far wall was, of course, her mauve velvet settee. The twin silver frames on her desk faced away from her. A tidy smile settled on her lips as she recalled the photograph in one of a dark young man with a high brow, wearing the uniform of a cavalry officer, which was autographed with the single name "Umberto." The second framed another dark young man, identically dressed. It puzzled Luisa that she remembered her husband like this most often, not as the overweight, bald, middle-aged Raffaello who had died of a heart attack twelve years before.

Her personal correspondence was piled in a letter tray directly in front of Umberto's likeness. Documents and letters containing her unequal struggle with finance were in the desk drawers, out of sight, if not out of mind. The latest addition to these was a demand for damages to an Aubusson rug belonging to her penthouse tenant, Penelope de Costa. Luisa's lawyer, Raimondo Gatti, had assured her the claim was shaky, since it was God's action that had driven the water into the Contessa de Costa's parlor. There was no question that His will would tip the scales of justice in the Contessa's disfavor, should the matter ever reach the *tribunale*. All the same, Luisa found the impudence of Penelope infuriating, and she pushed Avvocato Gatti's card under the silver bowl so as not to be reminded and let her thoughts seek solace once more in the silver frames.

It irritated her that her daughter-in-law refused to admit the resemblance of Raffaello to Umberto. It was not only strikingly evident to Luisa, and to all her friends when she pointed it out; it was confirmed by the historical fact that Raffaello and Umberto did have a remote ancestor in common.

Luisa felt a flutter against her rib cage and flattened her hand gently against her right side, determined to forestall a liver attack by considering her own behavior toward her daughter-in-law, rather than Caroline's behavior toward her. This preventive course led back nearly eight years, to summer and tea with Elisabetta Colombo, outside at Rosati's. Lorenzo and Caroline might have passed along the aisle of sidewalk between the rows of tables without Luisa's noticing had it not been for Elisabetta, who could spot everyone and everything worth spotting on the Via Veneto without seeming to move a muscle. To this day she resented Elisabetta's "Your son, my dear, and who is the pretty girl?" It was the first time Luisa had ever laid an eye on Caroline Morris, as Elisabetta knew very well. More than that, it was the first time Luisa had ever seen Lorenzo in love. It was unmistakable, as Elisabetta had been quick to point out. "How strange to see Lorenzo looking at a girl the way half the girls in Rome have always looked at Lorenzo," was the way Elisabetta had put it. It was easy enough for Elisabetta to guess that Caroline was an American. All the evidence was there. The long, slim legs, the wheat-colored hair, the wide-brown-eyed directness, the scrubbed skin, the antiseptic smile. "They are so utterly lacking in fantasy, American women," Elisabetta had sighed. "None. None at all."

Luisa's stare left the camel-back settee for the spent chandelier. To her credit she could tell herself that she had now lived under the same roof with Caroline for seven years without once criticizing her to Lorenzo. Before his marriage, it had been her duty to say everything that could be said to dissuade him from marrying a foreigner. And she had said it. His answer had been that Caroline could adapt to a way of life and a point of view alien to her own because she was "highly intelligent," an argument so novel that she had finally been convinced that Caroline's hold on him was unbreakable. She had tried to imagine one Italian male from Bolzano to Palermo who might possibly name intelligence as a quality to look for in choosing a wife. Clearly her son was not only in love with an American; he was thinking like one as well. It had amused her to speculate on how Caroline's superior mind would cope with Lorenzo's return to Latin normality. Now she was beginning to doubt that Caroline's intelligence was even average. In the past two weeks Lorenzo had telephone five times to say he wouldn't be home for lunch. Monday of this week, she and Caroline had dined alone, and it had been nearly two in the morning when she had heard Lorenzo drive into the cortile. And again tonight—he was still out. She had noted that Caroline's antiseptic smile gleamed as usual and that no furrow marred the composure of glowing brow. Any Italian woman would have known.

The tidy smile returned to Luisa's lips and she reached for her carafe. She took a pill from the larger of the bottles dispensed by the Moriconi pharmacists, covered the night lamp with a lavender chiffon scarf and sank back onto her pillows. Before she closed them, her eyes glazed on the Venetian blackamoor which stood behind her desk. The blackamoor's head was crowned by a feathered Indian hat belonging to her grandson, sent to him by his American grandfather from a place called Evanston, where the man was a university professor in the impossible beige wastes of one of the United States called Illinois.

It was long past midnight before Luisa fell asleep. She slept now, with her mouth open, dreaming the rain fell down through the roof and the upper floors to her own, dripping away at the purple flowers in her rug, wetting her bare feet. In the conscious world, something like this, if less disastrous, actually was taking place. The top of her hot-water bottle had come unscrewed. Small drops were falling on a purple flower, while others dampened the sheet under her feet.

Caroline Morris Salvini started taking inventory of the various routes by which she might conceivably get through the endless night without being reduced to lunacy. Lorenzo had just rolled from his back to his side, taking her share of the sheets and blankets along with him. She could lie on as she was, knees drawn up so that her feet came under the hem of her gown, arms tucked into the sleeves of her bed jacket, refrigerating. Lorenzo had come in at two-thirty, and she judged about an hour had passed since he had tiptoed from his dressing room and eased in beside her, while she pretended to be asleep. In the five hours before Carmela came in with their coffee there would be ample time for pneumonia to set in, in which event the solution of her problem would be out of her hands for all eternity. Lorenzo's mother would summon the idiot doctor. If he didn't mistakenly diagnose her condition as being in her liver instead of her lungs, which he was almost certain to do, she still had the prospect of being killed off in his clinic by incompetent nurses. As befitting a wife of a Salvini, she would be hauled off behind six plumed black horses to the family tomb in Piazza Verano. Lorenzo would leave immediately for the villa in the country, taking his motherless children along. While he was away, Luisa would have the servants remove her "effects." The rooms that had been hers and Lorenzo's within the domain of Luisa's small empire would be restored. The great feet of outsized gilt tables and chairs would return to claw the marble floor of her sitting room and the magenta brocade canopy would be rehung to sift the bed with lethal, medieval dust. By the time Lorenzo returned, there would be nothing of her to remember. Except her portrait, which now hung in Lorenzo's study. It would be moved, she presumed, to some corner of the gallery to fade into the past long with the others, a respectful distance from the jolly Cardinal Andrea and the pinched Cardinal Raffaello, whose eyes were too close together and who had come so near to being pope. "That's my last Marchesa," Lorenzo could say. He would be poised in that special elegant way of his, one leg forward, his body somehow reclining on the other. "That's my last Marchesa painted on the wall. . . ."

She rejected the comfort of self-pity with a panicky gasp, and settled her wobbling chin in tight jaws. She must not cry. She must not. Above all else she must not lose control. For the past week or so, dozens of times each day, she had blinked frantically and rushed to the bathroom to hold a wet cloth against her burning eyes. Somehow she had managed to get through the dreadful days dry-eyed, while the unshed tears gathered into larger and deeper pools, making her head ache with their weight.

Lorenzo coughed and Caroline held her breath, afraid he might have awakened, but he drew in the stone-cold air as rhythmically as before. How could he sleep? How dared he sleep when it was because of him that she lay awake? She strained to hear some distracting sound, but there was none, not even the monotonous fall of the rain. The shutters were hooked against the night. The long windows were fastened inside the shutters, and over them pale blue damask fell from the ceiling to the floor. She had been amazed to find out, after their marriage, that Lorenzo shared the horror of night air with the rest of Europe, and it had taken her months to accustom herself to sleeping in a closed room. Not in years had she had such a desire to yank back the draperies and fling open the windows and shutters. Supposing she were to do it? How just that he be lashed into consciousness by the rain, chilled to the marrow. Why should she be the one to die of pneumonia? In the light of this reasoning, she sat up and tugged at the covers Lorenzo had bound to him by an arm.

"*Che c'è, tesoro?*" Lorenzo asked in half sleep.

"Nothing. Nothing at all. Except that you have all the covers and I'm freezing to death." She gave the sheet another hard jerk.

Lorenzo relinquished his hold and she rolled to the edge of her side of the bed, covering herself. She stiffened as she listened to him turn and punch his pillows to conform to his new position. He gave a guttural sigh of contentment, typical of the state of those who have left sleep just long enough to relish the pleasure of returning to it, and then his hand searched for her hip and came to rest on it. She tensed her muscles, hoping to feel a stone to his touch, but he was already fast asleep again.

Outrage seized the reins of her control and her mind galloped away unbridled. There was nothing between the bare flesh of her hip and the contaminating hand of this man who was now a total stranger to her but the icy satin of her nightgown. She had that to be grateful for at least. God only knew what depraved depths that hand had explored in the past two weeks. She pictured it creeping under the short, tight skirt of the teen-age prostitute of the Ponte Matteoti, who looked like the Delphic sibyl and was reputed to have bought three apartments in Parioli on her earnings. The frame changed and the gold ring with the crest of the Salvini on Lorenzo's finger disappeared beneath the lace brassiere that sponsored the on-screen, off-screen exhibition of Clara Canali's pneumatic breasts.

Now, now, she mustn't let herself be absurd. If Lorenzo had ever felt anything for a prostitute it was contempt, and the film star didn't live who could keep him awake for the full length of a movie.

It had to be someone he knew. Someone she knew, too. He and Giovanna Colombo had practically grown up together. He considered her a fool for her many lovers, but he found her no less amusing than most men did. How naturally Giovanna must have responded to Lorenzo's incestuous caresses. In a huge carved bed of some country inn Giovanna knew of, a place "deliciously discreet, my dear, where one eats magnificently well," Lorenzo stroked Giovanna's alabaster thigh, and Caroline heard the throaty laugh before Giovanna turned to face him and they commenced the artful game of making love solely for the pleasure of the act, bound by the rule that all taking is fair and any giving a violation.

Of course it wasn't Giovanna. It wasn't anyone she knew. It wasn't anyone Lorenzo had known for long. It was someone new to him. A woman dark and sultry with long secret eyes and endless mystery. No. That sort of woman would make him laugh. A girl. Fair and sweet and challengingly innocent. Like Livia Del Bosco, who looked like an angel. And even played the harp. She remembered, though, that when she had observed that Livia belonged to the eighteenth century, Lorenzo had attributed her impression to his belief that Livia was mentally retarded.

Lorenzo murmured in his sleep and his hand slid down the curve of her hip into the small of her waist. He mumbled, and Caroline eased her head up from the pillow, straining to isolate a name from among his words, but they were quite unintelligible. She felt his fingers knead the hollow below her ribs for a second and then they were still.

What difference did it really make who it was? What mattered was that it was. Suddenly and surprisingly composed, she fixed her thinking at this starting point and headed it down the cool, clear path of reason. She made note of the vital statistics of their seven-year marriage with the objectivity of an accountant. She had been married at twenty-four and she was now thirty-one. Lorenzo had been married at thirty and he was now thirty-seven. Andrea would be six in August and Beatrice had just turned three. She repeated these figures a number of times, experiencing a kind of scientific excitement in the promise they held to add up to something. When they didn't, she tracked back to their first meeting.

It had been her second week in Rome, on assignment for *Today* to do a feature on Italian designers. She was at a cocktail party on Simona's terrace. A pudding of guests, as she had anticipated, the familiar democratic dish based on financial interdependence, cooked up according to the internationally foolproof recipe. Generous proportions of men in trade and women with careers, a coloring of celebrities pinched in for flavor and the pedigreed creamily frosting the top. Simona had been dressed in one of her own inspirations, copies of which were shortly to transform a large percentage of the world's women into sack-race contestants.

Simona had piloted her from small sea to small sea of small talk, introducing her, and then beached her beside the terrace's waist-high outer wall. She had been thankful to have it to lean on, and for the splendid view of the Forum with which to occupy herself until she could safely make a polite getaway. She was directing a smile at the Arch of Titus, she remembered, aware of the crosscurrents created by the artificial leveling of the socially incompatible in the little seas behind her. She remembered because it was right afterward that she had seen Lorenzo for the first time, several yards to her left, draped so that the wall supported his left elbow and the palm of his hand held his chin. He was watching her steadily.

She looked back long enough to observe that he was deeply tanned and that his hair was the color of wet sand in the sun. Latin blond. Without fairness. He was, she assumed, bent on hypnotizing her. In novels, sleepy, raping, velvet eyes had their way with inhibited schoolteachers, and heroines of films were suddenly and unaccountably mesmerized by a sort of Mediterranean myopia. Her own eyes had renewed contact with the Arch of Titus, resigned to the certainty that he was about to address her. Not that she felt in the least threatened. Her skill in discouraging advances and cooling ardor during the three years she had been divorced from Julian had developed to a point where she could have conducted a seminar on techniques.

"You were smiling," he said in English, walking toward her, and then coming alongside, "but I do not believe you find it amusing, this party."

"Honestly, no," she had admitted without intending to.

"I am Lorenzo Salvini."

"I'm Caroline Morris." His attention had gone from her eyes to her nose, to her mouth and back to her eyes, during which interval she could think of nothing to add. "How did you know I don't speak Italian?"

"I did not know. But I knew you spoke English because you are an American," he said, without interrupting his study of her forehead and hair.

"And how did you know I was an American?" She had smiled indulgently, anticipating the customary flattery.

"By your shoes," he had stated matter-of-factly, and his eyes had strolled off across the Forum up through the pines to the

Palatine. "I do not like these parties either. Cocktail parties are an Anglo-Saxon invention, quite unsuited to the Italian temperament. I was persuaded to accompany a friend who detests them as well." He smiled and shrugged, returning to her from his wanderings. "But likes very much a model he was told would be here."

"Oh," she said, for want of something better. Of her whole wardrobe she had been surest about her shoes, and now she felt as if she were wearing sneakers.

"He is down beside the fountain talking to her. Perhaps she is someone you know."

She had glanced in the direction he had indicated. "Oh, yes, Penelope Perkins. I do know her. Not well, but we've met at parties in New York."

"You are perhaps a model, also?" He rocked backwards and took her in as a whole.

She had stood naked at parties before. But in childhood dreams. She saw her opportunity to take the dominating role in this little comedy. "No, I am not a model." She gave each word equal emphasis, meanwhile feigning interest in the geraniums that spilled over the wall. He would now ask what she did and she looked forward to telling him she was an editor. It was invariably intimidating, a position that held the ominous prospect of dreary intellectual debate, the final dampener, she had discovered, to the spirit of conquest. She liberated a blossom from a tangle of leaves, curled her lips in a smile and turned back to him. Chagrined and dismayed as an actress facing a deserting audience, she found that he was no longer looking at her at all, but totally absorbed in the view. The babble behind her contrasted strangely with the awkward silence in which she suddenly felt enclosed.

"What a beautiful city," he observed at last.

"Incredibly. Especially at this hour. It's the color. The gold." She wondered how she could be short of breath when she was saying so little.

"It isn't gold," he corrected her. "People are always saying it is gold, but it is not at all, actually. It's the ochre. Look well and you will see."

As commanded, she looked well. And she saw. An ochre shroud fell softly on the dying day. "You have always lived in Rome?"

"Most of my life. I was born here. My father, also. And his." He moved his head to follow the course of a swallow and the ochre twilight set his profile in relief.

Senatus Populusque Romanus. Like the head on an ancient coin, she had thought, and behind him an ancestral assembly seemed to shadow the curving ascent to the Capitoline. Tribunes, centurions, consuls, senators, emperors, gods. S.P.Q.R. It was etched in the twentieth-century cement curbings and, in her first days in the city, she had reverently avoided stepping on the memorial lettering as in childhood she had superstitiously kept her mother's back intact by hopping over the cracks of Evanston sidewalks. A sudden breeze cooled her temples, and Lorenzo's nostrils thinned to draw it in.

"*Finalmente*," he said. "*Il ponentino*. It comes from the sea to refresh the city on summer nights. Late sometimes, but it always comes. It will return again shortly. Be attentive, and you will feel it."

Again, as commanded, she had been attentive. Seconds later, she had felt the ponentino once more, fussing her hair and rippling the hem of her dress.

"I think it would be pleasant to dine in Frascati," he said, not long after, abruptly, and to himself. And then to her, "You have plans for dinner?"

"No, but you see . . ." she began.

"Good. I'll tell my friend, de Costa, we're leaving. Now where has he gone?" His eyes darted from one group to another.

"As I was saying," she had insisted, aware that he wasn't listening and determined that he must, "I'm in Rome to . . ."

"Ah, there he is. Excuse me. I'll be right back." He touched her arm lightly, as one does a child's, and strode swiftly away. A few minutes later he was striding back. "Come," he commanded, taking her hand.

It was nearly three in the morning when he had taken her hand again. To say good night. To hand her out of his car and into the door of her hotel. She had been seduced without a kiss. Under an ochre sky. Beneath the vine-covered pergola of a country *trattoria,* fragrant with the mingled scents of roasting lamb and night-blooming jasmine. On the imperishable cobblestones of the Appian Way. Crossing the millennial Ponte Sisto. Before the Pantheon and pagan gods. In St. Peter's moonlit piazza with all the saints bearing witness. To the cry of Neopolitan heartbreak on the strings of a guitar. To the Tiber's whispered lullaby to the sea. To the rusty rhythm of oleander leaves orchestrated by the ponentino. He had taken possession of her spirit and laid future claim to her body.

She had made her last defense under the worst possible conditions. She was endeavoring to twirl her second bite of a special pasta Lorenzo had ordered for her onto an obstinate fork when it was initiated.

"Now then. Tell me. You are in Rome to do what?" he had asked, deftly subduing his own pasta and bringing it to his mouth.

Her brow had smoothed in astonishment. The vivid hues she had believed to be her true colors had faded so subtly that for an instant she couldn't even remember.

"You were saying earlier, at the party, that you were here to do something. What is it?" He inserted his laden fork between his lips with enviable neatness, as she watched.

"But I didn't think you heard me," she said, renewing her efforts to discipline the strands on her plate.

"Of course I heard you. It was simply that I was anxious to get away from that bloody terrace. *Allora?*" he prompted, taking another mouthful and chewing it with satisfaction.

"Well, what I happen to be is an editor." She succeeded in

transporting a doll-sized portion from her dish to her mouth and busied herself with obtaining another while the information made its impression.

"Look," he said, reaching across the table and taking the spoon from her hand. "Not with a spoon. One doesn't eat spaghetti with a spoon and fork. Like this. Watch me." He gave his plate a little jab and rotated his fork.

"But I've always been told . . ." she protested.

"That's it," he encouraged her, signaling the waiter to refill the wine glasses. "Excuse me. You were saying?"

"Nothing really," she sighed, at least abandoning any idea she had had of overwhelming him with a detailed itinerary of the roads over which her career had led her to Rome. Using his system, she wound a sphere large as a golf ball. "It's all very dreary."

"Oh, then don't talk about it," he advised kindly. "It's remarkable for an American to admit she finds her work unpleasant, although they must, of course. There is only one career for a woman, you know."

"You mean marriage."

"Of course."

When she had come back to her hotel room from lunch the next day she had found his card tucked in a mass of yellow roses which the chambermaid had stuffed into a too-small vase. As they had faded, so had her memory of what he looked like. The fourth day she told the maid to throw them out, and she felt the relief of a discharged hospital patient as the drooping yellow heads nodded through the door. Thank God his telephone call for which she had longed had never come. The fever had taken its own sweet time in breaking, but she was herself again.

She had changed the delicate, handmade pumps that had been delivered to her the evening before for a pair of loafers, seized her pocketbook and made for the elevator. She prayed that the table with the top of antique marble would still be in the shop window. She had been a fool not to buy it on sight, expensive as it was. It was much too large for the small hallway of her apartment, but there was no earthly reason why her career, which was going so well, shouldn't go even better. In two years she should be a senior editor. The vision of the sort of apartment she would be able to afford then brought a smile to her lips as she handed the key to her room to the concierge, and turned to face Lorenzo.

"What good luck," he said, taking her by the hand and leading her toward the main door. "I was afraid you might be out."

"But I am just going out. On an important errand." Her loafers took a firm hold on the lobby carpet.

"Shopping," he guessed.

"For my New York apartment, not myself. There's a lovely marble-topped table I've coveted ever since I came to Rome, and I've decided to buy it."

"Tomorrow will do just as well," he said, looking over her shoulder.

"*Ciao*, Lorenzo," a girl's voice came from behind her.

"*Ciao*, Lelia." His eyes followed whoever it was for a second before coming back to hers.

"They may sell it. Furthermore, I have a million things to do tomorrow because it's next to my last day here."

"All the more reason for coming to the country with me. *Su. Forza*." He took her hand again.

"What does that mean?" she asked, suspiciously.

Lorenzo laughed. "That my car is parked double in front of the hotel and if you don't hurry I'm going to get a ticket."

"Where are we going in the country?" she had asked after their route had twisted through narrow Roman streets and finally emerged on an asphalt road that had scarcely any traffic.

"To our villa. I suppose in America you would call it a farm. This is the Via Tiberina. It follows the course of the Tiber, and the farm is twenty kilometers ahead in this same valley."

When they came to it, Lorenzo had observed that the main gate was wide open. "Which means that Domenico is in the fields," he said.

"Domenico?" she had asked, her eyes lifted to the cypresses that bordered the long, narrow drive leading up a hill from the public road.

"He's our *contadino*. In your language, our tenant farmer who directs the other workers. That's his house. There," Lorenzo pointed, "between the stable and the chapel." He completed half the circle that terminated the driveway and stopped before the villa's front entrance. "I'll need a half hour or so to talk with him. Meanwhile, you take a look around. Domenico's wife will be in the kitchen. I telephoned to say we'd be coming for lunch." Lorenzo got out and came around to her side to open the car door. "There's a bathroom off my bedroom, which should be in order, but the other rooms aren't made up." He pointed to a corner on the second floor of the three-story building. "There, where the shutters are open, is my window."

It was through the same window that a shaft of light from the setting sun had entered to awaken her later. Her eyes had followed the course it had taken in reverse, across her bare breast, down and over Lorenzo's extended fingers, outside to the villa's park, where the silhouettes of the cypresses and pines seemed giant open and closed umbrellas in some enchanted garden.

Before they had fallen asleep, Lorenzo's lips had brushed the hollow of her throat and the lids of her closed eyes. "Our house in Rome is filled with marble-topped tables," he said, and she had opened her eyes to look at him smiling down at her. "I will love you all my life," he had added with great tenderness.

Caroline dwelt on the memory of that moment another perilous instant, and then it was too late. She thrust her forefinger between clenched teeth and bit hard, but tears rushed after tears to irrigate the arid waste of self-pity, until the bed heaved with her sobbing.

Lorenzo emerged from the depths protesting. "*Madonna*." he complained. "*Dio!*", his irritation mounting, he appealed to a higher authority. Fully awake and concerned at last, he asked, "*Che c'è, amore? Dimmi.* Caroline, *dimmi che c'è?*"

"Don't touch me," Caroline gasped.

"But what is it? Tell me," he demanded in English with more hope of an answer, sitting upright and reaching both arms toward her.

"Leave me alone," Caroline screamed, leaping from the bed. "I'm sick. Can't you understand? I don't want to talk. I'm sick."

And so she was, she believed, as she ran through the dressing room to the bath. She slammed the bathroom door behind her and leaned against it, folding her arms about her aching abdomen. Of course she was sick. Gravely so, she told herself. He had broken something deep down within her, and she was bleeding inside.

The weary heavens had worn themselves down to a drizzle, Pippo La Rosa observed with satisfaction as he stepped out of his father's car before the entrance of the Palazzo Salvini. He inserted his key in the lock of the iron *cancello,* folded back first the gate's left side, then its right, returned to the car and drove it into the courtyard.

He was displeased to see that the parking place nearest the entrance, from which a flight of stairs led to a mezzanine floor accommodating a suite of rooms that was his father's law office and another that was the family apartment, had been usurped by the Porsche of the wretched American beatnik. He took a brief flight in fantasy during which he drove the Porsche along the Via Veneto and beguiled a dazzling blond Swedish tourist to share it with him, as he maneuvered his father's sedate Fiat into a position alongside a similar Fiat that belonged to the Marchese Salvini.

The tower clock of Santa Maria del Portico announced the morning hour as three as he turned off the ignition. He synchronized the gold watch that had been the gift of his parents on his twenty-first name day with the tower bells and admired its fine lines by the light on the dashboard. It was four years old and as handsome as ever. He pulled out the ashtray, which contained a number of lipstick-stained butts, among others, sprang from the car, crossed the cortile and emptied the tray just under the door of the Porsche's driver's seat. He went back to the car and replaced the ashtray. He took a folded flannel dust cloth from under the sun shield, flipped it open and flicked out the ashes that had fallen on the seat and floor. He refolded the cloth, put it back in place and surveyed the car's interior as a whole. Something in the corner of the back seat caught his attention and he reached inside again and brought forth a pair of bikini-cut, turquoise panties, trimmed with black lace. He looked about the cortile a while before his eyes came to rest on a rear window of the Marchese Salvini's Fiat. It lacked an inch of being tightly closed, and he stuffed the panties into the opening, poking them through with his forefinger until they dropped onto the seat. He smiled contentedly, locked his father's car and went on into the palazzo.

Pippo crossed the pitch-dark La Rosa living room, fleet and sure of foot as if the overstuffed sofa and chairs and the gleaming veneer of contemporary adaptations of an eighteenth-century sideboard, table and chairs which composed a dining area were visible. He placed the car keys on top of the upright piano, took off his shoes and went down a hall to the bathroom. After closing its door, he turned on the light. He took a hair net from the pocket of his robe, which hung on the back of the door. As he stood before the mirror adjusting the net to direct the flow of waves from his forehead to the nape of his neck, he hummed softly.

In defiance of the common rule, he had mixed business with pleasure that afternoon and evening with extraordinary success. The test film he and Sergio had shot that afternoon had been quite a warm-up for the real film they would shoot tomorrow. His hair net in order, he seized his toothbrush, decorated it with a long ribbon of paste and brushed furiously. He rinsed his mouth thoroughly and studied the results in the mirror. Maybe he should have kept the turquoise panties as a souvenir. No, it had been better to get rid of them, and where better than the Salvini car? His grin widened around his flawless white teeth. The compelling depths of his dark eyes he owed to the mysterious Sardinian origins of his mother. He was indebted to his Neopolitan father for knowing how to use them to advantage. It was almost enough to be young and handsome, he thought, as he guaranteed the set of his waves with a pinch of his fingers. But, by the end of the summer, he would also be rich! He frowned suddenly as a related thought crossed his mind.

Several weeks before, he had participated in a disquieting discussion with four of his friends at the Bar Flaminia. Its subject concerned the number of times it is allotted a man to make love before impotence sets in. It had never before occurred to Pippo that there were any limitations to sexual activity this side of senility, except, of course, in cases of sickness or accident. He still doubted Sergio Rea's contention that the male mechanism could sustain no more than six thousand experiences without going kaput. Even so, to be on the safe side, he had decided to keep count until he had the opportunity to consult some doctor he could trust. He had estimated as nearly as possible his number of amorous adventures, beginning with his first with the family maid at the age of thirteen, up until the night the question was raised at the Flavia. Since then, he had used his little black diary as a check. He took it from his jacket pocket and made a mark beside the day's date. It would, he reflected, be a tragedy to be rich and not be able to enjoy it. But even if it should develop that Sergio's alleged authority was correct, he could still continue at his present tempo without reaching the fatal day until he was past fifty, an age when the body was so bereft of physical attraction that eroticism became ludicrous anyway. Happily, that time was a long way off. His teeth flashed again in a smile, and he turned off the light.

In his room he undressed in the dark. He hung his jacket around the back of a chair, took off his trousers, turned them upside down, joined one leg neatly to the other and suspended them from the top drawer of his bureau. He threw his shirt on the floor. Still wearing his socks, underpants and a short-sleeved T shirt, he slid between the cold sheets. A few minutes later he was fast asleep.

Beppe Bonaccorsi, the *sagrestano* of Santa Maria del Portico, mounted the iron stairway to the belfry. He had already swept the dust from the chapels, aisles and vestibules out into the Via della Scimmia, transported the required utensils from the sacristy to the altar and laid out the vestments for Father Ignazio. There was another ten minutes to go before he was to ring out the summons to six o'clock Mass. The tower was circular, and eight narrow, rectangular windows were spaced around it at regular intervals to bring in the light. Beppe went at once to the one of these that looked directly on the penthouse americana of the Palazzo Salvini.

He looked first at the sky above. It was gray and moody, less angry than it had been an hour before, to be sure, but still undecided whether to cheer up or go back to wailing. It seemed to Beppe that it was a shade brighter over St. Peter's, always a good sign. His eyes slid from the noble dome, crossed the Tiber and came down to the terrace of the penthouse. Its yellow tile pavement was splattered with mud and mats of rotting leaves. It was hard to remember it summer-clean and sparkling under the sun. The terrace ran the length of the palazzo roof, and onto it doors opened from the apartment's living room and three bedrooms. However, it had a depth of less than three yards. The Via della Scimmia had been considered a sweeping thoroughfare when it had been laid out in the sixteenth century, but it was little wider than most modern alleys. Consequently, the distance between the bell tower and the quarters inhabited by the Conte and Contessa de Costa was such that Beppe could observe life within the penthouse without the slightest optical strain. It was a diversion that had filled the leisure periods of his working day since the de Costas had taken occupancy of the roof two years before.

The American Contessa unwittingly cooperated with Beppe's

observations of her private world by sleeping with the window of her bedroom open. The morning that Beppe had seen her for the first time he had jumped to the conclusion that she was either an invalid or the victim of some accident. He had even imagined that she might be blind, because of a black mask that covered her eyes. Now, of course, he knew that she used the mask to shade her eyes from the morning light and that what appeared to be white gauze around her cheeks and chin was actually a strap that was designed to keep the jaw line firm and youthful. His moment of illumination regarding the latter had occurred at the cinema. The heroine of the film had slept in an identical device.

During the long rains the Contessa had been forced to keep the *serranda* of her bedroom lowered three quarters of the way, and so it was now. The sleeping Contessa was partly visible; above the waist she was in darkness. She was covered, as Beppe was accustomed to seeing her when the nights had been chilly, with the leopard spread, sleeping on her side with one arm stretched along the line of her hip outside the cover. What Beppe could see of her arm was clothed in red, and from this he deduced that she was wearing her *tuta*, a flaming flannel affair that was very like his own long-legged winter underwear. So attired, it was impossible for Beppe to identify the Contessa with photographs he occasionally saw of her in the newspapers, which described her as an ex-model internationally famous for her good looks and fashionable dress.

He could see the legs of her dressing table, but nothing of the bottles and jars and tubes and brushes and pencils that covered its top surface. On a small bench before the table lay a rigid black lace undergarment. The Contessa possessed others of identical design, but in pastel colors, and Beppi had watched her encasing her nude torso in one of them more times than he could count. It was remarkable to behold the transformation as she hooked the contraption up the front. Her slim hips rounded, her waist diminished and her breasts, which were no larger than those of Beppe's eleven-year-old daughter, even swelled a bit above the padding. Trussed up, she was still a long way from Beppe considered voluptuous, but he did have to admit there was a definite improvement in her proportions.

As usual, the door to the Conte's bedroom was shut tight. Beppi had several theories as to why the de Costas slept in separate rooms. One was that they had a difference of opinion over the matter of open and closed sleeping quarters. Another was that they made love in her room or his but preferred separate beds thereafter. As his own schedule didn't permit surveillance of the penthouse at night, he had no way of knowing. He favored his third conjecture, which was that they didn't make love at all.

He looked at his wristwatch, held it to his ear to be certain it was functioning, and went to untie his ropes.

The whole thing was cockeyed, but Randy was determined to get it straightened out, even if his head split wide open. It was Sunday. That was for sure. Because the Congregational church bell was ringing. But what about his dad? There he was sitting on the patio dressed in a business suit. With his briefcase on the glass-topped table, and his hat on top of his briefcase. On Sunday, What kind of a screwy thing was that? And besides, how come he could see the patio when he was in his own room and the patio was downstairs and across the living room and through the study and outside? Christ, but his head hurt. His dad was reading *Il Messaggero*. He could see it was all printed in Italian, except for the way "June" was spelled. In English. June, Not "Giugno." And right before the date it said, "Greenwich, Connecticut." The swimming pool was way off now from where it was supposed to be. It was about two hundred yards from the patio, instead of fifty. One side of it was sandy like the seashore and the water was washing up on it in waves and going back and washing up again. His father wasn't wearing the business suit any more. He was wearing shorts and he was taking his tennis racket out of its press. The church bell was making so damn much noise. And he was so hot. When his mother came to take his temperature it'd probably be 104. Jesus! His head. And his arm. There was something heavy on it. It was all numb.

Randy's conscious mind grudgingly took charge of diagnosing the cause of his physical discomfort and prompted him to move his arm from under whatever weight was upon it. When Randy involved his shoulder muscles in this endeavor without success, the mind advised him to open his eyes and determine exactly what it was he had to cope with. It was only then that Randy realized he had been asleep. But it was the only fact about which he was at all clear. He cautiously raised his lids, regarded the ceiling an instant, and hastily lowered them. He was not in Greenwich, Connecticut. And his father hadn't been reading *Il Messaggero* on the patio. Back home the pool was just as near the house as it had ever been and it was cement, as always, on four sides. The only truth in his dream was that his head hurt like hell, and now he knew it was because he had a hangover. And his arm hurt too.

Reluctantly, Randy advanced a step further into the world of reality. He opened his eyes again and they fixed on the area where he felt his arm to be, but it was entirely concealed from view. The naked body of a strange dark-skinned female lay over it. The back of her right shoulder rested awkwardly on the front of his left shoulder, and her head, capped by crisp black hair cropped close to the scalp, lolled back in the hollow alongside his neck.

A number of Randy's reflexes went into action promptly. His eyes blinked, his stomach billowed, his heart palpitated fiercely, and the nerves and muscles of his right side tensed to the call for the liberation of his imprisoned left side. He was on his feet in seconds. Lisa slept on. How he knew it was Lisa was that his hand had come away from her, tangled in something furry. It was a red wig. He shook it off furiously and it fell on the floor beside his stockinged feet. He had the sensation that it was a live thing and then, worse still, that it was something dead. His eyes riveted on the netting to which the strands were fixed and his stomach churned violently. He clapped his hand across his mouth, raced for the bathroom and bent over the toilet.

As the fires in his stomach died down those in his head rekindled. He closed the toilet seat, sat down on it and folded his arms on the basin to pillow his head. He tried to bring some order into his thinking and was eventually able, more or less, to sort out what he had dreamed from what he remembered of the night before.

But what monstrous things might he have done in between that he couldn't remember? An icy paralysis crept into his fingers as the recollection of Lisa's arm around his neck and her hand lifting his chin emerged from some murky level. And after that what? He sat up and pressed his fingers to his temples, but his brain stayed glued to the moment. Christ! Surely she hadn't kissed him or something. He wouldn't forget a thing like that. After all, Charlie had been there. No. Nothing could have happened with Charlie there.

He enjoyed a short period of reprieve and reassurance before doubts set in again. Yeah! Sure. *If* Charlie was there. Charlie had been slumped in the big chair for a long time. He was certain about that. But who knew when he had left? It could have been any time. While Lisa still had her clothes on. Or after they were off. It seemed to him unlikely that Lisa would have stripped and stretched out on the bed beside him after Charlie had gone home, or wherever he had gone. So, it meant that Charlie must have been on hand for the disrobing. Unless, incredibly, he, himself, was the only witness. Or even the instigator. Or. Oh, good God, no. His eyes widened to their farthest limits and glazed on the caked soap dish. Maybe undressing Lisa had been a joint project. Maybe he and Charlie had both even . . .

He shot to his feet, hurriedly unbuttoned his shirt and just as hurriedly buttoned it up again. Next to wanting to go back to sleep most of anything, he wanted to take a shower, but there wasn't any time to lose. He had to get Lisa out of the palazzo before people started waking up and everyone in the place found out she had been there all night. He filled the bowl and splashed cold water on his face, massaging it in vigorously. Next he brushed his teeth and combed his hair. At last he forced his shaking hand to take hold of the doorknob.

The shock of seeing Lisa's pink-brown nipples and high-riding hips a second time was no less electric than the first, particularly since he now had to consider the possibility that he had had intimate contact with who-knew-what parts of her body. Her legs gave an involuntary jerk and her head turned toward him, but she didn't wake up. He quickly crossed the cold terra-cotta floor and eased the India print spread up from her feet until it covered her shoulders. He looked down at her face intently, hoping to provoke some memory. Asleep and without the wig she looked a lot younger. Not more than fourteen.

He was wondering what would be the best way to go about waking her up and was startled when she unexpectedly opened her eyes. She stared at him for a few seconds, and then her eyes slowly searched the room as if they were seeking something lost. It was going to be even worse than he had anticipated, Randy told himself. He kept hoping she'd say something and, even more, that he would think of some opening. She lifted her hand and passed it slowly over her head, frowning. Her eyes were so dark and moist that he couldn't decide whether tears were rising in them or if it was part of their normal process of awakening. Surely she wasn't going to have hysterics or a feminine fit of some sort. He had assumed that this was one of the many times she had found herself in a strange bed, but maybe not. It could be that all the sexy come-on was as phony as the wig.

"Well, hi," he said, when he could bear the silence no longer.

Lisa's moist eyes held his. "What time is it?" she said finally.

"It must be about twenty after six," Randy said, judging the passing of minutes since the ringing of the church bell. With his wristwatch in hock he had come to rely on Santa Maria del Portico for the hour.

"I ought to go home," Lisa said.

"Yeah. Well, yeah, in a way I guess you really should." He tried not to sound too eager. She lived in some *pensione* way up by the station, Charlie had told him, and he supposed he'd have to give her his last thousand lire for a taxi. She couldn't very well get on a bus in the silver dress that was coiled on the floor beside the bed.

Lisa sat up slowly, clutching the India print to her chest, and her eyes took another forlorn excursion around the room.

"The place sure is a mess, isn't it?" He gave another nervous smile, hoping she'd return it. When she didn't, he went around to the other side of the bed and picked up the wig. "You can dress in the bathroom if you want to," he said, laying the wig beside her.

Lisa's long silver nails picked at the red nylon threads and she lowered her head.

Oh, brother, Randy moaned within. She was going to cry after all. "Boy, is this room ever a super-mess," he said, moving about with sudden energy. He swept up an empty fiasco from the floor and a couple of dirty glasses from a table. "I'll take some of this junk out and leave the coast clear for you."

He sped to the kitchen and leaned against the wall. Light years seemed to pass before he heard Lisa close the bathroom door. He went back into the living room and sank into an armchair. Tiny tom-toms were beating above his eyes. He didn't know how much of this he could take. He had known for some time that the day of reckoning was due, but its dawn was bleak beyond his worst imaginings. It had taken him exactly nine months to write one hundred and fifty pages of a novel he was pretty sure was lousy, make an ass of himself over a wop bitch, wash every penny of the five thousand dollars his father had given him when he graduated from college down the drain and wake up, still half-smashed, in a crumby bed in a beat-up apartment in a foreign country with a naked girl who was also, as they said these days, black. It must be some kind of a record. She'd be out any minute to make God only knew what kind of scene. If he had a choice he'd prefer rage to tears, but the way he felt, if he just died right this minute of a heart attack he'd be happiest of all. He stood up as the door opened.

Lisa had tamed the wig to the extent that it looked almost like the hair of a human head, and her eyes were heavy with mascara once more. She narrowed them and then, to Randy's horror, her body ground around inside its metallic prison keeping time. "Tall and tan and young and lovely, the girl from Ipanema goes walking," she sang.

Randy's panic subsided as he realized she was exaggerating the emphasis of the words and her accompanying gestures, making a parody of herself of the night before, to hide her embarrassment. It was an exhibition so pitiful that he involuntarily held out a restraining hand.

Lisa stood still, and her arms went limp and fell to her sides. "Guess it's time this gal from Ipanema went walkin' ", she said with a shy smile. "You can say that again. I don't even have bus fare."

Randy dug the thousand lire out of his pocket and thrust it into her hand. "This will get you home in a taxi."

"Oh, no," she protested, offering it back. "It's too much. I can take a bus."

"Please. I'll feel a lot better if you take a taxi." He thought of the time again. Even now the maids were due to arrive for work.

"Okay. I'll give it back to you the next time I see you." Lisa stuffed the money into the worn satin pocketbook that bulged with cosmetics.

"Forget it." Randy shrugged and started toward the front door.

"You probably don't remember last night very well, do you?" Lisa asked from behind him.

Randy stiffened. Well, what the hell, it was bound to come sooner or later. He took a deep breath and faced her.

"Do you?" she repeated.

He could be wrong, but it seemed she was hoping to hear he didn't. "Not very," he answered.

Some of the strain eased from the corners of Lisa's full lips. "I didn't think you did. You passed out early. I was pretty stoned, but I remember that you just slept on and on. Even . . ." Lisa glanced aside and her silver nails fluttered up and brushed at the red bangs. "Even with the music playing . . . and all."

He remembered the music now and staggering across the room to the bed. And afterward he had slept on and on. Through it *all,* she had said. He'd been pretty sure all along, but Christ, what a relief to be certain.

"Gee, I sure apologize for, well, for bein' here so late."

"Hell, it could happen to anybody," Randy said.

"Charlie shouldn't have left me here," Lisa added.

"Charlie's a goddam jerk." Randy looked forward to telling him that and a lot more. "Okay, you ready?"

Lisa nodded. Randy went outside, looked around and signaled for her to follow.

There were only two witnesses to their furtive flight across the cortile. Gino, for one, left off sweeping the broad stairs that led to the piano nobile to lean on his broom and shake his head.

Caroline followed Randy and Lisa's exit through the palazzo gate from the nursery window. Two weeks ago she would have been stunned. No longer. Randy's behavior was consistent with what she had come to expect, a testimony to the seamy, clandestine nature of all men. As his mother had requested, she had kept an eye on young Alexander Palmer when he arrived in Rome, and when his money began to dwindle she had persuaded her mother-in-law to rent him the dank apartment on the ground floor for practically nothing. She and Alice Palmer had worked together on *Today* and had been good friends. Furthermore, Randy had impressed her as serious and sensitive and deserving. But before her eyes was the evidence that he wasn't what she had thought at all. What he was was a dissolute sneak. No one was what he seemed to be, and least of all herself.

She stood on at the window motionless, numb and one with the gray stones and gunmetal sky. An hour or so more and day would begin officially. But what did one who had lost all identity do with a day? What direction was there to take when there was no going back and no going ahead? Her isolation from the past had begun the moment she became Lorenzo's wife. For Lorenzo her marriage to Julian Lowell was annulled because it was a pagan rite performed outside the Catholic Church and had never had the slightest validity. The fact that the ceremony was conducted by a justice of the peace reduced the two years she had spent as another man's wife to an adolescent escapade. During the years before this pardonable burlesque she had been a child. In those that followed, it was Lorenzo's opinion that she had been somewhat less than a woman, thanks to the mores of her country, where the differences between the sexes were scarcely defined. There was no confusion of the roles in Lorenzo's mind. The proper raising of a family and the supervision of a household was a full-time career for any woman. The provision of life's necessities and the likes of marbled-topped tables were male responsibilities. She would be his wife and the mother of his children. And he would be her husband and the father of her children. He would lead and she would follow. It was the natural order.

She had taken place in this matrimonial procession eagerly and soon discovered that keeping it wasn't as easy as she had expected it to be. In the beginning she was forever charging ahead or lagging behind, blissfully unaware she was doing either until Lorenzo brought her sharply to attention.

She had broken rank the first time in Athens on their honeymoon. She had been Lorenzo's wife for three weeks, and the metamorphosis which marriage effects in all women was working its subtle way toward completion. Shedding the cocoon named Caroline Morris Lowell had been as painless and satisfying as pitching out a hastily and thoughtlessly selected dress that had never quite fitted or been becoming. Scarcely aware that it was happening, she had become conditioned to respond automatically to her new name, sign it without hesitation and recognize it as being her own, on first and not second sight, on the letters that had arrived for her at the Grande-Bretagne, where she and Lorenzo had stayed. Instructing the hotel valet on the manner in which Lorenzo liked his trousers creased and the sleeves of his jackets rolled came as naturally as if three weeks had been three years. The words "my husband" no longer succeeded an awkward pause and a slight flushing.

On the morning of the twenty-second day of her existence as Caroline Salvini, she had stood in the center of the sitting room of their suite, looking down into a wicker laundry basket that rested at her feet. On the opposite side of the basket a squat man with head and neck all of a piece watched her with flat, expressionless eyes.

"My husband wants no starch in his shirts. I told you that. None. Absolutely none. Look," she commanded, pointing down.

The valet's stare flattened on one of the half dozen of Lorenzo's linen shirts that lay in the basket, rigid as cardboard, but he gave no sign of comprehending.

Caroline lifted a shirt from the basket and held it near the man. "Soft." She bent the collar and it made a little cracking sound. "This is like a board." She gave the collar another crack. "Not like this. Like this." She pinched the cuff of the chambray blouse she was wearing. "Soft. No starch. And here . . ." She ran her finger over the tiny crown and initials low in the shirt's left side. They had been pressed down so hard they seemed branded rather than embroidered on the cloth. "On the other side." She flipped the shirt over and passed an imaginary iron above it. "You understand now, don't you?" She sought a spark of the sort of intelligence that had illuminated the ancient Hellenes and then remembered that Lorenzo had told her that modern Athens was largely inhabited by Balkans. All the same, a slight mist seemed to lift from the man's dull Slavic eyes.

"No starch," he said. "Soft." He bobbed his head up and down.

Caroline nodded back. "My husband will be very, very angry

if they aren't right next time, especially since I told you 'no starch' when I gave them to you before. These will all have to be done over."

"Yes, madame," He glanced again at the cuff of her blouse as if to set the example firmly in mind, lifted the basket and went through the door, which she closed behind him.

She felt the elation of a meticulous housewife who has put her small world in order early in the day. Except for the shirts, Lorenzo's wardrobe was as tidily and conveniently arranged as that of a star theatrical performer beset by a demanding role calling for frequent and rapid changes of costume. She had surreptitiously studied what pleased and what irritated him. Once she had observed that the insertion of cuff links into their narrow slits caused him to groan with exasperation, she made it a point always to undertake the task of threading them through for him. As she bent to this work, he invariably rewarded her by kissing the nape of her neck. When she discovered that getting the bulk of a handkerchief in the little pocket of his jacket was a struggle that caused him to roll his eyes with vexation, she made it her business to see that he always found one already tucked in place. Once, when she had held the sheet-sized hotel towel for him to wrap around himself as he stepped from the shower, he had enfolded her inside it next to him. The silk of her slip had clung to his dripping body as they made love on the floor of the steamy, talcum-scented bathroom. She no longer pitied Oriental women. She imagined them afire with passion behind their inscrutable masks, and longed for the chance to pad paces behind Lorenzo on silent, softly slippered feet.

Her gaze fell lovingly on the chair to the right of the table before the long window. It was where Lorenzo sat when they breakfasted, she across from him. Their apartment had struck her as cold and leaden when they were ushered into it the afternoon of their arrival. Now it was warm and personalized by memories. At her request, the maid had shoved the senselessly dispersed furniture around to form intimate groups. The icon

Lorenzo had bought for her and which would hang over their bed in Rome had temporarily replaced a lithograph of the temple of Zeus. She kept fresh fruit heaped on a terra-cotta platter on an end table alongside the sofa, and fresh flowers on the coffee table in a black glazed-pottery vase, which they had recognized as a replica of one dug up in Crete when they visited the national museum. It disturbed her to note that the bouquet she had arranged only the day before was already dying. It was the first week in September, still fiercely hot from sunrise to sunset. Lorenzo had gone to be shaved and have his hair cut, and there was time to run out to the flower shop before he came back.

Fifteen minutes later she was making her way through the sun's platinum mist around Constitution Square toward the hotel entrance.

She carried a mass of yellow roses that had reminded her of those Lorenzo had sent after their first meeting, a copy of *Il Tempo* from Rome for Lorenzo and a copy of the *Herald Tribune* from Paris for herself. Keeping step at her side was Captain William Rogers of the United States Air Force. The captain was dark, taller than Caroline by a head, and his wilting uniform accentuated the fact that he was built to the most exacting American specifications. He, too, was carrying a copy of the Paris *Herald Tribune*. Indeed, it was their common taste in what English journalism the newsstand had had to offer that had brought them together.

"Boy, this heat is really beginning to get me down." Captain Rogers gave the visor of his cap a push and it tilted back. "How come you manage to look so cool?"

"I don't feel cool." Caroline smiled. It was true. But it was also true that she loved the heat. It provoked an atmosphere of primitive sensuality. Sightseeing was out of the question except in the morning. One risked sunstroke being about in the afternoon. Following lunch, she and Lorenzo went at once to their rooms. They passed the torrid hours with the curtains drawn, in an artificial twilight, in feverish delicious indolence condoned by the heat, their damp bodies coming together, parting in sleep, coming together again. Lorenzo maintained that lovemaking was at its best in extreme temperatures, and he had promised to prove his theory to her the following winter on a feather bed in Austria, where they would go to ski.

"I rather like the heat," she added. She smiled again, to herself more than to him.

"Not me. I never have been able to take it. It's being from Maine, I guess. A hot day there is like Christmas compared to this." The captain took a handkerchief from his hip pocket and mopped his brow. "Where're you from?"

"Well, I . . ." Caroline paused. She wanted Lorenzo to meet this man. He was the kind of wonderfully friendly, uncomplicated American who made her proud. She felt personally responsible for the outrageous horde of conducted tourists, men in porous nylon shirts and women bulging in slacks, they had seen clambering over the Acropolis as if it were Disneyland.

"Don't tell me you don't know," he laughed.

"Of course I know," she said. "I was born in Chicago."

"That can be pretty rough in summer, too, they tell me."

"Terrible," Caroline remembered and shook her head.

"You here with the Embassy?"

"No."

"On vacation?" He stuffed the handkerchief back in his pocket.

"Yes."

He adjusted his cap and looked at her directly. "I might as well get the sixty-four dollar question over with right away. You married?"

Caroline disengaged the fingers of her left hand from the rose stems and fluttered them.

"Nice ring," the captain observed dryly. "Well, it figured. That's my kind of luck." He gave a good-natured shrug. "Your husband from Chicago, too?"

"No. He's from Rome."

"He's Italian?" Captain Rogers regarded her as he might a trusted subordinate caught taking leave without permission. "Well, what do you know," he said finally.

It now seemed to Caroline as important for the captain to know Lorenzo as for Lorenzo to know the captain. "I'd like you to meet him."

"Very happy to," said the captain politely, but without enthusiasm.

"If you're not doing anything before dinner, perhaps you'd like to come have a drink with us." Their own sitting room appealed to her as the most suitable setting for this confrontation. She could have drinks sent up from the bar and the delicious unseasoned almonds on a mound of ice that went so well with the ouzo she and Lorenzo liked. She would seat Lorenzo and Captain Rogers in the two armchairs, facing each other across the coffee table. She would take a position midway between them on the sofa, a vantage point appropriate to the mission of establishing sympathy and harmony between the world she had forsaken and the one she had adopted.

"You don't think your husband would mind?" the captain had asked.

Caroline floated on above the steaming street, playing hostess for Lorenzo for the first time, her pretty tapered nails freeing a chilled almond from its delicate skin, admired by the captain, adored by Lorenzo for having brought them together as twilight cooled the Parthenon.

"I wouldn't want to intrude," the captain added.

"But don't be silly," Caroline reassured him radiantly. "He'll be delighted."

Lorenzo had reacted with delight less promptly than she had anticipated. "I'm afraid I did not understand correctly what it is you have told me." He had raised his voice to carry to the bathroom, where she had gone to fill the black pottery vase with water.

"Just a second, darling," her voice had lilted back above the open tap. "I want to get these in water quickly," she explained, hurrying back through the door into the sitting room. She poked at the flowers and puttered about the low table a considerable time, humming as she did so. "There," she said at last, straightening up and standing back. "It's a pity I had to cut so much stem, but don't they look pretty?" She cast a glance behind her at Lorenzo. He wasn't looking at the roses. He was watching her. Intently. "Oh, sweetheart, forgive me." She spun about and circled his neck in her arms. "Now then. What I said was that I invited this nice American to have a drink with us." She uttered each word slowly and distinctly like a kindly foreign-language teacher trying to get through to an obtuse pupil.

"That is what I understood you to have said. And who is this nice American?" Lorenzo underlined the word "nice."

"His name is William Rogers."

"Ah. His name is William Rogers," Lorenzo repeated. "And . . ."

"And he's a captain in the Air Force." A premonition stirred and threatened her state of euphoria.

"Is he?" Lorenzo left off staring intently at her to stare intently at some spot above and beyond the back of her head. "You have never mentioned to me this William Rogers. He is someone you knew in New York?"

"Oh, no, no." Caroline hastened to make things right again and knit her fingers together tighter at the back of Lorenzo's neck. "I never saw him before in my life. Darling, I'm not about to drag someone from the past in on you. I met him just now. At the newsstand."

"Ah, really. This man is then a stranger?" Lorenzo smiled, quite warmly it seemed to Caroline.

"A complete stranger," Caroline beamed as the road to understanding brightened before her. "You see, I stopped to buy papers. I reached for the *Herald Tribune* just as he did and we found ourselves holding ends of the same one. He laughed and apologized and I laughed, too. And then we each bought separate copies and he sort of walked along beside me and we talked and that was how it was."

"It was so. Like that?" The mysteries of the encounter were clearing for Lorenzo.

"Yes. It turned out he was as nice as could be. So . . ."

"You were able to tell this in only a few short steps," Lorenzo encouraged her.

"Tell what?"

"That he was so very nice." Lorenzo underlined "nice" for a second time.

"Yes. After all, it's the sort of thing that doesn't take very long to discover."

"Oh, not at all long," agreed Lorenzo. "And because he is a person so nice you asked him for a cocktail."

"For you, darling. Because I thought it would be fun for you." The fires of her mission were beginning to blaze anew. "He's the sort of American I think . . ."

"For me."

"Well, I . . . why, Lorenzo . . ." She stopped short, struck dumb by the lightning change in his expression. Near as he was, she had the impression he was regarding her from afar, seeing her for the first time and backing off. A few seconds later he actually did unknot her fingers and make a swift exit through the bedroom door.

She replayed her mental recording of the little scene they had just enacted, settled on jealousy as his motive, smiled to herself and followed him. "*Amore*," she called at the doorway and immediately regretted her choice of endearment. It was calculated to flatter him because he was anxious for her to speak Italian, but somehow the foreign word had sounded artificial on her lips. "Darling," she amended, taking note as she crossed to where he stood before the dresser that the desired mixture of reproach and indulgence had come through in her own language.

Lorenzo continued briskly marching a set of military brushes over his hair, deaf and mute to her bilingual appeal.

"I simply never dreamed you'd feel this way."

Lorenzo put one of his brushes at ease on the dresser top and held the other poised in mid-air as he surveyed the results of his attack on his new haircut in the mirror.

"It's easy enough to call off," Caroline told his reflection. "We left it that he'd telephone at six, just to make certain it was all right. I can make some excuse. You see, darling, what I thought was . . ."

Lorenzo slammed the brush down beside its twin and wheeled around so abruptly that Caroline sprang back with a little cry.

"I know what you thought," he hissed through clenched teeth. "You have already told me why you wanted me to meet this fine example of your society. Because he is so nice."

"But not only that . . ." Caroline protested in a small voice. "I also wanted him . . ."

"No doubt to meet me. Because I am too so nice. Because not to meet me he believes you to have married possibly a member of the Sicilian Mafia. Or a Sardinian bandit. This is what you thought."

Caroline blinked the shadow of guilt from her eyes. "Lorenzo, please . . ." she tried again.

"So, you arranged for me this hour of cocktails. For me. For me you made an appointment with someone I do not know and someone you, too, do not know. Not consulting me. Ah, no. In complete command. In full suffragette form. Running from that room to this room to the bathroom. The flowers in water. The ashtrays placed so. The stage set." Lorenzo flung his arms high. "*Ma . . . porca miseria . . . per carità di Dio. Ma sei matta?*" He questioned her sanity with vibrating fingers.

"I'm sorry," Caroline murmured.

"A woman does not arrange my schedule and select my company. I put in order my social activities. I don't want a wife full of initiative. I want to live with a woman, not a militant suffragette. I am a man. I am your husband. And I command." Lorenzo stiffened his forefinger and pointed to himself. "*Comando io,*" he repeated in Italian. "I thought it was understood."

Caroline had the impression his message was coming to her over amplifiers, that the whole hotel and half of Athens had heard. "I know, Lorenzo, I know. I was wrong," she managed to get out at last, "but you see, in America it's the women who usually invite people for dinner and cocktails and . . ."

"*Ma che mi frega dell' America,*" Lorenzo's voice soared again as he shot past her into the sitting room. "If how you wish to be married is in that way, that's where you should have stayed." He swung his jacket from the sofa and in its flight across the coffee table it caught the yellow roses, and water drenched the cushion of the chair she had destined for Captain Rogers. "In America," Lorenzo shouted, disappearing from her sight down the corridor toward the elevator.

She had wept wildly for paradise lost and her despair had deepened as the afternoon and early evening passed without hope of regaining it. When darkness came she had dressed in her lemon chiffon, which was Lorenzo's favorite, and he had finally taken her to dine at a terrace restaurant above the harbor, where they had ordered and then sat in silence, looking down at the anchored boats and up at the stars and out at the secret night sea, stiffly polite as strangers opposite each other in a diner on a train. The orchestra had flogged away at some soulless composition until it went into a convulsion from which it eventually perished. There was an interval without music and then it commenced again. The new melody had a relentlessly sensual beat. They had bought a recording of it the day before and played it over and over during their long afternoon. Caroline stared down at the plate the waiter put before her, took up her fork and listlessly picked at grape leaves which enfolded little lamb patties; but the music insisted, and her eyes met Lorenzo's. Their gaze held while he put his napkin on the table and stood up and reached for her hand. She had floated into his arms, weightless, submitting to the ardent demand of the music, to the hard authority of his body, following where he led, and the natural order had been established again.

In time, sustaining it had become habitual with her. She had relinquished all thought of independent action. Without regret. She had yielded to him. Without reservation. She had wanted no identity other than the identity he gave her. To be his wife. To be the woman he loved. She had been happier than she had ever imagined possible. And, like a fool, she had never suspected that it might not last forever.

Only a fraction of her brain registered Randy's return. She supposed he had conducted his unfortunate victim to some conveyance in which she was now rattling through the drab morning to wherever she lived in her shocking wig. As he hastily passed across the middle of the courtyard, he lifted his head and glanced about in what seemed to be a survey of the palazzo windows. It was possible that he had caught sight of her, although it was hard to tell. She vaguely wondered whether she ought to give an honest answer to Alice Palmer's urgent appeal for news of her son that had come in yesterday's mail, but the response to the thought refused to take any sort of concrete shape. There were no answers anyway. To anything. So what was the use of questions? Of wanting to know? Know what? There was nothing to know except that nothing mattered. Nothing. Nothing at all. Except the children. The children mattered, of course.

She turned from the gray shades outside the window toward the bright blues and greens and yellows that decorated the nursery, but even these seemed sad and subdued in the dreary light. Across from her the door leading to the outer hall was closed. To her left were two interior doors which opened into the children's bedrooms, and these were slightly ajar. She went to the one nearest her and looked in. One of Beatrice's arms was flung through the slats of a chair back that was always put alongside her bed to prevent her falling out. Miss Vaughn, the children's nurse, slept on the opposite side of the room, at the moment on her stomach, covered so that nothing of her was visible except a bit of her forehead and a great puff of her red hair. Caroline eased the door shut and went to look in the other. Andrea had kicked off his blankets, drawn his bare feet up and lowered his head to make a little circle of himself. She tiptoed to the side of his bed and uncoiled him gently. He rolled over on his back and opened his eyes. A few seconds passed before he smiled. "*Ciao*, Mommie," he said, his eyes bright and wide awake as stars. "Is it time to get up?"

Caroline put her forefinger to her lips and shook her head. She took off her robe, and Andrea's smile broadened as she lay down beside him and pulled up the covers. "Go back to sleep, darling," she whispered, holding him close.

"You, too?" he asked eagerly.

"Yes. Me, too." She kissed his temple and rolled her cheek against his fair, silky baby hair. His legs made the series of intermittent jabs and jerks with which small children resist the fall from wakefulness before he was still. After a bit her own breathing matched the easy, even tempo of his and she slept, too.

The sun made a serious attempt to break through at quarter past seven. Beppe Bonaccorsi, who was crossing the Largo Argentina, had looked at his wristwatch only a second before. He stopped and leaned against the railing that enclosed the ruins of Republican temples in the center of the square, a leg-breaking drop below street level. Wide streamers of misty sunlight slanted down from the heavens onto the crumbling altars and columns. It made Beppe think of the climax of films he had seen in which the hero, or heroine, or sometimes both, walked, chin on high, into some promised land, their way lighted as the ruins were now, while violins accompanied a celestial chorus. Beppe felt his own spirit take sudden flight and soar up along one of the slanting streamers to where he imagined angels waited, but his mystic experience was brief. A cloud cut him back to earth. In shadow again, the excavation looked its age and one of the dozens of cats to whom it was home gave up his idea of mounting an altar for a sun bath and slunk back to his refuge under the *portico*. Beppe went on across the square to the kiosk and bought the morning's *Paese*

Sera for himself and *Il Messaggero* for Gino. During the five minutes it took him to walk to the Palazzo Salvini, the sun managed to drop more misty streamers to the earth. Although clouds continued to cut them down, it was Beppe's bet that the sun was going to take over control of the sky before long. He announced this as he crossed Gino's threshold.

"*Magari,*" Gino hoped, casting his eyes toward the ceiling.

Zia Ida lifted her hands out of the dishwater and made the sign of the horns with dripping fingers, and Signora Elena, Gino's wife, made the sign of the cross with her right hand while she adjusted the damp cloth on the pants she was pressing with her left. An angry whirring sound came from the next room, and Beppe jerked his head toward the closed door and questioned Gino with his eyes.

"It's a phone for drying hair," said Gino. He took one of the newspapers from under Beppe's arm, saw that it was the organ of the odious left and impatiently exchanged it for his own.

"Ersilia is dressing Anna's hair in the latest fashion," said Zia Ida, tossing her own crown of gray braids high.

"A style Signor Michele invented for the daughter of the English ambassador," Signora Elena added proudly.

"French," corrected Zia Ida.

"Oh, yes. French." So much splendor had recently come into her life by way of her daughter that it was no wonder she was confused.

"The Contessa de Costa has four wigs," Beppe said.

Zia Ida looked at her sister-in-law and lifted her chin. "What did I tell you?"

"She keeps them on wooden heads that have faces painted on." Beppe's eyes sparkled as he waited for that to sink in.

Zia Ida and the Signora Elena both clucked and shook their heads.

"The Contessa has made a *causa* against the Marchesa Luisa," Gino said.

"No!" Beppe couldn't imagine the Contessa capable of any action that was so demanding. "How do you know?"

"Mario told me. The Marchesa had him call Avvocato Gatti."

"But what for?" asked Beppe.

"She claims that the rain came in and ruined her rug because of faulty construction."

"Is the rug in the Contessa's living room or bedroom?" Beppe asked.

"Bedroom."

"Hm." Beppe filed the news away for future consideration and looked down at the newspaper which Gino had opened to the sports page. He had already made his selections for the weekly football lottery, except for one. "I may be crazy but I believe I'm going to bet Naples to win over Milan," he said.

Gino shrugged.

"I've just got this feeling that . . ." Beppe began and then dropped the subject. He knew Gino didn't like the football lottery. He had explained why to Beppe many times. It was too impersonal. Not scientific like lotto, which was Gino's gambling weakness. One selected lotto numbers through dreams, so of course there was a direct connection between the player and his fortune.

"Gino dreamed that Il Duce came to Anna's wedding," Signora Elena said with modest pride.

"Did he speak?" Beppe asked.

"Oh, yes," Signora Elena answered.

"Mmm. *Il morto che parla,*" Beppe mused. "Forty-eight." Although he himself never played lotto he was familiar enough with the symbolic numbers to know that forty-eight represented a dead person who speaks.

"He was in uniform," Gino said. "I didn't catch sight of him until we were leaving the church. He was standing just inside the door. I saluted him and he saluted back, but he didn't speak until we were outside the door, standing on the step just above the street. You know, the wide step?"

"*Sì, sì.*" Beppe bobbed his head impatiently. As if he needed to be told about steps he swept every morning of his life.

"Well, we just stood there a while like old friends, without speaking, and then all of a sudden he looked down at the street. It was filthy. Torn papers. Old cardboard cartons. Little hills of garbage. Orange peels and egg shells. Chicken bones."

"*Ma che schifo.*" Beppe uttered his disgust. "And Il Duce? What did he say?"

"Ah!" Gino shook his fingers toward Beppe. "What did he say? If only you could have heard. What he said. What he said!" As Gino's voice rose he followed it up from his chair onto his feet. "He put his hands on his flanks. So." Gino illustrated. "He looked right. Then left. And he said what you just said, '*Ma che schifo.*' And then! Then he threw back his head and roared. He was a lion in the zoo. His face was red with the rage. And the muscles here . . . here." Gino poked at his neck with his thumb. "These muscles stood out. Way out. He must have roared one minute without taking a breath before they came running. They poured in from every street around. Via Giulia. Corso Vittorio. Up from the Campo dei Fiori . . ."

"Who?" Beppe, who had followed the story anxiously, was distressed at losing the thread.

Gino gave him a look of disdain. "The *spazzini.*"

"Oh, of course," said Beppe, instantly picturing the Via della Scimmia swarming with street cleaners. "And then what happened?"

"I don't know," Gino sighed and sat down again in his chair. "I woke up."

"He made them tidy every inch. Be sure of that," Beppe said.

"Ahha. Of that I have no doubt." Gino recaptured the dream's glory briefly and added a scene in which Mussolini sent the spazzini scurrying with brooms and shovels, to fill their trash containers that were mounted on little wheels and push them out of the Via della Scimmia on the run.

"In the days of Il Duce Rome was a mirror," said Zia Ida.

"And now look at it." Signora Elena banged down the iron to emphasize her scorn. "The fight Gino has just to make them leave the palazzo entrance decent."

"Communists. All Communists. No one wants to work any more," Zia Ida summarized.

"The delinquent American boys woke me up or I'd have finished the dream. They were drunk . . ." Gino considered the presence of his wife and sister and beckoned with his finger. Beppe bent over and cocked his ear toward Gino's cupped hand.

"*Bella?*" Beppe asked at the conclusion of the whispered confidence.

"So-so." Gino shrugged. "Nothing to compare with that other, certainly." A beautiful American *negra* who had occupied an apartment on the Via della Scimmia the year before had caused Gino and Beppe to conclude that what they read of racial prejudice in the United States exceeded the limits of sanity.

"Well, I've got to be on my way," Beppe slapped his newspaper against his thigh and inclined his head toward the two women. "It's going to be one of the greatest pleasures of my life to know that Anna will be coming across the street when I ring the bell at ten, Signora."

Signora Elena gave him a smile, wet her finger and touched it to the iron.

She had never been a woman to talk much, Beppe reflected. It had been years since he had really looked at her, and he was astonished to realize that nothing actually remained of her original beauty but her stupendous eyes. But then twenty years had passed since Gino had taken the week off and gone to his native Veneto to bring her back as his bride. "It seems only yesterday that Anna was too little to cross the street. I remember how she would wave to me from the gate, and I'd warn her to stand well inside because of the automobiles."

"Time passes," Gino sighed.

Beppe checked this fact with his watch. "It lacks ten minutes of being eight." He opened the door. "Until later . . . *arrivederci.*" He stepped outside and stopped short. "Gino," he shouted. "*Il sole!*"

The sun was out. Luisa Salvini hadn't yet opened her eyes, but she knew it all the same. She could hear it. The sounds that came from outside were the unmistakable beginning of the clamor of Rome's awakening to clear skies. Little by little she was able to isolate specific vibrations from the general ferment and identify them. The spazzini were shuffling around directly under her window. Trash cans clanked against the metal lip of the garbage truck, the great maw devoured its ugly breakfast and the monster moved on down the street with the spazzini trailing after it. They were singing. All during the rains they had snarled about their work like bad-tempered animals. It could only be the sun. She subsequently heard the rasping cry of a broom vendor. The sun always brought them forth. Someone was beating a rug, a chore never set to in bad weather. A Vespa tuned up and took off at jet speed. A screech of automobile brakes coincided with the Vespa's arrival at the corner and she held her breath in expectation of a metallic impact. There was none. Instead there was laughter, an evidence that nerves were already beginning to iron out, after which the Vespa made a fresh start and the gears of the automobile shifted to regain lost momentum. The thoroughfare traffic along the Tiber and Corso Vittorio was humming a gayer tune than it had in weeks. An iron overhead door of one of the shops below rolled up. She rightly guessed that it was the smith. Beaten metal rang and rang and Luisa opened her eyes. If the smith was at work, it was eight. She reached up and pulled the bell cord to summon Carmela.

Luisa planned her morning while she waited. She would send for the plumber and discuss the project for the new furnace. And she would call the carpenter to come estimate the cost of repairs needed on the glass veranda. The apartment to which the veranda belonged was vacant, and she would never be able to let it until it was set right. She would also advise Gino to let her know if Penelope de Costa went out. During her absence she would go upstairs herself and see how much truth there was in the story of the rug.

She commissioned Carmela to alert Gino to this vigil as Carmela poured her coffee.

"But," Donna Luisa, it is the day of Anna's wedding. Gino won't be here," Carmela reminded her.

Luisa frowned and took the coffee cup from Carmela.

"If you could see Anna. Her cousin has rolled her hair on spools big as my wrist." Carmela limped to the window. She had broken a leg in childhood, and the country doctor, instead of resetting the bone in the conventional fashion, had joined the fractured ends side by side, on the theory that the juncture, once healed, would be twice as strong. Carmela attributed her robust constitution to the genius of the man. She pulled the cord and the mauve velvet curtains separated. The room brightened several shades. She unlatched the shutters, and as she pushed them outward the sun rushed in and beat a bold path across the flowered rug.

Luisa blinked and shaded her eyes with her free hand. "Not all that way, Carmela. It's too bright."

"Ah, you have seen what a beautiful day. I am happiest of all for Anna. It is for her that the sun has come back. It is the answer to prayer." Carmela adjusted the shutters to admit less light and shut the window. "Donna Luisa, you will not object if I go to the ceremony? I would be away not more than an hour."

"Sì, *sì*," Luisa conceded wearily and held out her cup to be refilled. "If you get on with your work, that is, instead of wasting time babbling about nothing. Attach the heater and run my bath. And then take that feathered thing and that box of blocks to the nursery." Luisa submitted her liver to a test, poking at it with her thumb; while Carmela listed about fulfilling her orders. It was definitely improved. "And ask Miss Vaughn if Andrea carried off my letter opener. I can't find it anywhere," she said as Carmela went out the door. It was only after Carmela was out of hearing distance that she remembered the hot-water bottle.

"You did not screw the top of my water bottle securely,"

she said upon Carmela's return and noted with satisfaction that a rush of color tinted her servant's cheeks.

"Oh, signora, I was careful . . ."

Luisa threw back the covers and stepped into her slippers. "Look," she ripped off a bath towel and pointed to the spot. "Everything must be changed," she said, going toward the bathroom. "The letter opener. Did you ask Miss Vaughn?"

"She has not seen it." Carmela passed her hand over the damp area and shook her head unhappily. "She will ask Andrea, but he is still sleeping. And, a curious thing, Donna Luisa. His mother is sleeping with him. She came in some time during the night. Why, do you suppose?"

"Why not? It's perfectly natural." Luisa locked the bathroom door, bent over the tub, took the water's temperature with her elbow and added more hot water. She waited until she was stretched out in the tub and submerged to the neck to think. It was, of course, anything but natural for Caroline to go sleep in the nursery. She didn't know when Lorenzo had come in, although she did know it was some time before three. It had been exactly that, by the tolling of Santa Maria's clock, when she had awakened to find her feet soaked and gone into the bathroom for the towel and heard the motor in the cortile and looked down from the narrow bathroom window and seen it was the La Rosa creature. Lorenzo's car was back, and the La Rosa had been standing between it and his own car, fooling around at one of the windows. In any case, there was a good chance that Lorenzo had returned quite late and some sort of drama had been enacted, but if it had she felt certain it had taken place inside Caroline's head. Caroline would never make a scene. The trouble was that there was no telling what action women of her kind resorted to instead. It was all too vexing. She would have expected Lorenzo to behave with more discretion, but that was not the sort of criticism he appreciated hearing.

Luisa sat up and squeezed her big lavender sponge against her neck. A river of soapy foam ran down between her flat breasts. She lay back again and lifted her right foot above the water. During the rainy spell her toenails had grown and carried the nail polish a half centimeter from the cuticle. She rearranged her morning schedule. She would go to Arden's, have her hair done and her nails and a pedicure. The furnace and veranda could wait. More pressing emergencies threatened. If a drama had started that was to have successive acts, she wanted to be prepared for her role in it by looking her best.

The car situation turned out to be exasperating, as usual. She had foolishly waited until she had dressed and telephoned to Elisabetta Colombo, who had decided to go along with her to Arden's, to have Carmela tell Mario she wanted to be driven into town, only to be told by Carmela that Caroline had taken the children and Miss Vaughn in the big Fiat to the Gianicolo. The little 600 Fiat was out of the question because of Elisabetta's weight, which would soon forbid her easy entrance into anything smaller than a truck. And yet she still gave herself the airs of the great beauty she had once been. Luisa passed the palms of her hands over the beige tweed that covered her fleshless rib cage and down along her flat hips as Carmela bent and plucked a loose thread from the hem of the skirt.

"She should be back any minute," said Carmela, straightening up. "She told Mario she was just dropping the children off to play in the sun with the Casano children and would be right back because of the wedding, and it had been arranged that Signorina Vaughn and the children would be driven back in the Casano automobile."

Women had no right to let themselves go. Elisabetta claimed that she had no trouble with her liver, ever, but Luisa felt certain it must be the size of a melon under all that fat. "Hm, what?" There were times when she had to restrain herself from hitting Carmela for her habit of repeating the same information in a number of different ways. "Oh, yes, the wedding." Caroline had offered to represent the family at this ordeal. The lives of the servants and of the peasants at the villa had a fascination for her quite beyond Luisa's understanding, doubtless a result of the democratic doctrines her country held so sacred. "I'll go down and wait in the cortile. Tell Mario to meet me there at once. Oh—and tell Don Lorenzo he will have to take the little car."

Luisa saw that Mario was already waiting outside the gate by the street when she came through the palazzo's front entrance. He was holding under his arm the cap he wore when he drove, and his bald head, which always seemed polished, was shinier than ever in the sunlight. It would be days before the cortile was dried out, she thought, as she picked her way around little iridescent pools formed by rain and oil from the cars in the hollows where the stones were worn. She smiled, remembering that last year Andrea had called it "walking on rainbows," but an instant later she came under the window of the La Rosa boy's bedroom and frowned. He was evidently talking to someone on the telephone. She would have imagined it was too early for him to have opened his great, sly eyes, considering the hour he had got to bed.

"Ah, *buon giorno*, Donna Luisa," Mario said as she came up beside him. He inclined his head in a little jerk and got his feet, which had been spread apart, close to each other. "*Bello oggi*, eh?"

"Yes, yes. Beautiful," said Luisa and saw the car just turning into the Via della Scimmia. Caroline drove up in front of them, and Luisa was disappointed to see that she was wearing dark glasses. Since it was a bit premature to make such a defense against the sun, Luisa reasoned that they must be hiding eyes that couldn't bear close examination.

As they drove along the Tiber, Luisa thought how baffling life was in many ways. For instance, she knew the back of Mario's head intimately, every crease of his neck and turn of his receded hairline, from staring at it hundreds of times over thousands of kilometers. Yet she had never seen her own, except in a mirror. As they turned into the Corso, a great limousine cut them off and caused Mario to make an emergency reorganization of clutch and gears. Little white curtains had been fitted in the back windows of the limousine, a fashion among the members of the Senate. How had it really come about, she tried to think, that the power had come into the hands of these upstarts? They rode in limousines with those ridiculous cottage curtains, while she could just barely afford to keep up two Fiats and had to share her house with the likes of the family La Rosa. It was pointless to search for answers, she concluded, as they turned into a courtyard of the Palazzo Colombo. She took some consolation from the fact that Elisabetta had as hard a time as she did keeping things going. The courtyard looked downright seedy. Well, anyway, if Lorenzo was up to something with anyone they *knew*, Elisabetta of all people was sure to have heard who it was. She waved. And Elisabetta, waddling out from between columns, waved back.

The red-cheeked country girl who had replaced Anna as maid of all work in the La Rosa household placed a tray with Pippo's breakfast on the table beside his bed. Pippo sat up and balanced the telephone receiver between his jaw and collar bones, so as to have both hands free to deal with his morning meal.

"Of course I love you," he reassured his fiancée on the other end of the line. He smacked his lips against the mouthpiece making sounds to imitate a series of kisses, while he tore a brioche in half and buttered it. "*Tesoro, amore,*" he whispered. He spread a thick layer of marmalade over the butter and stuffed the bread into his mouth. He chewed, half listening to the declarations of devotion that were pouring into his ear. The other half of his attention was on the movements of the maid, who was shuffling around in felt slippers gathering up his clothes that needed washing or pressing. As she bent over to pick up his shirt the wide spread of her hips widened even more. Pippo reached out, flashed his hand lightly over the girl's buttocks and picked up his coffee cup all in one motion. She straightened up and looked behind her, and he stared innocently into space. Once he had given her the full benefit of his eyes at their most endearing, he lowered his lids and sent her a sensual impulse through his long, thick lashes. She blinked and swallowed. They always did. He winked, and she turned nervously back to the pursuit of her chores.

"And I missed you," he said into the mouthpiece. "I worked with Papà way into the night." He kicked off the covers, pulled off his socks, dropped them on the floor and covered up again. "It's a very hard case Papà is working on. I wouldn't feel right not helping him all I can," he confided to his fiancée, meanwhile pointing to his socks to convey to the maid the message that they were to be taken to wash with the rest of the bundle she had collected. "No, no, we're not half finished. He's gone to court this morning, but as soon as he comes back we've got to lock ourselves away from everyone in his studio and work all afternoon. And perhaps tonight," he added to be on the safe side. One never knew what the day would bring.

Actually his father wasn't even in Rome. He was in Milan on business, but there was small chance of Donatella's discovering it. She wasn't sneaky and prying like most girls, which was one of the reasons she had been chosen from the multitude. There were reasons of equal importance. Her parents and his parents were friends, so he was not only sure about her background but comfortable in it. She was twenty-three now. They had been engaged officially since she was eighteen, and he could be absolutely certain that she had never known another man. Moreover, he could be absolutely certain that she never would. She was submissive and sweet and devoted. She was pretty enough, although inclined to be heavy, which was all to the good. She was built for comfort, and what else did a husband want of a wife? The attractions of girls who looked good in bikinis and on the dance floor were strictly extramarital. As he had said the other night at the Bar Flaminia, there were two kinds of women, the kind to go to bed with and the kind to wake up with. Sergio Rea had observed that the latter category was getting smaller each day. And he was right. Pippo pictured his partner of the night before in pursuit of various domestic activities, overcooking the pasta, filing her long nails while some slovenly maid put carelessly ironed shirts with missing buttons into his drawer and pushing a carriage which held his son, a sublime being created in his exact image. *Mamma mia. Che schifo!* Not that a girl of that sort would ever be capable of producing such a splendid creature. He, himself, had made his entrance into the world between two solid pillars of flesh, and there was a great similarity in the way Donatella and his mother were built. He did not plan to marry for another four or five years, but under the house of Pippo La Rosa there would be no sand that might shift.

"And what are you going to do today, *tesoro*?" What name could be more appropriate? She was a treasure and one to be guarded with care. He finished his coffee as he listened attentively to her schedule. Shopping for dress material with her mother, lunch, and then the dressmaker with her mother again. Late afternoon she was going to her cousin Bianca's and because the weather was so nice perhaps they would take a walk. Pippo wasn't in favor of the walk, although he didn't say so. On the first beautiful spring day the number of motorized Romeos trying to pick up girls on foot would reach a menacing high. Not that he didn't trust her, but all women were given to behaving like geese, heedlessly wandering off after bait that was thrown out to them and getting lost before they knew it. Even the best of them needed constant control. Their flightiness was by no means confined to their relationship with the opposite sex. The way they flitted from one counter of a department store to an eye-catching display on another making impractical purchases revealed a bird-brained appreciation of economics that could quickly drive an unwary man to the poorhouse.

"Look," he said, "don't go for a walk until you hear from me. Papà may want to take a break and if he does I can pick you and Bianca up and we'll drive around until I have to come back. All right?" He didn't really need to ask. If there was any hope of seeing him she'd never stray out of earshot of the telephone. She would be at his disposal if he should want her and safely indoors if he didn't. He had no sympathy for cuckolds.

It was simple enough to keep women in line. Men who wore horns deserved to. "*Ciao, tesoro, ciao.*" He transmitted another series of kisses and hung up. "My shoes," he reminded the maid, who was on the point of exiting. "In ten minutes polished and back," he commanded as she left.

He took off his hair net, put it on the table and reached over to the chair to take his little black book from the pocket of his jacket. In his crowded agenda, business came first. He telephoned the camera shop that was developing the 35-millimeter film that he and Sergio Rea had made the day before and was told that it would be delivered to the palazzo around one o'clock. True, it was only a test, but it would be important as a guide for the real thing they would make that afternoon, and he insisted again to insure its delivery. Next he called the workman who was in charge of a small crew that was packaging their product. Choosing a name hadn't been easy, but they had finally decided on Go-Go Grow because it sounded up-to-the-minute as well as if it were an American import. He was told that the bags, except for a last few dozen, were stacked in the garage they had rented and ready to go. Pippo put the receiver in place, sank back on the pillows and closed his eyes, and a sea of Go-Go Grow sacks, filled to their plump two-hundred-pound capacity, flowed onto trucks which sped out of the city south into the countryside toward the small farming communities in Lazio, Campania, Puglie and Calabria, where they stopped in the main squares. The red-lettered posters flamed in the sun. The loud-speakers prophesied agricultural miracles to come, and on a screen set up on the truck's platform a film testified to many that had already taken place. Eager farmers waved lire notes in the air and fought for place in long queues. The trucks emptied as the little metal cash-boxes filled. Two hundred percent profit! When he and Sergio had made the calculation, deducting the expenses of labor and materials, and come up with the net figure, he had been truly frightened by the brilliance of his idea.

Looking back, it seemed so simple, but then he supposed so

did all inspirations of genius. The wonder was that the idea hadn't come to him sooner. He had simply been leaning against the bar at the Flaminia, the same as he had hundred of times, year in, year out, drinking a *cappuccino* and idly watching Luciano, who worked the *espresso* machine. Luciano had wrenched the little coffee container off the machine and banged it clean of the used grounds, which fell into a receptacle behind the bar. The disposal was nearly full. Pippo only half put his mind to the ultimate end of the dead grounds, assuming that they might be dried and, in diluted form, reused for some purpose. Coffee-flavored ice cream tasted only vaguely of coffee, and perhaps this was the source of the flavor.

"What do you do with those old grounds?" he had asked.

Luciano had shrugged. "Nothing. We throw them away."

There must be an Everest of coffee grounds somewhere, considering the hundreds of thousands of cups Romans consumed in a day. "Where?" he had asked.

"The spazzini take them."

Luciano had banged another little circle of grounds into the disposal, and Pippo had leaned over to examine them closely. They looked so neat. So clean. In fact they were clean, even sterile, because of the boiling water that had dripped through them. They definitely did not look like refuse. What they reminded him of was rich, dark soil. And it was right then that the idea had come to him in a sort of brain-scalding flash. Fertilizer! Ready-made, costless fertilizer. Costless to him, that was. To be sure, something would need to be added to disguise the true identity. A white powder seemed indicated. Plaster of Paris might do. It was cheap. What difference if it hardened and caked on the fields? He'd be miles away before it was ever discovered. Proper precautions would have to be taken against legal repercussions, naturally, but he wasn't in his final year of law school for nothing.

The telephone squealed and Pippo lifted the receiver, his eyes still closed. "*Pronto*," he answered, slowly returning from his kingdom of the future. "Eh. Sergio. *Ciao.*" He had given Sergio equal partnership in Go-Go Grow, even though it was all his idea, but then Sergio was his best friend, as close to him as any of his four brothers, closer in many ways, since his brothers were all married and tied to wives and children and desk jobs. It had been Sergio's idea to make the little film. Apart from being a sound selling gimmick, casting for the girl who was to take the leading and only role had afforded them weeks of inexpensive diversion. Nine of the marks in his little black diary represented interviews during which the obligations of aspiring actresses toward a producer had been clearly understood. Sergio had had six successful encounters. Not a bad average, considering that they had interviewed a total of thirty-five leading ladies. Ordinarily, Sergio's schedule was less flexible than Pippo's, but luckily the dealer in foreign cars for whom Sergio worked had been away for the past week, so his time was more or less his own. And so, during the day, were the automobiles the firm used for demonstration. Some of the credit for their success with the fledgling actresses was due to showy transport. It was curious how fast the virtuous pretensions of females broke down in a Jaguar. In a 600 Fiat hours had to be wasted in argument.

"Sì, *sì*," he said, in complete accord with a plan Sergio suggested to pass the time until after lunch, when the shooting of the film was to begin. They would drive in a Jaguar or a Mercedes to the airport and hang around for a while to see what dropped out of the sky. Gianni Sarti a friend of theirs, worked for an American airline there, and on fine days they frequently drove out for the screening of incoming female tourists who were traveling without escort. Gianni couldn't jeopardize his job by official introductions of any sort, but the very fact that they appeared on intimate terms with a trusted employee was enough to quell the misgivings of timid travelers. "I'll be waiting for you down at the gate at eleven," he told Sergio. In a Jaguar or a Mercedes they could speed down the Via del Mare and be in Fiumicino just as the heaviest international traffic would be coming through customs. "*Ciao,* Sergio. *Ciao, caro,*" he said and hung up.

He leapt out of bed and crossed the hall to the bathroom. He squatted on the bidet and lathered himself well, meanwhile giving thought to what he would wear. Whipcord pants, he decided, a cashmere sweater and his tweed jacket with the leather elbow patches. He would seem to be idle and rich, whereas in a conventional suit and tie he would look employed or, at best, in dogged pursuit of some profession, not at all in keeping with the spirit of airport scouting. No, no. The more casual the better. Lorenzo Salvini never wore a suit in the daytime. Not that the Salvinis were rich. He happened to know from his father that they just about made ends meet, but nevertheless Lorenzo Salvini looked rich and had the attitude of a rich man, which counted for a lot. Lorenzo Salvini was the first man he had ever seen wearing elbow patches. He had copied the idea, not because he admired the man in any way, but because he had recognized the effectiveness of it. An ordinary middle-class wage earner wouldn't dare risk looking poor. Only the rich could afford to look seedy. Or, in the case of the Salvini, only a man who came from a privileged background. Not that he envied that, certainly. The aristocrats had a past. There was no refuting that. And they could keep it. What good was a past? He had something that had real value. A future.

He turned on the spray of the bidet, and as the water washed away the soap, his male organ and the dense forest of black curls surrounding it emerged in dewy, downy freshness. He held it tenderly in his hand and peered closely for any signs of deterioration. Movable and stationary parts all seemed to be in perfect order. It was a muscle, for the love of heaven. And any fool knew that the more a muscle was exercised the stronger it became. They had all decided that in their teens. He had to laugh, remembering that Gianni Sarti had taken the theory so seriously he'd got himself caught in a milk bottle and had to summon the doctor. He hadn't thought of it in years. He'd bring it up later at the airport and it would be good for a few laughs. He pulled the plug and the old pipes gargled and choked and gargled and choked as they swallowed the water and suds. His voice rose above them in song as he started to shave.

Nothing about the ceremony was in any way as Anna had imagined it would be. The lace that trimmed Father Ignazo's surplice had never figured in her thousands of projections of the moment she was now living. But it was the lace she was seeing most of all. It was so close that the pattern was enlarged and defined as if she were observing it through a magnifying glass. It had been mended in one place. She tried at least to keep her attention on an area where the design was uniform, but it kept coming back to the mended place. The lace moved away and its pattern became indistinct. She lowered her eyes and saw her own hands. Waxy, clasped, dead hands. In her fright she pressed her palms even closer together and her hands whitened the more. She slanted a glance to her right. The ivory brocade that she saw covered her own arm. The blue serge that was almost touching it covered the arm of Riccardo. She tried to give the materials and the arms they clothed some relationship to each other, but she couldn't think above her rising panic. Father Ignazio was speaking; his words had no meaning. She should look up but she couldn't move her head. She felt herself slipping away from herself. She closed her eyes and fought to keep from sobbing aloud for the Anna that was forsaking her. She was terrified of this unfamiliar being she was becoming. She wanted herself back. She wanted the Anna she had always been. If she ran from the church, across the street, through the gate, into their door, she could be that Anna again. She could be safe in her bed in the corner while her father and mother slept in theirs behind the curtain, so near to her. Here in the church they weren't with her in any true sense. They were behind her, far behind her, in such a way that they could never again catch up with her. When she was seven years old her father's father had died, and they had gone on the train to Vittorio Veneto for the funeral. The train had been crowded, so her father had found a place for her and her mother in one of the cars, and he had gone to sit back in another car behind them. She had awakened in the middle of the night and cried and rubbed her wet eyes against the rough sleeve of her mother's coat because she was afraid the car her father was in would never catch up with theirs and he would be lost forever.

It was like that now. As it had been on the train, the three of them were fixed and moving at the same time. And she was ahead. And it would be so forevermore. Behind her some place her father sat in his stiff, dark suit with his arms folded, his eyes on her. Beside him was her mother in her navy silk with the white dots, her hands in her lap and her fingers twined in the rosary. And never again would it be the three of them together. They were there and she was here ahead of them, and it would be that way always and always. They were back there with each other and she was here ahead of them. Alone. Alone with Riccardo.

Another time the lace on Father Ignazio's surplice came nearer and nearer and she sought the place where it was mended. As long as she looked for it she needn't think of Riccardo. During the seconds she searched for the mended spot she could stay detached from the dreadful fear that was turning her to stone. Concentrating on the lace she could almost forget Riccardo's presence. Riccardo. Father Ignazio was marrying her to Riccardo. Now. Now while she looked for the mended spot, Father Ignazio was marrying her to a man named Riccardo Lauria. The man was here beside her but she couldn't remember one of his features or the sound of his voice or the feel of him. Or how he smelled. She leaned just slightly to the right, so slowly it couldn't be noticed. She took a deep, secret breath and identified the incompatible odors of moth balls and after-shave lotion. She drew back and her body stiffened as it sometimes did during her most fervent prayers. Father

Ignazio was questioning Riccardo Lauria and Riccardo Lauria was making his affirmative answer with the voice of a man who had only that instant learned to speak. It was a voice she did not recognize as one she had ever heard before.

And now Father Ignazio was addressing her. The time had come when she was compelled to look up. The weight of her head seemed too great for her neck to support and lifting it was torture, but little by little she managed to raise her chin. Her eyelids were heavy as if they had been closed in a profound sleep. She knit her fingers together so tightly that the bones touched through the skin, filled her lungs with the perfume of incense and opened her eyes wide. Father Ignazio was smiling down at her, gently nodding encouragement. She murmured her reply, but she couldn't hear it above the sound of her pounding heart. Her heart was thundering out the seconds that were left and when the final moment came she knew it would burst. It roared in her ears and deafened her to what Father Ignazio was telling her to do. She felt a touch at her elbow and her head made an involuntary jerk to the right.

Riccardo. Oh, Riccardo, she sighed to herself within herself. You are here. I am not alone. I am with you. We are together. Her pulse beat slackened and the terrible ache in her shoulders eased away. *Amore*, Riccardo, *amore*, she sighed within herself again. He had nicked his chin shaving and a fine line of dried blood was just barely visible under a coating of talcum. *Amore mio*, she whispered to him through closed lips, and the hand she held out scarcely trembled.

Riccardo slid the wedding band over the nail Ersilia had tinted with polish of the faintest pink. The ring caught the light from the long tapers and she watched the rays spread out and out until all the world seemed washed in purest gold.

Thank God it was over. Caroline side-stepped out of the pew and headed for the door. The Protestant God of her childhood would have struck her dead for the thoughts that had boiled around in her head during the ceremony. At its start she had tried to emerge from her state of shock and establish the mood of reverence and romance the occasion wanted. A sweet girl who looked as if she had been created after a design by Raphael was marrying a man who might have been her twin. They were in love. This rite represented the beginning of something quite wonderful. She knit her brow to tie these facts together, but the ends kept coming loose. Each time a bobbing altar boy rang a little bell she felt a snap somewhere behind her forehead, and she finally gave up. What she was witnessing was the beginning of nothing but the end. If that poor deluded kneeling girl had the remotest inkling of what was in store for her, she'd flee screaming. It was not a sacrament. It was a sacrifice. How fitting that she be robed in white as she was offered up.

As she neared the door, she saw that the sun was doing its best to penetrate the dank confines of Santa Maria del Portico, but it had advanced only a few inches beyond the threshold, and she knew it was destined to reach no further even in midsummer, since the entrance lay at the bottom of the canyon formed by the Palazzo Salvini and the church itself. She had noticed that on gray winter days there was no perceptible difference between the atmosphere within the church and that outside, but today as she went through the door she stepped abruptly from one season to another.

Even so, it was still too early for the sun to have gained full strength. Members of the wedding party and guests stood about in album-like groups, looking like overexposed photographs in the bright white light. She went up to the bride and groom and shook Riccardo's hand. "I know you'll be very happy," she told Anna, and felt like Judas as she kissed her on each cheek, remembering how she had babbled on about the spiritual blessings of marriage and the rewards of motherhood when Anna had shyly announced her engagement to Riccardo. She shook hands all around, uttered the usual optimistic prophecies, smiled until her jaws hurt, and escaped at last.

She crossed to the palazzo gate and looked into the courtyard. The 600 was gone, so Lorenzo had evidently left some time during the ceremony. He had another urgent business conference and wouldn't be home for lunch, he had told her, and she had smiled her sweetest smile before he kissed her forehead farewell.

She went briefly into the palazzo. Once out through the gate again, she turned and headed up the Via della Scimmia toward the Corso Vittorio. She walked briskly and her thoughts kept pace. Since she had never lied to him before, Lorenzo had had no reason to doubt her excuse of an upset stomach and bad dreams the night before. Finding her asleep with Andrea in her arms had brought such a mist of tenderness to his eyes that she had been half disposed to believe that his faithlessness existed only in her imagination. She had even determined to re-examine the evidence against him as they had their coffee in the nursery with the children. It *could* be that he was really involved until the small morning hours of these last two weeks with the men who wanted to buy a parcel of land belonging to the villa to make a golf club as he had professed. It *might* be that he had been telling the truth about intending to have lunch at the villa and then changing his mind and eating instead in a trattoria near the villa with the prospective buyers. It was highly irregular for him to have had lunch near the Villa and not to have gone to the villa itself, as she had found out from Domenico when she had telephoned there that day, but there *could* have been a good reason.

She had put the two teaspoons of sugar in his coffee and stirred it as she always did, and as she had started to withdraw her hand he had caught it and kissed her wrist. She had lowered her eyes and gone back to her thinking. The men who coveted the Salvini acres *must* exist, as it would be impossible to invent a group bent on so ridiculous an enterprise. Rome already had one golf club of sorts, which had always struck her as being as out of character as a football stadium in the Fiji Islands or a tennis club in Lapland.

Beatrice had had a fit of coughing while Lorenzo held her on his lap, and he had looked from her to Miss Vaughn, sincerely alarmed. When she refused to drink the hot chocolate she ordinarily bolted down, he began to wonder if the doctor shouldn't be called. Could it be that a man who loved his children so would take risks with their future happiness? She was condemning him solely on circumstantial evidence, she warned herself, almost convinced that her wretched, sleepless night was due to physical indisposition, as she had told him. The more she had thought about it, the more she had realized she had nothing concrete on which she could base a verdict.

And, if it hadn't been for Andrea's tricycle, perhaps she never would have. Thank God she and not Miss Vaughn had loaded it into the back seat of the Fiat. It had given her a chance to poke the loathsome, tacky bit of trash down along the side of the seat, from which it might easily slither onto the floor. She had first planned to fish it out and dispose of it somewhere as she drove back from the Gianicolo, but somehow her mind had gone blank until she reached the palazzo, and then Luisa had been waiting.

She found a taxi at the stand before Chiesa Nuova. "The American Consulate on Via Veneto," she gave the address, got inside and, as they drove off, took off the little pillbox she had worn for the wedding and crammed it into her pocketbook. She combed her hair and made a critical appraisal of her face in the hand mirror. Miraculously, there were no circles under her eyes. They were blue and serene and even appeared rested, for all the slight burning she still felt underneath the lids. And her color was good. She snapped the mirror back into its little case and closed her bag.

"You are American, signorina?" the driver asked.

You bet I am, she thought to herself and aloud said, "Sì." There had once been talk of her giving up her citizenship and passport. Bless her father for having persuaded her not to and for having suggested she go through the necessary formalities of registering each of the children as American citizens when they were born, because if it was their birthright to have dual nationality he felt it was wrong to deprive them of it. Lorenzo had grumbled about it, but finally given in. This was the only argument with Lorenzo she could remember ever having won.

The taxi pulled up where the American Embassy and the American Consulate stood side by side. She paid the driver, crossed the sidewalk that was the property of the Italian State and, as she stepped through the Consulate gate onto soil that was officially American, felt a distinct and vigorous stirring of roots, long hibernated. Her chin automatically inched forward and up.

The elevator rose as if borne on wings, and she thought contemptuously of the groaning, creaking cage in the Palazzo Salvini. The doors slid noiselessly back and she was conscious of the crisp, efficient workings of American know-how behind the doors that gave off the reception hall. The young man at the desk, an Italian, remembered her from times of passport renewals.

"Good morning, Marchesa Salvini," he said. "What can we do for you on this beautiful day?"

"I should like some information about passports. For my children. I'm thinking of taking them home on a holiday." She faltered a bit trying to sound offhand, but he didn't seem to notice.

"Of course," he said. "Just one minute and I'll see if Mrs. Aiken is in."

While she waited she took apart the features of Richard Nixon, whose photograph hung behind the reception desk, and then reassembled them.

"If you'll be seated for just a few minutes," the young man said upon returning, "Mrs. Aiken will be free."

She sat down on a small sofa covered with gray plastic and treated the American flag to the same examination she had just given the President. It had never looked quite right to her since the stars had been rearranged to accommodate the addition of those representing the new states. It would be better not to prepare the little talk she would have with Mrs. Aiken. She had rehearsed her request to the receptionist beforehand and it hadn't come off at all as she had planned. It certainly wasn't the first time an American mother had applied for passports for her children. She crossed her legs, which had taken to shaking at the knees. The young Italian's eyes slid away from the paper on which he was scribbling and traveled along the floor to her feet and up over her ankles. When he got just past her shins, she uncrossed her legs again and placed her knees together and resumed her research on the flag. Which was the last state that had been admitted? Hawaii or Alaska? It was quite shocking she didn't know, come to think of it.

"Mrs. Salvini, Mrs. Aiken can see you now."

Caroline looked up at a girl who stood in the doorway through which the young Italian had gone to and fro shortly before. Ah, thought Caroline, there's someone who knows about Hawaii and Alaska and the population of the capital cities of all the other states, to boot.

"You are Mrs. Salvini, aren't you?" The girl's nasal voice minced out accusingly through thin lips.

"Oh, yes. Yes, I am." Indeed that was who she was here, and even Mrs. Lorenzo Salvini, as she had been occasionally on letters that had come to her from the United States, always to Lorenzo's dismay, for as many times as she had explained to him that an American wife also takes her husband's given name he had never been able to make it stick in his mind. "Thank you," she said, a little nasally herself and, she hoped, democratically, and went inside.

When Randy woke up for the second time he felt almost good. The more he thought about it the less sense it made. All yesterday's problems were still unsolved and he had even added a couple of new ones. Now that he had given Lisa the thousand lire he was really flat broke. In the back of his mind he had always thought that if worst came to worst he coula borrow from Caroline Salvini. Now that was out. Maybe she hadn't seen him take Lisa out to the taxi, but then with his luck she probably had. When he first caught sight of her in the window he had thought it was Vespa Virgin Vaughn, which would have been more or less okay, since he and Charlie had caught her on her day off riding on the back of a Vespa, holding on for dear life to a creep with a longish tangle of black curls, not exactly the type Lorenzo Salvini would approve of as the kind of company for his children's nurse to keep. She had come to them practically in tears and asked them not to tell as if they would have anyway, and sworn that she got lost and asked the creep the way and he had offered her a lift and that there was nothing "between them." He and Charlie had figured there probably was or she'd never have brought the subject up. The black, apy creep with all that hair and Vaughn with that pinky-white English skin that some people thought was so great but always looked to him like the girl was running a slight temperature. Jesus. It was a mating worthy of a horror story.

In any case, if it had been Caroline at the window and not Vaughn, that was something he had to get squared away fast. All he needed was for her to write a letter to his mother, and his mother would be on the first plane for Rome. Maybe even his father. His mother was usually okay about not telling his father things, but this would be enough of a blow to make her cry and his father would want to know why, and before she could get hold of herself it would come out.

He didn't know how he would go about convincing Caroline, but he'd think of some way. It was funny, but he had a weird feeling that it was one of those days when things would work out. It'd been a helluva long time since he'd had that kind of hunch. The number one reason was probably because he could see a patch of blue sky through the high window. He'd nearly forgotten what blue sky looked like. He could take a certain amount of bad weather, but day after gray day had really depressed him. That and the booze. He'd gone to bed stoned practically every night for a week. It was a miracle that his head no longer ached, nor his stomach, which was growling around to be filled. His neck was a little stiff from sleeping in the armchair, but he would work that out in the shower. Once he had shaved and dressed and gone to the corner bar, where he could get coffee and a brioche on the cuff, he'd take a walk somewhere and sit in the sun and think. Heading the list of what he had to think about was Maria Pia. He'd had all the crap from her he was about to take. He took it as an encouraging sign that he was even now thinking of her with detachment, whereas she had heretofore always entered his mind accompanied by the urges of a sex maniac.

He thought he heard someone banging on the door while he was under the shower, and he turned the water off and listened and decided he had been wrong and turned the water on again. He soaped himself thoroughly, beginning with his head and working down. He rinsed, repeated the process, tested his hair for soapless squeaks and shut the water off. Someone was banging on the door now for sure. He grabbed a towel, wound it about himself loin-cloth fashion, jammed his feet into rubber beach sandals and stepped lightly out of the bathroom and across the living room to the door. If it was Caroline Salvini he wasn't yet prepared for the encounter, and he'd pretend to be out.

He put his ear to the crack and waited for some sound other than his own breathing. A moment later Charlie's voice pierced the keyhole at about his heart level and he jumped back. "Hey, Ran. Ran!" He heard Charlie thump some object against the outer door handle, which responded with a metallic cry, and then shuffle away several paces and call out, "*Auguri, saluti.*" He was either yelling at someone in the cortile or he was still drunk. Both, probably, Randy guessed with disgust. He clutched the towel ends tighter with his left hand, ground his teeth behind stretched lips, drove his right hand at the door in a fist and then opened his fingers and jerked the creaky, iron latch. He held the door slightly ajar and craned his neck around it, keeping his body out of sight.

Charlie was facing away from him, brandishing an opened beer bottle. A second, unopened bottle was tucked under his arm. Courtyard center, Anna's wedding party posed in tight formation for a photographer who had fixed his camera on a tripod. Even the most fashionable wedding photographs struck Randy as looking old-fashioned, but this had a peasanty quality that made it seem even more so. Gino was so rigid in his black suit that he seemed upholstered, and his wife and the old-maid sister wore dresses with hemlines at least six years behind the current style. Charlie's Porsche in the background looked as if it had mistakenly gone into reverse and backed into another century.

"*Auguri!*" Charlie made the liter bottle of Nastro Azzuro circle and flash in the sun high above his head.

Randy craned his head out further and hissed and Charlie spun around. "Jesus, I thought maybe you were dead in there," Charlie said. His eyes were bloodshot but focused, so he wasn't drunk. "Come on out and drink a toast to the bride and groom."

Randy longed for arms that could extend the four yards that separated him from Charlie, and his hands actually itched to encircle Charlie's neck. "Get in here." He measured his words to travel the distance between them and land with force so accurately that his cheeks hurt.

"Okay, okay." Charlie put on his amiable smile. "What big teeth you have, Grandmother." He passed through the door and around Randy and headed for the armchair, at ease as an emperor approaching a throne. His jeans rode low to the falling-off place on his protruding hip bones, and his shirttail hung out below a rusty-brown pullover.

Randy conducted him to the chair with a look of loathing and went back to the bathroom without a word. He took a can of spray deodorant from the shelf over the basin and shook it against his ear to detect some sign of life.

"I brought you a beer." Charlie put the unopened bottle on the table beside the chair.

It was one of the rare times in his life that Randy hadn't the good manners to acknowledge a gift, and he stole a glance out of the corner of his eye to see what effect it would have on Charlie. It didn't surprise him that it had none at all. Randy aimed the deodorant tin at his left armpit and pressed down. The little spigot spat out a thin spray. Randy bore down again, but the pressure was spent and only a few drops drooled from the little lip. Randy distributed these over the area under his left arm and banged the can down. He went into the other room and opened the top drawer of a bureau, his back to Charlie.

"My head feels like it's about to explode," Charlie said.

The odor of musty old wood rose up from the drawer. Randy picked over a nest of socks that were coiled in one corner. He believed he had succeeded in matching a good pair until he noticed that one had a hole in the toe. By the end of the day his nail would have it worked to the size for his toe to fit through and he'd be out of his mind. At the rate it was warming up he didn't need socks anyway. He zigzagged the swollen drawer shut and zigzagged the one below it open.

"It feels like it's liable to crack right down the middle," Charlie said.

Randy stared at the two dress shirts that clothed little cardboard corpses the laundry had laid out complete with paper bow ties. He had worn them a time apiece, one to the opening of the opera to which he had escorted Lorenzo's cousin, Patricia Salvini, a terrible girl with flying hands who had run squealing from one group to another during the intermissions, dragging him by the hand and introducing him to lounging louts with crazy names like Gigi and Fuffo and Buby. Fuffo's father, it was explained to him later, owned the other half of Rome that the Vatican didn't own. His title wasn't really "good" but it was clear that his father's holdings went a long way to making up the deficit.

He had worn the other shirt to a Christmas party that Elisabetta Colombo had given. The place had been lousy with footmen and waiters in knee pants. The chandeliers sparkled and there were candles all over the place, and the way they lit up the frescoed walls and painted ceilings, he had to admit, was pretty great. It made it easy to imagine how the palazzo must have been in its heyday. The Gigis and Fuffos and Bubys and girls with flying hands were thick as flies and went flitting from one salon to another. There was an orchestra in the big main reception room. It was pretty Meyer Davis, but then half the guests had a foot in the grave, so it figured. He danced with Patricia Salvini and a couple of other girls just to be nice, but he could only speak a few words of Italian then, so he had mostly sat on a skinny-legged gilt settee talking to an American woman who was there he'd never understand why, except that Italians seemed to have no standards for judging Americans aside from money.

"They really are gorgeous people," the American woman had said and asked him if he didn't agree, and he'd said he did. *Principesse, duchesse, marchese* and *contesse* were dripping with necklaces and bracelets and had tiaras and ornaments and things stuck in their hair. The Principessa Colombo was so weighted down with jewelry she looked like a hippopotamus about to submerge. "Fabulous," the American woman had said three times. The spectacle had plainly taxed her vocabulary to its limits. She told him her name was Study. Cora Study. Cora! Good God! Mrs. Study, as if he might have it in mind to make a pass at her if she were Miss Study. She had a diamond about the size of a paperweight on her left hand and a black dress with a lot of involved panels that his mother called a "better-lady's dress" that they bought on those hushed floors in department stores like Saks and Bonwit's where no one else ever got off the elevator.

About midnight there had been a fanfare, and a character who was the ringleader in one of the monarchist parties that was hoping to reinstate the king had babbled something, and a solemn quiet had fallen and glasses had been raised.

"They're going to drink a toast to the king." Cora Study had blinked her mascara in rapture. "Yeah, of the Golden River," he had answered. The mascara had lowered in disdain and she had pursed her lips so that the little spokes that flew out from around them deepened and she had lifted her glass, too. You, Cora Study, of all people, he had thought. Under a monarchy women who say "fabulous" and "gorgeous" get sent back to the scullery, and fast. He had looked about and observed that the candidates for the funny farm were in the minority, but not by a lot. Those who weren't had worn indulgent smiles and scornful smirks, and Lorenzo Salvini had pin-pointed the proposer of the toast from under lowered eyelids, as if he were sighting him down a gun barrel. The screwball toastmaster had smashed his glass, and Cora Study had realized just in the nick of time she wasn't to follow suit and that the one glass was symbolic for all. He'd made his escape about the time the footmen were due to be turned back into mice, and gone to the Pipistrella. It was the night he had met Maria Pia.

"As usual, it's the fault of The Bitch," Charlie said. "No. I couldn't sleep this off in peace. She's got to call me from Paris at nine. Nine A.M."

There were ten clean Brooks shirts in two stacks in the drawer with the dress shirts. Two of them his mother had sent at Christmas and had never been worn. Maria Pia had screamed and covered her head with the sheet the first time she had seen him Brooks-shirted and pantless. He hadn't had a clue as to what had got into her. A few seconds later, she had thrown off the sheet and jumped out of bed, wearing nothing but little lace panties, and made circles around him like a savage who has just captured his first missionary. She had pulled the shirt out in back until it bulged like a spinnaker and run around to the front and done the same and clapped her hands and thrown back her mane of hair that was the mixed-up colors of autumn leaves and laughed with her mouth open so wide he could see all the way to her back molars and noted for the first time that she didn't have one single filling.

"I wish you'd tell me what's so damn funny," he had said and, still laughing, she had ducked down and come up inside the shirt next to him, her head through the front opening. He had wrestled her over and onto the bed and kissed her laughing mouth shut, tearing hell out of the shirt, naturally, and then demanded she tell him what it was all about.

"But it ees so *buffa*, your shirt, like the shirts very old men wear at night, only short, ees *buffa, ridicola.*" He worked it out that *ridicola* must mean ridiculous, but he still hadn't seen why. That was one of the things about her. She was only seventeen and he was twenty-one and she always managed to make him feel he was about six. She had snatched the tail of the shirt and ripped it all the way up the back. "Ees too big, ees big enough for you and me to get in it." And, of course, fool that he was, she had him at a shirt maker's the next day getting measured up for a form-fitting shirt like the wops wore. She made him get six, and they had cost him ninety bucks. And then she had carried on about his shoes, how they were so thick-soled and heavy he looked like he was going hunting, and she had caused him to fork out another fifty bucks for two pairs of shoes. When he made his first appearance in the shirt and shoes, plus some pants she had insisted on that covered his ass like Scotch tape, she had slithered her eyes up and down him in ecstasy. "You look so sexy," she breathed. "And also like I'm about to do the tango," he had said.

"Maybe if I hold some ice on my eyes," Charlie said.

Well, screw Maria Pia. All six wasp-waisted shirts were dirty and in a heap on the floor of the *armadio*. He took a light blue Brooks shirt from the drawer and started to unbutton it.

"Yeah. Ice." Charlie got out of the chair and shuffled toward the kitchen.

Randy renewed a resolution to ignore him. Sooner or later it was bound to penetrate his thick skull that he was carrying on a monologue and the faster he got the hell out the better for him. Randy thrust his arms into the sleeves, and as he pulled the body of the shirt down over his head an ominous cracking sound came from the kitchen. His chin emerged above blue poplin and squared with apprehension, which was almost immediately justified by a thundering crash that set off successive waves of lesser tinny crashes and breaking glass. Charlie uttered no sound, and Randy approached the kitchen door cautiously, preparing himself for the sight of blood, even death.

Charlie was leaning against the sink examining a cut on his finger which Randy saw at a glance was little more than a scratch. The door of the refrigerator swung open wide and the entire freezing compartment lay on the bottom level of the box. It had cut through the metal slats of the shelves, and jagged chrome edges stuck out at wild angles. He took a step forward and a sticky piece of glass which had been part of a marmalade jar ground beneath his rubber sandal. A trickle of what seemed to be blood oozed from the refrigerator wall and dripped onto the floor, and Randy gave Charlie's wound a second look and then realized that the substance was ketchup. A wicked tangle of wires had been pulled loose, and one of them was still attached to the compartment, which was so covered with frosty ice it looked like a miniature igloo.

"I wouldn't touch anything," said Charlie, with all the calm of a police inspector. "Those wires are probably still connected."

"Christ," Randy said. "I just can't believe it. It's just too goddam much." He stared at the refrigerator and then at Charlie and then at the refrigerator once more. The incredible part of it all was that he had frequently wondered if the whole freezing unit, which seemed to be so precariously suspended in old-fashioned machines of this sort, ever did fall, and now it had actually happened.

"I could have lost my finger," Charlie said. "Or even my whole hand." He held his finger under the tap and ran the water. "Have you got a Band-Aid?"

Randy leaned against the wall. He truly felt the need of support. "Would you mind repeating that?" he said.

"I asked you if you had a Band-Aid." Charlie flicked the water off his finger and dried it carefully on the tail of his shirt.

"Do you realize what you've done? Can it be possible that

anyone who isn't completely one hundred percent off his rocker can have deliberately demolished a huge goddam refrigerator and half a kitchen and stand there and calmly ask for a Band-Aid?"

"Whatta you mean 'deliberately'? I simply pulled the stupid ice-cube tray and the whole damn thing came crashing down."

"Absolutely, completely destroyed a big expensive thing like a refrigerator. No one would believe it. You just couldn't get anyone to believe it."

"Oh, for God's sake, Ran, come off it. It's a crappy, crumby old thing that's about a hundred years old. They haven't made Frigidaires like that since I was a kid."

"That's not the point," Randy shouted. He seldom raised his voice, and whenever he did he surprised himself more than anyone else.

"Well, what is the point?"

"The point is that it's not mine. Whether it's a hundred years old or brand-new has nothing to do with it. I rent this apartment and am solely responsible for everything in it."

"Okay, so we'll . . ."

"But of course you wouldn't understand that. Not you. You never felt responsible for anything or anybody in your life. It's beyond your comprehension." Randy's spine stiffened as he stood up straight. The best way to win this kind of an argument was with a few well-placed punches.

"Not at all. I understand perfectly. This precious antique belongs to the old fart of a Marchesa and you're worried that she'll think you busted it, and . . ." Charlie sighed and went on complacently investigating his wound.

"You think you can go through life banging up cars and furniture and doing whatever you goddam please and get away with it, don't you?" The refrigerator was emitting a cold, rancid smell. He glared at the top of Charlie's head and considered the satisfaction it would give him to lift him by his fine, pale hair and shake him like a puppet. "Don't you?"

"Oh, brother." Charlie rolled his eyes upward in mock martyrdom. He laid his injured finger in the palm of his hand and shuffled past Randy out of the room.

The refrigerator made a croaking sound and then another as what Randy judged to be *rigor mortis* set in. He had no idea what the cost of a new one might be, but the sum of two hundred dollars came to haunt him. He left the kitchen and shut the rancid smell behind him. Charlie was enthroned in the armchair once more swigging on the beer bottle, and Randy lunged across the room. "Stop drinking!" He had meant to yell but his throat was so constricted with fury it strangled the words. He snatched the bottle out of Charlie's hand and slammed it down on the table.

"Well, look who's talking." Charlie folded his arms and leaned back. "It wasn't me who passed out last night, if you'll remember."

"Don't make the mistake of thinking I've forgotten last night." The red wig jumped its flimsy mental block and glued itself again to Randy's fingers. "I ought to kill you for leaving that girl here."

"What have you got against Lisa?"

"I haven't got anything against her. I'm not talking about Lisa. I'm talking about you."

"You're just pissed off because she's black. Supposing it had been some girl like Maria Pia? That would have been different, wouldn't it?"

The trouble with talking to lunatics, Randy reflected, was that there was just enough truth in their arguments to distort the issues. "As a matter of fact it would have been different. Because a white girl wouldn't have the disadvantage of being colored."

"The way I see it, colored girls and white girls are just the same. I never even think about Lisa's being black."

"The hell you don't. You think about it all the time. And she thinks about it too. You get a big bang out of walking down the Via Veneto with your arm around Lisa, shocking the wops and the American tourists. You don't give a damn for

Lisa. And that goes for all the other self-appointed promoters of equality like you. If any of you really cared about Negroes the last thing you'd do would be to drag them to parties and places where everyone else is white and they are in the minority but good, and everyone sneaks stares at them or puts on the big act like you that they don't see any difference at all."

"Who says it's an act?"

"Nobody. Naturally not. That's the whole deal. To keep up the farce. The white people all bend over backwards being super-polite and trying to act natural, and the poor Negroes put up a big front, talking too much or laughing too loud to make it seem they feel at home, or else they stay in some corner and keep quiet so people won't say they're pushy. And no matter how they play it they can't win. And all the time nobody's kidding anybody."

"That's the way you see it." Charlie wet the cut on his finger with his tongue.

"Because that's the way it is. How do you think that girl felt when she woke up this morning? Just the same as any white girl under the circumstances, I suppose. Especially since she was minus the crazy wig and stark naked. The first thing a white girl would think was that she was a tramp or if she didn't give a damn she'd laugh it off. But the first thing Lisa thought about was that she was colored and I was white. And that goes for me, too. Christ! That wig!"

"White girls wear wigs. Are you going to tell me Lisa hasn't got a right to wear a wig just because she's black?"

Lurking around in the back of his mind Randy was pretty sure there was an answer to this but he refused to be side-tracked. "What I can't understand is why they let themselves in for things like this. Jesus, if I were a Negro you'd have to drag me to a white party in chains. And if people like you were so all-fired interested in them as you pretend to be, you'd have the decency not to shove them into situations where they get embarrassed and humiliated. Anyone who isn't demented can see that all it does is set back their cause about a hundred years. But the thing is, you're *not* interested in them. Deep down you couldn't care less. What all of you are interested in is yourselves. A lot of goddam show-offs, getting attention. Leading your own little half-assed private rebellions. Against everything and for nothing behind a lot of phony togetherness." Although he continued to glower down at Charlie, the urge to beat him up had gone. The funny thing was that he didn't feel like himself. It was uncanny, but who he felt like was his Old Man. He even felt that he looked the way his Old Man looked in the morning sometimes when he'd come storming out of his bedroom half dressed, wearing a Brooks shirt and no pants and sounding off about something that had made him sore. Randy looked down at his legs, almost expecting to see long black socks secured by regimental-striped garters.

"Why don't you move to Mississippi?" Charlie asked.

"Why don't you wash your hair?" He saw Charlie across a long span of suddenly accumulated years.

"Get Mr. Clean. He's mean," Charlie chanted.

"You've worn that same stinkin' shirt and that rotten sweater for about a month."

"He hates dirt," Charlie chanted on. "He's mean, Mr. Clean. And also he won't let me have my beer."

Randy snatched the beer off the table and plumped it into his hand. "If you're determined to become an alcoholic, that's your affair. And be my guest." He took the bottle Charlie had brought for him and shoved it into Charlie's other hand.

"Mr. Clean is a reformed drunk, it would appear." Charlie took a long swallow and then put both bottles back on the table. "I realize we've about exhausted the subject, but how did Lisa get home?"

"On my last thousand lire, that's how." Randy turned and walked briskly toward the armadio to get his pants. His hunger pangs were digging in.

"Oh, gosh, well . . ." Charlie pulled a small wad of lire notes from his pocket and disengaged one. "I guess the least I can do is square that. And I'll get the world's first Westinghouse or whatever the hell it is fixed or get a new one or something. I didn't know you were broke. The hell of it is I'm just about broke myself. I've gotta use this for gas, but when The Bitch gets here . . . Jesus . . . " He looked at his watch. "Christ, I'm late. I'm supposed to meet The Bitch at the airport in about fifteen minutes. I won't get there on time and she'll be wild, after calling me all the way from Paris. Oh, hell." He got up and shot to the door. "You don't want to come along, I guess."

"No, thanks. I've got a lot to do."

"Yeah. Well, okay. So long." Charlie stepped outside and then stopped and spoke over his shoulder. "See you later."

The poor jerk is actually waiting for an answer, Randy told himself. "Sure, sure," he said. There he went again. Winding up as usual feeling sorry for someone he'd wanted to kill. The day had certainly started out lousy enough, but even so he still had the hunch things were going to work out.

The sun had already laid hand to the terrace of the penthouse and dried large patches of the yellow tile pavement. The serranda was raised and the double doors of the bedroom were wide open. The Contessa de Costa's breakfast tray was on the foot of the bed. It was made of pink wicker, and the little troughs at each side which held the Contessa's mail and the newspaper were empty. The morning's Paris *Herald Tribune* had been perused and dropped on the floor, and opened letters were scattered over the leopard spread. The door to what Beppe knew was the bathroom was closed. Ordinarily Beppe resented the intermission of the Contessa's bath and waited impatiently for her to reappear wrapped in her robe of white toweling, but her absence from the stage gave him the opportunity to pursue his investigation of the rug without the usual precautions.

He leaned far out over the Via della Scimmia, and his eyes traced the rug's design critically. Familiar as he was with the Contessa's boudoir, he had been unable to recall what her rug looked like when Gino had mentioned the lawsuit. Now he understood why. Garlands of faded flowers lay on a dusty background, a sad spectacle that reminded him of a sun-beaten August garden. No wonder it had made so little impression on him. The rug undoubtedly had value as an antique like the tapestries that were hung from the windows of the Palazzo Venezia on festival days, but he wouldn't give it house room. He squinted and peered more closely. True enough, there was an area extending about a half meter in from the door sill that was several shades darker than the rest of the rug, and it was edged by a jagged, rusty border similar to the boundaries on maps which marked the divisions of countries. Most certainly the rain had damaged the rug. But would the rain have entered if the Contessa had slept with the serranda and the windows closed as was customary? There were technicalities involved that warranted discussion. Not that he liked to take sides, but it would be wrong for him as a possible key witness in a forthcoming lawsuit to withhold evidence.

The door to the bathroom swung open, and Beppe very nearly lost his balance in his hurry to get back into the shadows. The Contessa was quite naked. She had a towel wound around her head like a turban, and her face was covered with a thick, white paste, as if she had fallen head first into a tub of freshly mixed plaster. It wasn't the first time he had seen her without clothes, but whatever she was up to now was a decided novelty. He had once seen her apply a like substance of sticky white to her legs. His sleuthing out the answer to that riddle had eventually led him to a pharmacist who had suspected it must be a product to remove hair. Could it be that the Contessa was bearded like so many of the women of southern Italy? His mother had had quite a mustache as well as a heavy growth of leg hair. It was a condition that he had seen exaggerated, but a certain amount of hair enhanced a woman's attraction. He had once caught his wife trying to shave under her arms with his razor and had strictly forbidden her ever to touch it again. The hair had grown back in, stiff at first as the bristles on a boar, but it had softened up as it lengthened.

The Contessa bent over the bed and riffled through the letters and papers with her right hand while she scratched her buttock with her left. She found what she was looking for, a sheet of paper that looked as though it might be directions such as are enclosed with medicines, and darted back into the bathroom.

Beppe would have liked to linger a while to see what change the treatment made in her, but he was also anxious to get to Anna's wedding dinner. Guests would soon be pouring into the Trattoria allo Spiedo, and the late-comers risked getting substitute dishes if rations ran short. He had gone with Gino to plan the menu a month before. The first course was to be Tullio's special *lasagna* made with spinach and *ricotta*, so light it fairly flew from plate to mouth. The very thought of it was enough to set his feet in motion.

Luisa would have preferred having an *aperitivo* at Babbington's or the Caffè Greco. Both were only a few steps away from Arden's. Going to the Via Veneto meant loading Elisabetta into the car for the trip up and unloading her once they got there. But Elisabetta had insisted, and Luisa had had to agree that it would be a shame to sit inside on the first day of sunshine.

Mario took the road winding up past the Casina Valadier to the Pincio, where a sight-seeing bus from Dusseldorf was groaning under a packaged tour and blocking the turn into the Villa Borghese.

"It's started," sighed Elisabetta. "Look at them. Packed in like heifers."

"They're always the first. The Germans," said Luisa, sliding her eyes along the bus windows at the women in printed cotton dresses whose beefy pink arms always looked to her as if they must feel sore. "Have you ever noticed that they wear cotton no matter what season of the year they come in?"

"Oh, I've noticed," Elisabetta said. "As if Rome were in the tropics. And the men wear socks with sandals. They are easily the least aesthetic race on earth."

Mario squeezed past the bus at last and turned at the huge circular flower bed, into which gardeners were setting pots of purple and pink and lavender and white cineraria toward the Porta Pinciana. The mechanized legions of modern Rome were storming the Aurelian wall with horn and bumper when they reached it. Accelerators roared with frustration and exhausts fumed poisonous gas. They were ten minutes getting through the narrow archway and onto the Via Veneto.

Mario double-parked and hurried out and around to open the door. Elisabetta was nearest it, and he helped her with her exit, a complicated performance which she executed sectionally. Her right foot went outside first, and when its toe touched ground, her right hip billowed and popped through the opening like an escaping balloon. Her left hip was third in the line of succession, and then, almost as if it were an afterthought and she had forgotten she had another leg, she reached back inside and took hold of it just under the knee, hoisted it out and set it beside its mate. No small amount of thigh was exposed in the process. and Luisa wished again that she had been firm about Babbington's.

"We will be a half hour or so," Luisa told Mario upon alighting. She consulted the clock on the street corner. "It's midday now, so right at this spot promptly at a quarter of one." The sun danced on Mario's ivory head as he inclined it, and she had taken a half-dozen steps toward the table she and Elisabetta spoke of as "ours" when she heard him call her name.

"The Principessa's scarf," he said, nearing her. "It had fallen on the floor of the car."

"Oh, thank you, Mario." She caught an end and flipped the scarf lightly from his hand. It surprised her that Elisabetta, who did have her shortcomings but unquestionably had exquisite taste, should have bought a turquoise scarf trimmed in black lace. And nylon lace at that. She smiled and it dangled from her fingers, fluttering back and forth as she stepped between the crowded tables. It took the shape of something other than a scarf slowly, like a bit of silk a conjurer puts into a hat and pulls out magically changed into a flag. A loop in the material had concealed what it really was, and she put her pocketbook under her arm and used both hands to straighten it out. But they are too small for Elisabetta, she thought, and then her blood rushed from her brain to her cheeks and her mental processes ceased entirely.

By the time their drinks came Luisa had persuaded herself that no more than a few seconds had elapsed between realizing what she held extended, clothes-pinned by thumb and forefinger, and ramming it into her pocketbook. It was madness to suspect she had occupied center stage in a bustling café for as long as it now seemed displaying a pair of women's underdrawers. Nevertheless, the tips of her ears continued to burn and reject most of Elisabetta's chatter.

"Who is it that allows all these disgusting signs to be put up?" Elisabetta toured the world at the invitation of TWA, Pan Am, Lufthansa, Swissair and BOAC and returned to her chair outraged. "Do you know?"

"Know what?" Luisa was trying to remember the expression on Caroline's face when she had brought the car back earlier.

"Why all this propaganda is allowed? Who is responsible?"

"Lorenzo says that enormous sums are paid to the city." Caroline was wearing a light blue suit, she did remember that.

"It used to be forbidden. It gets worse each year. Look. They even have ugly little signs scattered through the flower beds."

As Caroline was driving and the drawers were in the back of the car, she probably hadn't seen them at all. "They're beautiful," she said.

"Beautiful! You mean the beds, not the signs, I hope."

"Of course I mean the beds." She reached back and patted the fat white head of a hydrangea and wondered briefly how it was the gardeners contrived to keep the flowers along the street in full bloom, never in bud and never fading the whole year long. Miss Vaughn or one of the children could have found the thing and asked about it, though. That might easily have happened. Children found everything. "The signs are hideous."

"Isn't that the American boy who lives in your house?" Elisabetta asked.

"Where?"

"There. At the table in the sun below the kiosk."

"Oh, yes. Yes, it is." Luisa was reminded that Randy was two weeks behind in paying his rent, which she was counting on to cover the light bill.

"Ah, Elizabetta. Luisa, my dear." Francesco Casano raised Elisabetta's hand and then Luisa's, meanwhile taking in an exceptionally pretty pair of legs belonging to the girl at the next table. "How beautiful you're both looking."

Luisa was well aware that he was addressing the legs. It was a trick of his youth, and ordinarily Elisabetta reprimanded him with a weary sigh, but Elisabetta was clawing at the cellophane packet of almonds that had been served with the drinks. Thirty years ago Elisabetta and Cesco Casano had been wildly in love, and Elisabetta's nails would have been clicking to claw that girl's cheeks. Ah, now it came back to her. Caroline had been wearing dark glasses.

"Cesco," trilled Elisabetta, interrupting phase two of his ancient art of conquest, eyelids at half-mast and nostrils thin. She patted the chair beside her and he sat down.

There was no use speculating, anyway. Lorenzo had gone too far. Her role was clear. He must be stopped. And short of any climax.

"She's a very pretty girl, my love," said Elisabetta, "but you must have noticed that she is about seventeen. And you are . . ."

"Seventy," he said, eyelids again at half-mast, but in mourning.

Elisabetta covered the liver spots on the back of his hand with plump fingers, and the great sapphire she wore flashed in the sun. He smiled at her and put out the light of the ring with his other hand.

Was he remembering giving it to her a lifetime ago, Luisa wondered? And the invented story that it had been left her by an aunt? And their plans to run off together? But he had stayed with Amelia and the children, and poor impotent Guido Colombo had died believing in miracles, never knowing that Cesco was Giovanna's father. How quickly their passion could have turned to bitter ashes instead of this warm glow. Not that this little adventure of Lorenzo's could be compared. Luisa lifted the clasp of her pocketbook and peeked inside. What hideous, vulgar things they were, but better so. A girl who could have bought them wasn't to be taken seriously. It was certainly no one they knew.

The day was as near ideal as Pippo could have asked. It was too early in the season for the airport to be crowded. In another six weeks it would be steaming with guided tours and misguided tourists who had the misfortune to believe that the summer months were best for seeing Europe or to have their vacations coincide with the heat, a bedlam of baggage and bustle that precluded anything more than a hurried and superficial study of the potentialities of unattended female arrivals. Winter was worse, though. The few women who traveled alone were almost without exception on business, buyers for American stores and journalists from American newspapers and magazines, immediately identifiable by outsized pocketbooks with myriad compartments out of which stuck appointment books and notes and correspondence and the other trappings of their trades. Pippo gave them a wide berth, having once paid twelve-hour court to a woman named Vera Crumer who had told him she was a fashion coordinator. To this day he hadn't the remotest idea what a fashion coordinator might be, and far from a clear idea of what Vera Crumer had been. At first sight she had appeared to be about twenty-eight, brunette, average as to height and somewhat above average as to feature and figure. But, as the day wore on, and she had led him from one atelier to another with unsmiling determination, scratching down memorandums, fixing prices and consulting her wristwatch like a clocker at some sporting event, she had seemed to grow taller. Distrust of claims made by the artisans and manufacturers with whom she dealt had transformed the blue of her eyes to a steely gray, and suspicion that promised delivery dates would not be kept had pinched her nose and narrowed her lips. She had returned to normal at lunchtime and invited him to her suite at the Hassler. To eat, he imagined, and make love. Once there, she had explained that there was only time for a sandwich and that as soon as a telephone call came through from New York, it was back to work. He had assured her that no one worked until after the siesta, but she had proved him wrong. An appointment had been fixed for her for three before ever leaving New York, and he had exchanged commiserating looks, when they arrived at that unheard-of hour, with the ceramic manufacturer who was as groggy for want of a nap as he was, although certainly not as famished. A sandwich and a Coca-Cola. *Mamma mia!* At midday the La Rosa table creaked under the weight of heaping bowls of pasta. He and Vera had made a sexual contact of sorts along toward midnight in the back seat of his car on the Appia Antica. He could never have called it making love. It was more like the collision of two foreign bodies in outer space. Vera had clanked her teeth against his and shot her thin dry tongue back and forth at them like the fangs of a snake. He had been injected with enough venom to carry on to a conclusion and she had squealed with more pain than pleasure. It was the nearest he had ever come to a homosexual experience, he had told Sergio later.

The cream of the tourist crop chose spring and autumn. Every plane-load held the prospect of one or more subjects of interest who were not handicapped by tight budgets or committed to careers and fixed itineraries. Alitalia and Air France flights were due in, and Pippo searched the sky for a breakthrough. He found the observation deck at Fiumicino exhilarating in all seasons, and it never failed to revive the dreams he had had in his teens of becoming a pilot, of his triumphant entry into the airports of the world in uniform. Most any uniform other than that of a street cleaner fascinated women. In a way he still regretted never having realized that ambition, but in his fantasies he had always been on the ground, either leaving a successfully accomplished flight mission or walking with his copilot over the runway toward a challenging new one. The humdrum hours aloft between take-off and landing hadn't interested him. When he had thought of them at all, they were spent reading a mystery novel while his supreme authority was delegated to his first officer or the automatic control. He had been obsessed with his future in aviation for a year before its less attractive side was actually presented to him. It was on his first plane ride, a trip from Rome to Milan with his father. He had never known such terror before or since. Strangely, it had been a smooth passage through clear skies, but his panic had had nothing to do with weather. As nearly as he could remember, it was the result of his divorce from the firm ground on which he had always walked and the hopelessness of escaping the unnatural environment he had exchanged for it. A newspaper account he had once read of a plane that had exploded in mid-air had raced through his mind just before he fainted dead away. His father had sent him back to Rome by train, and he was at the moment as near to a plane as he had ever been since, or ever intended to be.

There was a scream from the sky as the nose of a jet ripped through it. The great silver fish streaked to earth and touched down with grace and then, out of its element, jerked along spasmodically like a hooked marlin.

"I wonder why other countries don't paint their colors on planes?" said Sergio.

"Because we thought of it first," Pippo said, casting a patriotic eye at the green, red and white fin. The ladder had been wheeled up and the belly was opening. Pippo put his theory to the usual test. It was that basically no one really enjoyed flying much more than he did. He had yet to see anyone on an incoming plane who didn't exit smiling. The sky shrieked again and an Air France jet plunged down.

"Let's go," Sergio said.

When a single plane-load came through customs, Pippo and Sergio surveyed the scene standing side by side, but they had learned it was better to take up separate stations when there were multiple arrivals. What one missed the other was likely to see. Since they couldn't very well communicate in words, because of the distance and din, they had worked out a system of signals. Pippo sent one now to Sergio, who shook his head and crossed his eyes. Sure enough, what was unmistakably a husband took the elbow of a blond girl Pippo had thought was alone. It was just as well, since Sergio had now spotted a much prettier possibility. Her attractions were special enough for Pippo to desert his post and wander over to Sergio's station for a joint appraisal. "No, no," Pippo said, following a quick study, and tapped his wrist. The woman was wearing a watch. Vera Crumer had worn a wristwatch. That alone was enough, but even before Vera he had detested women who were preoccupied with the time. He sauntered back to the Pan American enclosure and leaned against the counter. The backside of a small brunette held promise, but when she turned around she was disappointingly dish-faced. She gave him a twitching little smile as she passed by and he favored her with a wink, and then saw Sergio's eyeballs were rolling, a signal that he had caught sight of something really exceptional.

"*Una tardona,*" said Sergio, when they met each other halfway.

"Well, yes," conceded Pippo.

"How old would you say?" asked Sergio.

Pippo crooked his neck and squinted professionally. The woman was an unusually fine specimen of a breed that was familiar to him. He took in her shoes, bag and an armful of bracelets and hung a high price tag on all of them. Tall, slender, silver-blond, deep, deep tan. Skin firm and unlined. "Hmm," Pippo delayed his verdict. She carried a leopard coat over her arm, and her body moved beneath the loose silk-jersey dress as if it resented even that much confinement. "Thirty-eight." Pippo based his conclusion more on attitude than attribute. There were years of experience behind taking center stage as she had and perfecting that pretense of being oblivious of a gaping audience. "Maybe even forty."

"*Francese*," said Sergio, who had lived a year in Paris and was consequently in charge of public relations with French prospects.

"No. English or American." Pippo was certain. These were fields he handled.

"She's waiting for someone."

Ten minutes passed, during which a number of satellites went into orbit around the heavenly body on which Pippo felt he held first claim.

"Look at those cretins," said Sergio.

"Any minute one of them is going to try to pick her up." For the most part the competition was poor, but there was a well-dressed man about the age of Pippo's father who was a definite threat. "Wait for me at the car," he directed, and set out on what appeared to be a casual stroll. He was several yards from the woman when she took a cigarette from a gold case. He was only a few feet away when his chief competitor fumbled around in the pocket of his jacket and extracted a packet of matches. Pippo timed his steps to breeze past his adversary, extinguish the flame in the middle-aged hand and hope in the middle-aged heart, and flick on his lighter. The woman looked at him for quite a long interval before she raised her cigarette.

"Thank you," she said when the cigarette had caught on.

He had been right. She was American. "You are coming in Rome? Or leaving?" he asked.

She blew out a cloud of smoke and took another puff and

exhaled and watched that trail off before she spoke. "I'm coming in," she said at last. Her voice was slow and soft like the voice of a sleepy child. "From Paris."

"Ah," said Pippo, "I flew down from Paris myself yesterday. As a matter of fact, I'm out here to check on a bag that was lost on the plane." It was a story he had used many times before. Vera Crumer had been incensed by such inefficiency in handling baggage and had even written him to say that she had taken his problem up with an airline executive she knew in New York, but this was another sort of woman. She appeared not to have heard. She wasn't interested in lost luggage. She had already lost interest in the cigarette she had just lighted and tossed it away. She was interested in one thing only in life. Now he was positive of it. "You are waiting for someone?"

She wet her lips and nodded.

"Please allow me to introduce myself. I am the Marchese Salvini. Lorenzo Salvini." He took out his wallet, pulled a card from it and handed it to her. Months before he had found a small stack of Lorenzo Salvini's cards, secured by a rubber band, lying on the top of the rubbish Gino had put out to be collected. Some of them were yellowed, but he had salvaged a dozen or so from the center that were quite presentable. She dropped the card into her bag without looking at it, and Pippo made a mental note to retrieve it later. He had only a few left.

"I'm beginning to think the person I'm waiting for isn't coming." She craned her neck about to check on recent arrivals, and her breasts strained against their silken prison.

"I'd be very happy to give you a lift." He realized now that she wasn't wearing stockings, though when he had studied her from across the room, he had assumed she was, simply because her legs were so tanned. Furthermore, she wasn't wearing a brassiere. She was, he would have bet his last lire, absolutely naked except for her dress. "I think you can be fairly sure your friend is not going to come."

"He is very unreliable." She pulled the coat from her arm and swung it around her shoulder.

"Your bags?" Pippo asked.

"There's only this one." She touched a small satchel on the floor with the toe of her shoe. "I've come down for some fittings and I'll only be here overnight."

Pippo had a struggle concealing his astonishment. He thought of his mother's dressmaker, who came to their apartment, and the patterns and pins and material and thread that littered the dining table. This woman plainly dwelt on dizzy heights of luxury. He was glad he had chosen Lorenzo Salvini's identity instead of a half-dozen others that he could lay claim to with the cards in his wallet. He picked up her bag and gripped her arm. "You have an appointment then?" he said, guiding her toward the door.

"At four," she said.

"Ah, well. That's a long time off. I, too, have an appointment this afternoon. But meanwhile we can have a leisurely lunch." He waved the bag at Sergio as they approached the car. "No luck with my lost briefcase, but look what I found instead." Sergio, who had been leaning against the Jaguar, stood up and registered surprise and pleasure. It had frequently been observed that Pippo and Sergio complemented each other because Pippo was dark and Sergio was fair, and Pippo was garrulous and Sergio was quiet. It was also true that Pippo was bright and that Sergio's wits were ever so slightly blunted, and that this was the basis of their friendship. "My friend, Principe Borgia," Pippo said.

"Sergio Borgia," Sergio amended with aristocratic modesty. His responses weren't up to coping with a first name that wasn't his own.

"I am Amanda West," the American woman said in her sleepy child's voice.

"Sergio doesn't speak English, I'm afraid," said Pippo. "You speak Italian?"

"No. None. None at all." Amanda said.

"Ah, what a pity," he pretended. It was instead a great advantage to be able to converse with Sergio in a language she didn't understand. "Well," he sighed, "I shall have to act as interpreter." He got in beside Amanda and addressed Sergio in Italian. "You did bring the keys to the Fregene house. didn't you?"

"Of course," said Sergio. Like the car, the house in Fregene was the property of his boss, and he had been commissioned to supervise some repairs on it during the owner's absence. "They're right on this ring with the car keys."

"Sergio says you are very beautiful," Pippo told Amanda. "Smile at her," he told Sergio.

Sergio smiled at Amanda, who curled her lips sleepily. Her restless breasts struggled against the silk as she settled deeper into the seat. Sergio watched until they quieted down and then switched on the ignition.

"She hadn't got a stitch on underneath that dress," Pippo said, and Sergio ran his eyes along Amanda's thigh before he shifted into reverse. "I told her we'd take her to lunch, but it's early, so we have plenty of time to get around that." All the pleasure went out of their operations when expenses exceeded the cost of gasoline and an aperitivo or a cup of coffee. "We're discussing the best place to have lunch," Pippo placed an apologetic hand on Amanda's knee, and continued to Sergio, "I think the best plan is to tell her we're going to have lunch at Toni's. It isn't opened yet for the summer, so when we pass you can say that we'll go on to the house for an aperitivo, since it's really too early to eat anyway. Once we've got her at the house . . ." Pippo winked at Sergio over Amanda's head and gave Amanda an expurgated English version of the itinerary he had proposed.

"I don't think she's forty," said Sergio. "I'd say about thirty-six."

"What difference does it make?" They had long ago agreed that the relativity of age to sex was variable.

Sergio gunned the motor and the Jaguar took off with a roar which drowned out that of a departing jet. As they sped over the one-way lane leading away from the air field, the Porsche of the beat American passed them going in the opposite direction in the other lane. Pippo waved to the detestable creature at the wheel. It would do no harm for Amanda to believe they were friends of other owners of expensive cars. His greeting wasn't returned. Instead the beatnik hung his mouth open and stared, like the idiot he was. It didn't matter because Amanda hadn't seen the Porsche anyway. She was looking at him, holding a cigarette near her moist, parted lips, waiting for a light. He reached across her and pushed the lighter on the dashboard, and while he waited for it to ignite her breast rolled against his arm.

"She's not hungry anyway," Pippo said. "For food, that is."

Sergio laughed and steered the car right, onto the road that led to the sea.

Mrs. Aiken gave the forms Caroline had completed a final going-over, and used both hands to remove her glasses. They were attached to a chain that went around the back of her neck, and she buried them among the flowers and leaves that embroidered her green batiste blouse before she spoke. "Unless there is some urgency, your passport will be ready Friday."

"Oh. No, no, there's no urgency." Caroline had observed on entering that Mrs. Aiken belonged to the sisterhood of women who have chosen to separate themselves from the world by desks. Other members of the terrible sorority pursued their callings in such places of public assembly as libraries, schoolrooms and admission halls of hospitals. Their hair was either gray or graying, and if it hadn't been tightly curled by nature it was tamed by nets. They wore tailored suits in winter, shirtmaker dresses in summer and hand-embroidered batiste blouses off season. They had the power to read the past and alter the future of those who fell under their spell, and one who allowed them an intimidating second was lost. Caroline looked at Mrs. Aiken squarely. "That is, there isn't at this very moment. However, my father isn't well and I might have to leave suddenly." It was perfectly true that her father wasn't well. He had written that he had a bad cold. "I should like it as quickly as possible."

Mrs. Aiken chewed the problem around on her front teeth quite a long time before she dug her glasses from their flowery grave and reset them on her nose. She penciled a little note in the margin of one of the forms and reread what she had written before setting a period to the statement. "Since the children will be on your passport it isn't too complicated. You may pick it up any time after four." She attached the children's birth certificates and photos to the forms with a clip while Caroline complimented herself on remembering their existence and getting them from her desk after the wedding. They had been acquired in preparation for a family jaunt to Zermatt after Christmas, but they had come down with the flu one after the other, so it had been put off.

"Thank you very much." Caroline grasped her bag, feigned an intention of rising and then sank down again. "Oh, but I'm forgetting the form for my husband."

"What form?" Mrs. Aiken preferred answering questions to asking them and she frowned.

"Well, I assume there must be some form my husband must sign giving his permission for his children to leave Italy." Caroline widened her eyes in innocence.

"No, no." Mrs. Aiken put the palms of her hands together in the attitude of prayer and rested her chin on the tips of her fingers.

"In other words, I can take the children without any sort of written consent from my husband? It's enough that I have the passport."

"Of course."

"But I can't believe it." It was indeed too good to be true, and Caroline placed a hand on her chest and sent her features into shock to conceal her relief. "Are you sure?"

Mrs. Aiken was not accustomed to having her pronouncements challenged. "I am positive," she said with some irritation.

"But then what's to prevent an American wife or husband from skipping off with the children?"

"Nothing at all. It happens frequently."

"But that's shocking." A few more tugs, Caroline judged, and the wool would be well pulled over the evil eye. It would never do for Mrs. Aiken to suspect her true motive, for she had long ago discovered that it was a unique characteristic of Rome for a secret to remain a secret only so long as it is known by a single person. "Surely you don't think that's fair."

"It is not my business to judge. However, if you were unhappily married you might think differently."

"Perhaps, but all the same . . ." Caroline stood up.

"Of course, if the Italian parent has some objection to his children's leaving the country, he can naturally prevent their departure by appealing to the Italian authorities."

"Oh?" Caroline took a deep breath and held it.

"If he finds out in time, that is," Mrs. Aiken added and smiled.

Caroline froze her face in disapproval. "Oh," she said again and exhaled slowly as she took Mrs. Aiken's outstretched hand.

She fairly flew from the building while images provoked by Mrs. Aiken's terrible joke flashed around the walls of her mind like films from a speeded-up projector. Lorenzo returns from his sordid nocturnal wanderings to find her gone. His children gone. He is beside himself with terror. The lights go up all over the palazzo. The police are called. The *carabinieri* arrive. Find her! Where? Pursue her! How? She has left no note. She has vanished without leaving a trace. Lorenzo gives way to his despair. Guilt devours his nervous system. Remorse hollows his eyes and lines his cheeks. He realizes he has lost all that he really loves. Too late. Beyond recalling. Heartbroken, he falls across their bed, his body racked by sobs.

Since she had never seen Lorenzo cry, the ending left a good deal to be desired and, as she glided down in the elevator, a revision presented itself. Lorenzo races to the airport, accompanied by the "Italian authorities" Mrs. Aiken had spoken of, faceless men wearing dark felt hats and somber suits. They reach the exit to the runways just as the plane is rocketing across the field. Lorenzo watches it take off in a trance, and when the lights of the aircraft are finally lost in the night sky, he covers his face with his hands and the heavy fist of tragedy strikes to bow his head.

It was inconceivable that Lorenzo would ever cover his face, much less bow his head, in the presence of Italian authority or any other. As the door to the elevator opened at the ground floor a far more credible and gratifying climax unfolded. Lorenzo follows her to New York, a setting in which he is automatically at a disadvantage. The machines of his hotel laundry turn his shirts, which have never been touched except by human hand, into coats of mail. The spaghetti he eats in Italian-American restaurants, overdone and seasoned by cooks who have never been nearer to Italy than Brooklyn, churns in his stomach like a nest of vipers. He is as edgy as a drug addict because his customary daily ration of *aqua minerale* is cut off. She has resumed her old career on a level far higher than the one she left to marry him and has found a brownstone duplex with a garden in the East Sixties which is ideal for the children. Her job and her children make life worthwhile, and interesting friends make it exciting. Lorenzo's campaign to win her back is waged in her own living room, and it is pathetically one-sided. She comes home from an exhilarating day at her office to find him waiting. It is the dread encounter she has known all along must take place. She realizes almost at once there was nothing to fear. Now it is she who is strong and he who is weak. Now it is her nights that are filled with adventure while his are lonely. And he knows he has only himself to blame. She is kind but distant as she would be with any stranger. And she is compassionate because her own suffering has made her understanding of the suffering of others. She feels nothing more than this. Pity. Her love for him is dead. And he has killed it. He leaves and she watches him from the long window of her drawing room, a desolate figure disappearing into the night. It is significant that outside the degree of air pollution is particularly high. He fades from sight, and she smiles wistfully and sighs for what was and will never be again and then remembers she must dress for dinner and the theater. She moves briskly through pure, filtered air to the circular stairway that leads to the second floor. Her spirit rises with each step she takes upward. The past is dead!

As Caroline stepped back onto the Via Veneto, the visions of her ultimate victory brightened and whitened like the filaments of an exhausted light bulb before they abruptly burn out. She came to a start and a full stop, a foot short of a horse carriage that was parked at the curb, and she took root as the horse appraised her warily. Could it be that she had advanced so far into a state of lunacy that it was even evident to an animal? Quite likely. Surely the plot she was hatching was insane enough to give outward manifestations. What woman in her right mind could dream of secretly fleeing from one continent to another with two small children and no one to help? How was she to go about it? The carriage driver appeared with a feed bag and diverted the horse's attention from his study of her. Time was passing. She had to make a plan. She circled around the back of the carriage, crossed the street and passed the entrance of the Hotel Excelsior to the Café Doney.

The sidewalk tables were all occupied except for one, and she slid in behind it and ordered a Campari. By an unwritten treaty, this side of the street had long ago been ceded by the Romans to the American tourists, although there was considerable crossing of friendly borders, and she felt almost instantly comforted by the sound of her native language. At the table to her right a husband and wife were choosing a restaurant for lunch from a guidebook. The woman was resisting fading into her forties with admirable style. She was trim and slender and her hair was a subtle in-between blond shade that could or could not have been dyed. Her husband was slim and trim as well. Lorenzo would have said that he looked like a boy. According to Lorenzo American men had no middle age.

They were gray-haired adolescents at fifty and even sixty, and then, if they survived their quota of heart attacks, went immediately from youth to senility overnight. This phenomenal mutation was, of course, the work of the diabolical American woman, who had perfected the black art of arresting the psychic growth of the American male at puberty. In contrast to his emotional dwarfing, his physical development was fostered with painstaking care, a therapy based almost exclusively on games played with balls of various sizes and weights. As age increased, the dimension of the ball diminished. The American Man-Boy desperately kicked a watermelon of pigskin toward a goal fifty yards away and the American Boy-Man drove and putted a sphere of pock-marked rubber toward its grave and his own. These innocent diversions gave him the illusion that his life was full. It never crossed his mind, stunted as it was by the witchcraft of his mate, that what his life was really full of was work, that he ground around the mill of little and big business like a blindfolded donkey, deprived of his sight by the creature he had emancipated so she could make him her slave.

Caroline marveled that she could ever have listened to such rubbish as she followed the finger of the man at the next table move down the list of suggested gastronomical sanctuaries. The finger stopped and tapped decisively. "This sounds great," the man said to his wife and read, "Nino's. The accent is on food rather than froufrou. A favorite with the Roman because of steaks and service that are unexcelled in the city." He looked at his wife and anticipated her approval with a smile.

She answered with a patient smirk and took the book from his hand. "We can eat steak at home," she reminded him wearily, as if it were something she was repeating for the very last time.

"Yeah. Sure. I suppose you're right. I was thinking it would be nice for a change. It's not that I don't like spaghetti. That big fat kind we had last night was great. It's only that I get homesick every once in a while for a good thick piece of meat."

A mist of nostalgia separated him momentarily from his alien environment and he squinted through it at Caroline.

Caroline cleared the air between them with a sunny beam that urged him to stand up for his rights and refute the charge that Lorenzo would have made against him had he been present. The man squared his jaw instantly and turned her to stone. Though he continued glaring at her directly, it was plain he had actually seen her for no longer than a second. It was a reaction far more meaningful than the one she had hoped for. Here was a man who had promised his wife to love her always and meant it. It wasn't that he resisted the attraction of other women. They didn't exist for him. She was his wife and he was her husband and other women were excluded for all time.

"You really must stop calling every kind of pasta 'spaghetti.'" The object of the man's unwavering fidelity took a deep breath and let it out in a martyred sigh. "That was cannelloni we had last night. It's pasta. Spaghetti is pasta. Fettuccini is pasta."

"Okay, okay. Pick out some place where they have good pasta. It's all the same to me." He looked at his watch, wound it and folded his hands on the table. "It's twelve-thirty, though, and we ought to get going maybe."

"No one eats at twelve-thirty. The waiters would think we were crazy if we turned up at this hour."

"Well, I'm going to have another drink then. You want another?"

His wife declined with a quick shake of her head, gave her husband's arm an indulgent pat and flipped the guidebook to another page. She was so wonderfully self-assured and definite that Caroline was filled with awe and envy. Had she ever been like that? Could she ever be again? Or had she irrevocably traded her independent birthright for a mess of Oriental pottage? Caroline fitted the woman into her own shoes and the woman strode unhesitatingly into action. She stepped briskly to the street, commandeered the first taxi and sped away in it to the Banca di Roma on the Corso, where she withdrew Caroline's three thousand and sixty-eight dollars, which was all that was left of the six thousand she had accumulated when she liquidated her past to marry Lorenzo. She dashed back to the waiting taxi. Ten minutes later she was at the American Express, getting traveler's checks and informing herself as to plane schedules. There were no second thoughts. No doubts. No procrastination. She made the reservations and paid for the tickets on the spot.

That was the plan! Caroline rustled through her pocketbook for a piece of paper and pen to write it down before it escaped her. Depending on what flights were available, she would leave on a flight that night or one the next morning. The operation must be synchronized with Lorenzo's absence or Lorenzo's sleeping. It looked remarkably simple once it was in writing. Bank. Pick up passport. Tickets and checks. Pack. Leave. A troop movement divided into five neat, distinct sections. The first and third were as good as accomplished. If it weren't for the infuriating custom of shutting up shop for the interminable lunch hour, she would be able to cross them off her list within an hour. However, she would have to go home and come back again anyway for the passport. She read number four of the last two objectives and then number five and then read them again and again and again.

"Here it is," the woman at the next table cried out in triumph. "Here's the restaurant where Helen told us we absolutely had to eat. It's called 'George's.' I knew it had a strange name."

"Since when is George such a strange name?" the man asked the half-empty glass he held in his hand.

Lorenzo would have observed that the man was in danger of coming of age with alcohol. Alarmed that she might be condemned for life to seeing everything through Lorenzo's eyes, she bore down on the pen hard and underlined the word "pack." Pack what? Winter clothes? Summer clothes? Toys? They would jam trunk upon trunk, crate after crate. She emptied the drawers and closets of the nursery and her dressing room and amassed enough apparel and equipment to fill the entire baggage compartment of an ordinary passenger plane. There was such a staggering amount that she wouldn't wonder if there wasn't enough to take up an entire cargo ship just on its own. It was out of the question. She could take only the essentials. Even that was enough to make her heart sink with the thought of payments of overweight. Her three thousand and sixty-eight dollars dwindled away by one third before she even saw Kennedy. She dropped the pen from shaking fingers and laid her hands flat on the table to steady them. What had she ever done to deserve this torment. What fiendish fates were at work to drive her innocent children from their home? How could Lorenzo? How could he?

Strangely, she felt widowed rather than betrayed. She longed for the Lorenzo of that far-away summer day with whom she had lain in the great bed while sentinal cypresses in the villa's park guarded their first sleep. She yearned for the Lorenzo who had held her body as they danced as one beneath the stars of the glorious Greek night. But she mourned most for the Lorenzo who had stood at her bedside after Andrea was born, an inarticulate, anguished, adoring Lorenzo whose lips had parted to utter words that were never spoken. She had raised her arm to draw him near and he had taken her hand and pressed its palm softly against his cheek as he sank to his knees. The bed might have been an altar before which he prayed. His eyes had explored her own until they seemed to find the very depths of her soul, while his trembling hand eased the sheet clear of her body. The hospital jacket covered her to the waist and he had stroked the inside of her aching thighs and touched the pad of white gauze that covered the stitches in the tear between her legs with tentative, reverent fingers. Then he had bent over and kissed her abdomen and his tears had fallen on her naked flesh like drops of blood from a wound. It was true she had never seen Lorenzo cry. She had *felt* him cry. It was not possible that he could have forgotten while she remembered. This Lorenzo of the faithless nights was a lie. The man who had knelt by her bed and the man she had imagined had profaned it could not exist in the same body. There was only one Lorenzo. He belonged to her. She had invented the other. He was a phantom of an aberrant mind, a ghost to be exorcised by reason.

She returned to time and place, an exhausted, jubilant survivor of a long journey in hostile lands across perilous seas. The Americans at the next table had left. People were deserting other tables, going home to lunch. It was time for lunch. It was time to go home. Lorenzo would be appalled if he could see her. It was all very well for American divorcées to sit alone on the Via Veneto, but not his wife. She summoned the waiter and paid for her untouched drink. The sky was now outrageously blue and cloudless. The branches of the trees were misted in the new green that only spring knows. She floated forth on air that was like silk and sprang suddenly back under the protection of the café awning like one shot at from ambush. In her direct line of vision, not five yards away, Mario waited at the wheel of the Fiat for the lights to change. By some miracle, the all-seeing eyes in the lunar face of Elisabetta Colombo stared straight at her and didn't register. Her mother-in-law was obscured by Elisabetta's bulk, except for an arm that grasped the strap at the window. The loathsome scrap of apparel would be at Elisabetta's feet, perhaps even touching the toes of the silly, frivolous shoes into which she insisted on stuffing her puffed insteps. Caroline had actually forgotten about the incriminating turquoise evidence against Lorenzo for a little while and there was no way she could account for her lapse of memory, unless it had been for the same reason that the doomed are temporarily and mercifully relieved of the symptoms of fatal diseases of which they have learned they will die. And why, oh, why hadn't she got herself under control on her ride back from the Gianicolo to the palazzo and disposed of the thing?

The car rolled on and Caroline watched it out of sight. It

was getting on for one o'clock. Lunch would be around two. She wouldn't go home for lunch. Never had she telephoned to say she wouldn't be home. There had never been a reason. She had so little strength now to do what she knew she must do that she didn't dare expend any of it sitting alone another time at a table with Luisa. The bank would be open at half-past three. Then the passport, and then the American Express. There were two and a half hours to fill. How? Where in a city where everything was closed but restaurants at this time of day? Restaurants and hairdressers. Hairdresser—that's where she could go. There would be a whole blissful hour under the dryer with the whir shutting out all sound and where no one would ever dream she might be crying.

"I'm surprised a good-looking boy like you isn't with some gorgeous Italian girl on a day like this," said Cora Study.

Randy shifted his weight from one leg to another and managed to respond with something between a grin and a grimace. He was always hearing it said by Europeans that Rome was provincial, and today he understood why. In the hour he had sat on the Via Veneto he had seen almost as many people he knew as if he had been home in Greenwich. Patricia Salvini and Fuffo of the bum title and all the loot, both dressed in riding clothes, had emerged from the Hotel Excelsior and driven off toward the park of the Villa Borghese. Not long after that Caroline Salvini, of all people, had sprung out of a taxi and flown into the American Consulate. It had seemed funny, somehow, since he'd almost gotten to think of her as more Italian than American. Then the Marchesa and the Colombo, which had made him pretty nervous, since they reminded him of the busted refrigerator. And now Cora Study.

"Just to think that yesterday it seemed like the sun would never shine again. And now look!" Cora Study waved her red crocodile pocketbook on high. "Everybody's out. Not a care in the world. You must admit they are fabulous people."

Randy admitted it by inclining his head. His jaws were still locked. Cora Study had evidently put on her make-up under artificial light. Her skin was hidden under layers of a chalky-pink substance so that she seemed embalmed, and the stuff had filled in the spokes around her lips to turn her mouth into a crazy kind of sunburst. He supposed he should ask her to sit down, but the roll and coffee he had wolfed down had already reduced his thousand-lire capital by nearly half. Not that it wasn't a bargain. Where else in the world could you sit for an hour for eighty cents without having the waiters glare at you?

"They really know how to live," Cora Study proclaimed.

"Yeah, yeah. They certainly do," said Randy. Now that the matter was settled, she'd surely go on her way.

"You are going to the horse show, aren't you?"

"The horse show?" It was a new subject, at least. It could go on for a long time, so Randy crossed one ankle over the other and supported his weight by resting his hand on the back of his chair. "I didn't know there was one."

"Oh, for heaven's sake," Cora Study exclaimed and pursed her spokes in reproof. "It begins tomorrow. You mustn't miss it. They say it's the most beautiful horse show in the world. It's held right over there in the park." Cora Study swung her crocodile bag toward the Villa Borghese.

"I didn't know. I've been sort of busy," said Randy. Getting drunk. Getting laid, You know how it is, Cora Study. He supposed Patricia Salvini and Fuffo were to take part in the spectacle, since he remembered now that on that memorable night at the opera Patricia had asked him if he rode. "I'll certainly try to take it in."

"Oh, do," urged Cora Study. "It's not to be missed. I'll be going with the Princess Colombo. Rather she'll be going with me as my guest. Isn't she a fabulous person?"

"Yes, she is. Yes indeed," concurred Randy emphatically.

"You know I rent one of the apartments in her palazzo?"

"Oh, is that so?" Little by little he would come to know Cora Study's life story. There would be the chapters on Mr.

Study, "fabulous" tales of courtship and passion and lustful kisses on those spokes.

"Perhaps you'll come have drinks with me there some evening." Cora Study untangled her hand from crocodile straps and held it out.

"Well, thanks. That'd be great. Thank you very much." Randy dropped Cora Study's hand somewhat more hastily than he had meant to.

"Or maybe we'll see each other tomorrow at the horse show," Cora Study said and started off, throwing a little wave back at him.

"Oh, yes. Yes indeed." Randy waited until her bag-matching red crocodile shoes had clicked off a few yards, and then sat back down.

There was no little truth in what Cora Study had now said more times than he could bear to count. The Italians did know how to live. But it wasn't true they hadn't a care in the world. They had just as many cares as other people and then some. To hear people like Cora Study talk, anyone would think they were immune to contagious and fatal diseases and personal debts and national disasters. Jesus. Apart from far-out places like India and China, you couldn't name any place where more things went haywire. It was just a normal, everyday occurrence for the electricity to fail or the gas. About once a month the water in some quarter or other stopped altogether so it had to be lugged in from the fountains.

The great thing about the wops was that they didn't go to pieces because everything wasn't one hundred percent okay. They held together because of the fifty or forty or even twenty percent that was okay, because they figured that was about all anyone could expect out of life anyway. So what if they didn't have a Ferrari? They could still get to the sea in a 500 Fiat and the sunset looked just as good through one pane of glass as another. The last laugh was on tourists who criticized them for living in the present and putting off whatever possibly could be put off until *domani*. Who could be sure of anything but today? Like try to get through to them that the time for really living it up comes about seventy in some senior citizens' paradise, all ramps and wheel chairs. Or that it's pretty stupid to sit around enjoying the first day of sunshine when who knows but what the stock market will crash in the fall and it'd be better to be worrying about that. Or that it's better to get loaded and mope around about some girl than knock hell out of her, which was the way they handled women and the way they claimed women liked to be handled.

He had never hit a girl in his life, unless you could count the swipes he'd taken at his kid sister when they were little. Even then the only time he'd really let her have it was when he was sixteen and she was fourteen and she'd taken his record player to a clambake and got it so jammed with sand it never worked again. He'd smacked her once across the cheek and then she ducked and caught a second blow on the arm and let out a howl that he'd hit her in the chest and maimed her for life, probably. And his mother had given him a long harangue about how delicate young girls were and how no man who wasn't a beast ever laid a finger on one. From then on he had limited his defense against Suzanne, who had gone right on being a pain in the neck until she was about nineteen, to trying to uproot great hunks of her long hair. It hadn't been anything like as gratifying. Not that he advocated bone-breaking or bloodletting, but the wops really knew the score when it came to women. He'd seen them settle it more than once with the flat of the hand and not use one useless word. The nicer you were to women, the more they demanded, until they finally had you stretched out on the ground and were trampling all over you. In other words, it was you or them. And he had had it.

His appointment with Maria Pia was in the park of the Villa Borghese, and she would be approaching it just about now from the Piazza di Spagna, where she had a morning job answering telephones and questions in a tourist agency. It was, of course, only a temporary thing, she had explained. It could end any minute. It was simply a matter of meeting the right person, who was, naturally, a film producer who would automatically cast her in all the roles Sophia Loren and Gina Lollobrigida were too old to play. She would be internationally famous overnight and have the world at her feet. It was the kind of demented discourse he had heard from at least a thousand girls, but the difference was that she was a thousand times prettier than most of them. She was entitled to her pipe dream, but what burned him up was that he'd been left waiting in the rain on some lousy street corner about six times in the last few weeks while she pursued it. Excuses always came tinkling out of her mouth fast as coins from a slot machine pay off. Lies, every one of them. And when he'd catch her she never had an instant of remorse. Just like nothing had happened at all, she'd laugh and her hair would go wild and she'd fling her arms around his neck and run tingling fingertips up and down his spine and then dig in her nails until he felt as if strings of firecrackers were being shot off inside him. Afterward, he'd forgive her, of course. More than that, before his money ran out, he'd even reward her by buying some crazy bracelet or dress she'd see in a shop window and moon and moan for like some starving cat. When he thought what she had cost him. And the time! If he'd spent half the days and nights he had wasted wondering where the hell she was and what the hell she was doing, he would have a finished novel. Good or bad, it would at least be something accomplished, some evidence that his father hadn't given him his graduation money just so he could become a slob. But last night was really the last straw. If she hadn't stood him up, he wouldn't have got drunk. Now he had the memory of Lisa's head on his shoulder tattooed on his brain for all time. And God only knew what would come of Caroline Salvini's witnessing the final touching scene.

Randy lunged into the sparkling green of the Villa Borghese, gimlet-eyed and resolute as a jungle hunter bent on the kill. He sighted his prey some distance off, and much to his surprise, since it was the first time she had ever been known to meet him on time. She was more or less where they had arranged to meet. When he had said the statue of Goethe, he had meant at street level below it. The statue was set on a knoll, and Maria Pia had climbed up and fitted her own figure in alongside that of a kneeling marble youth whose nude backside represented the young Werther to a few people, nothing to most and, so he had been told by Charlie, seventh heaven to all the fags in Rome. Randy slowed down and cut into the shaded area of the sidewalk so that he could observe her as he advanced without her being aware of it. As he drew closer, he realized it had been an unnecessary precaution. She was as oblivious of her surroundings as her marble companions. She was much nearer to reclining than to standing. Her arms were thrown wide, her face was lifted to the sky and her inert body was draped over the stone as if she had been laid out in some mystic, pagan rite as an offering to the sun. The May breeze was lifting her short skirt to indecent heights and tickling the bare back of young Werther with strands of her hair.

It was a public display of private rapture that Randy was positive topped anything Cora Study had ever seen, and not surprisingly it had drawn a sizable audience. The steps of a pair of carabinieri had locked and their eyes had fixed in doll-like fascination under their Napoleonic hats. Randy thought they might be going to take her into custody, but they turned after a bit and marched on in perfect unison, as if some invisible hand had wound keys concealed in their backs. Some motorists only slowed down for a better look, but two drivers had drawn to a full stop at the curb. A man with frosted hair had settled glasses attached to a black ribbon on his nose and himself on a bench to view the tableau in comfort. Randy would have been willing to bet that the sculptured tribute to the poet hadn't had as much attention since its unveiling. Maria Pia, without a care in the world and, high above her on his pedestal, Goethe, who had never had anything but. Maria Pia without a glimmer of guilt for the night before and without an instant of repentance for all the other days and nights before that. Maria Pia making love with the sun, and a growing aggregation of slack-jawed jackasses making vicarious love to Maria Pia. Well, how about that! Yeah. How about it? Not a care in the world. Oh, really. Was that so? It would take him ten seconds to reach her, and she'd find out whether she had any cares in the world or not.

He bounded to the corner, sprang up and across the grass incline upon which the monument was set and sent Maria Pia's celestial paramour into a swift and total eclipse. Her eyes were closed. She made a brief protesting frown because of his shadow's intrusion, and then her brow smoothed and she slept on. Or so it appeared. He leaned over, suspecting she might be playing one of her games. But no. She was out, all right. Her lips were parted so that the cutting edges of her astonishing white teeth were visible and the pink tip of her tongue. It must have been how Eve looked before she bit into the apple. It was a combination of sin and innocence that would have had an ad executive with a toothpaste account in gibbering glee. If he himself were seeing her for the first time, Christ only knew what corny emotions he might be susceptible to. Instead, she was every tormented nightmare of naked public exposure he had ever had.

His teeth ground behind compressed lips, and his hot breath hissed through his nostrils like dragon fire. Weakening restraints that were still holding his arm muscles under control snapped like old fiddle strings. His hands turned into claws, and the claws pounced upon Maria's upper arms and circled around them like tight bracelets of steel. He jerked her to her feet so fast that her head took a leap forward to catch up with her body.

"Ohhhh." Maria Pia's brows knit in outrage and she made a sleepy attempt to shimmy free of his confining grasp.

"Shut up!" Randy commanded and stiffened her neck and spine with one violent, massive shake.

A cloud of alarm settled uncertainly on Maria Pia's face, which was not accustomed to entertaining such unbecoming expressions. "I was asleep," she pouted.

"That's not news to many people in Rome. I had to fight my way through the crowds that were watching you to get up here. Oh, you were asleep, all right. With your skirt up to your neck." Randy released her from his hold and folded his arms. "But then I guess you were tired. You probably had a late night," he suggested with caustic charity. Maria Pia's eyes shuttled from right to left, while behind them Randy knew she was ransacking her grab bag of lies and excuses for one she hadn't yet used. She apparently found something which seemed worth a trial, since she smiled sadly and Randy encouraged her with a warm wink.

"It ees true. I sleep not any. Where I call you from ees the *farmacia* . . ."

"You were buying medicine," Randy prompted. She was running out of material, repeating old stuff like a summer television show. This was going to be the one about her mother and the gastrointestinal attack. Unless it was the one about her father and her mother and her two sisters and four brothers all felled in one swoop because of an influenza epidemic that singled them out from all of Rome. It was her masterpiece and had explained a four-day disappearance during the holiday of the Epiphany. "Somebody sick?" Randy probed on solicitously. He was having no small amount of abdominal discomfort himself, induced by suppressed fury. Maria Pia nodded and trapped her lower lip with her remarkable teeth. She turned aside and fanned the marble bottom of the mourning youth with her long, dense lashes. Ordinarily, she was able to flood up like Niobe, at will, but an unaccountable drought plagued her, and she fanned and bit away without raising a trickle. The time had arrived to give her some help. Randy delivered it with lightning dispatch. He whacked her left and right and then dropped his stinging hands to his side like a cymbalist enjoying his fleeting moment of triumph. Shades of red from pale to rosy rushed to color the imprints of his palms on Maria Pia's cheeks as her eyes widened and rounded into expressionless discs. She was probably going to scream or keel over in a tantrum or some other goddam dramatic thing. She had an ear-splitting vocal range from contralto to soprano, and when she let go it should liven up quite a radius. The *galoppatoio* was set back from the opposite side of the street, and the thud of hoofs and an occasional squeal wafted over as Patricia Salvini and Fuffo and associates spurred their mounts over obstacles.

Something had to give, but Maria Pia showed no signs of emerging from her cataleptic coma. It could be that he had smacked loose some vital hinge in her head, unseated her medulla oblongata from its spinal rest. His hands were still stinging as if he had patted a porcupine. Maybe she was keeping her jaws clamped to hold in blood and uprooted teeth. He had an impulse to give her a little poke with his finger to bring forth some response. But supposing she toppled over the way fighters did, not on the moment of impact, but later when their legs got the news that their brains had been iced? Jesus, this was terrible. His mother wasn't one of those daffy dames who made things up. She had laid it on thick about fragile bones and vulnerable tubing and temperamental organs. He made a furtive comparison of Maria Pia's small, soft hand with his own. He thought of the times he had encircled her wrists with his fingers and of the inches there had been to spare. A splotch of angry purple was deepening under her right eye. Why didn't she move? Say something? Anything.

"*Amore,*" Maria Pia said.

Randy sprang back as if he had been addressed by the dead. Mouth agape, he watched her prolonged resurrection with the same dumbfounded absorption with which he had witnessed the awakening of Snow White when he was five years old. She smiled, not broadly, but wide enough for him to determine that the dental miracle inside her mouth was intact. She looked aside and then back at him, a calisthenic achievement not to be tolerated by a displaced medulla.

"Tesoro," Maria Pia murmured. Her hand fluttered forward and she touched him shyly on the arm. *"Amore mio. Amore. Ti voglio bene."*

Now that he was sure she was okay, self-reproach gave way to self-satisfaction. In his junior year at Yale, a girl named Leslie Cavanaugh had driven his libidinous longings up to a perilous peak and his first-semester average down to a critical low. The final battle had been waged with words. Leslie had walked off with the last one. If only he had known what he had just learned now.

"And you love me. You have hitted me." Maria cupped her cheeks in her hands and beamed with pride. "A man never hit a woman when he don't loves her."

There was a lot of rotten grammar and a disturbing amount of logic in the statement. It stood to reason that he wouldn't have worked himself up to clouting a girl about whom he felt indifferent. Maybe he did love her. And also maybe he didn't. The laboratories of the Roman institutes for advanced studies of male-female relationships were open around the clock. There wasn't any urgency. He'd postpone further research and get on with his other business of the day. Caroline Salvini. The igloo in his kitchen. No dough.

"Ees in your mind always I am with other mens. And ees not the true. Only I love you."

"Yeah. Sure, sure." What if Caroline *cabled* his mother! "I've got to go."

"*Amore*. Randee."

Randy blocked a pass she was making toward his mouth. "Cut it out, will you? Haven't you put on enough floor shows for one day?"

"I am sorry." She stiffened with prim obedience. "Tonight I come to you. Tonight I make you know is only you I love. My whole life. *Sempre. Sempre.*"

"Fidelis." Randy plumped out his cheek with his tongue. *"Sì, sì,"* he said and bounded down the slope to the sidewalk. He looked back before he turned toward the Pincio. Goethe

and his chums were alone, and she was already out of sight.

As he came into the cortile of the palazzo, he saw that Charlie's Porsche was parked, not surprisingly, in the space reserved for the Salvinis. Next he saw, not surprisingly either, that Charlie was parked on Gino's stool inside a cubicle that was a cross between a sentry box and a ticket window. Gino's office, the servants called it. There was a sliding glass through which Gino screened tradesmen and social callers. Charlie was wearing Gino's cap, which made him look like the Dutch boy on the paint can gone to seed, and was talking to a delivery boy in a black smock. Randy stopped and leaned against a pillar.

"Signor La Rosa is not in," Charlie told the boy. Charlie had a masterful command of the Italian language, Roman dialect included. "Just hand the package over to me and I'll see that he gets it the moment he comes back."

"It's a film," said the boy. "My boss told me . . . what I mean is I'd be responsible if it got lost."

"Ah, the film. Yes, yes. Signor La Rosa spoke to me about it on his way out." Charlie snatched the parcel from the boy's grasp. "Thank you. Thank you very much."

Randy waited until the messenger had passed out to the street and bounded across the courtyard. "Will you get the hell out of there?" he snarled murderously.

Charlie hung Gino's hat back on its peg and exited from the door that opened into the cortile. "This should be very interesting," he said, tearing away the paper. "I've got to get hold of a projector."

Randy caught the wrapping as it floated to the ground and made a grab for the negative, but Charlie ducked. "Hand it over, Charlie. I'm not kidding. You ought to be committed. Can't you keep your hands off things that aren't yours?"

"It so happens La Rosa's got his hands on something that isn't exactly his." Charlie tossed the roll of film up with one hand and caught it with the other.

"Meaning what?" Randy asked.

"Meaning The Bitch. That's what."

"I don't get it," Randy said. After Charlie had explained, he still didn't. Pippo La Rosa wasn't much older than he was. He'd never seen Charlie's mother, but she had to be about the same age as Cora Study. His stomach did a flip and sprayed his throat with an acid geyser slightly flavored with last night's wine. And those other guys who laid the old bag. How could they do it? The nose of the Salvini Fiat snorted at the gate and Randy swallowed. "It's the Marchesa. Get your car out of her parking place."

"I know who has a projector," Charlie narrowed his eyes nastily on the film.

Randy brought Charlie to attention with a sharp elbow jab. "I said to move that car. And fast. Beat it!"

"I'll bring the projector back here," Charlie called as he started the engine.

"Don't," Randy advised, even though he knew it was a waste of breath.

Mario docked the Fiat, and the Porsche howled out into the Via della Scimmia. The rusty hinges croaked rebelliously as Randy pushed his door open. The sun had long since gone to peer through other windows, and his room was dark as a dungeon.

Unless she called a halt, Luisa presumed her courtyard would soon be swarming with revolting, ragged beatniks like the lovely Spanish Steps, which now looked like a leper colony in Biblical times. She didn't believe at all that the subhuman being at the wheel of that expensive automobile was its owner, as Mario had maintained. He had probably stolen it. She considered delivering her ultimatum to Randy in person and decided against it. It would be less tiring to send a note in which she would also set the following day as the absolute deadline for paying his rent.

She went to her room, closed the door and opened her pocketbook. She rejected one hiding place and then another as being uncertain. There were the children. There was the ubiquitous Carmela. All three were strictly forbidden ever to open her bag. The underdrawers were better left where they were. She snapped the bag shut and sat down at her desk. Since she could never remember Randy's name, she began the letter without salutation and closed it without complimentary formality. There was a rap at the door as she signed her name, and she called out "*Avanti.*"

Carmela entered. Her hair was covered with a large white cap she wore to do the dusting, and she ploughed across the thick rug toward Luisa like a capsizing sailboat. "I didn't know you had come back in, Donna Luisa. Just now I saw Mario. There were some messages."

"From whom?" Luisa folded the paper.

As Carmela wrote with great difficulty and had even more trouble deciphering her own script, she had to rely on her memory in transmitting messages. "The first was from that American gentleman."

"What American gentleman?" Luisa put the folded paper in an envelope and tossed it on the desk. "What's his name?"

Carmela threw back her head and closed her eyes like a medium, and Luisa leaned back in her chair. There were frequently interminable intervals before the messages came through, and Luisa feared she might be in for one of them.

"Ah," said Carmela, suddenly wide awake. "He is the man of the card on the table beside your bed. He is of the Embassy of America."

"Mr. Fuller," Luisa said. He had come about the vacant apartment during her liver attack. He was evidently still interested, and it wasn't yet fit to be seen. A pity. He was a bachelor and held a position that didn't allow delinquency in meeting his financial obligations.

"I told him to telephone at the lunch hour and he might be able to speak to you. And then your son called to say that he would be home for lunch and your daughter-in-law called to say she wouldn't be home for lunch." Carmela shook her head like a spaniel happily returning to land after a swim through deep waters.

"I think you have it the wrong way round," Luisa corrected.

Carmela couldn't trust herself to make an immediate denial. She scowled and pressed her forehead with all the fingers of her right hand before she spoke. "No. No. He said he would and she said she wouldn't. I have told Bruna because she was attending to the table-setting since Mario was out with you, and then I heard her telling Mario . . ."

"Did my daughter-in-law say anything else?"

"Well, when I picked up the receiver I said '*Pronto*' and then she said '*Pronto*' and then she said "Is this you, Carmela?' and then I said . . ."

"*Basta!*" Luisa brought her palms down with a bang that set the twin silver frames to dancing. "What I want to know is whether she told you when she'd be back or where she was going."

"No. She didn't," Carmela replied and sealed off further comment behind thinned lips.

Luisa was certain now. Caroline had seen the underdrawers. It was easy enough to imagine how Caroline had felt. Very much as she herself had felt on that long ago afternoon when she had intercepted a note to Raffaello in French, postponing a rendezvous at "our usual place" until the following day and signed with a kiss in the purple-red lipstick that was the fashion then and no name. She had rushed to her mother, who had rushed to Raffaello's mother, and Raffaello had sped to her stuttering with outraged innocence, swearing vengeance on the malicious perpetrator of the joke and vowing his eternal love for her. Of course, although she had pretended to believe him, she had known there wasn't one word of truth in anything he had said. Except that he loved her. She was safely back in the matrimonial bed that same night, keeping well to her own side nevertheless. A week later he had given her the stupendous gray pearls that were the envy of every woman she knew, and almost nine months to the day she had given him Lorenzo. She was far cleverer several years later when he fell under the spell of Francesca di Bicci. God had given Francesca a head of rare beauty but he had evidently forgotten to fill it. It was agony to be with her longer than ten minutes, and Luisa had arranged Raffaello's schedule so that Francesca was seldom out of his sight. She saw to it that Francesca accompanied them wherever they went, except to bed, and in no time at all Raffaello was praying for deliverance from boredom. It was in her thirties, though, that she perfected a defense that was unerringly successful as well as diverting. Whenever she detected that Raffaello was entertaining the idea of straying from the connubial confines, or even that he had strayed, she pretended complete ignorance and simulated a simultaneous craving to explore green pastures herself. She purposely chose someone Raffaello detested as the hero of this fiction. She had once worked him up to such a feverish frenzy over her gynecologist that he had escorted her to appointments and sniffed and snooped at the frosted panes of the closed door to the examining room like a rabid mastiff. He inevitably left off betraying to devote full time to the prevention of being betrayed, to keeping his head from sprouting those horns that are for the Italian male the supreme ignominy.

It was too much to hope that Caroline would ever think of, much less employ, similar tactics. Whereas Italian women thought only of getting their husbands back, American women thought only of getting even with them. Very strange this sudden decision not to come home for lunch. Could it mean she was already charging into battle under her single standard, ready to lay waste to the family and ruin the lives of the children for the sake of her idiotic pride? Who knew what diabolical strategy she was planning for a future in which Andrea would develop into a delinquent like that beast who had shot out of the cortile in that stolen car and Beatrice into a member of that leper colony on the Spanish Steps?

There was a rumbling like distant thunder from the street, and the smith's door clanged shut. It was one-thirty. Luisa stood up and Carmela, taking this as a signal of dismissal, turned away.

"Wait, Carmela." Luisa rounded the desk. She was beginning to see how Caroline's absence at lunch could be used to advantage. She would have Lorenzo to herself. Oh, yes, yes. A bit of heightening for dramatic effect, perhaps. But it should go very well. He would be coming home any second, so there wasn't any time to lose. "I want you to tell Mario to lay the table for three."

"Oh, there's to be a guest." Carmela brightened.

Luisa looked through Carmela and then at her. It was not going to be easy. "There is not to be a guest."

"But I don't understand. If . . ."

"You don't need to understand. All you need to do is listen and do exactly as I tell you. Now then. Number one. Mario is to lay the table for three. Since my daughter-in-law will not be coming home, Don Lorenzo and I will wait a reasonable time and then lunch without her. Anyway that doesn't concern you. I'm only thinking aloud. Now. Number two. Hmmm . . ." Luisa longed for more time and knocked her knuckle against her teeth to speed up her thinking. "Let's see. Ah, I have it. Number two. The telephone will ring at fifteen minutes past two. I want you to answer it. Don't be off some place. Be right beside the library telephone at ten minutes past two so you can answer immediately. Do you understand?"

"I tell Mario to lay for three. At ten past two I go to the library telephone and wait for it to ring. And I answer it."

"Very good, Carmela. Excellent. Now, number three. When you answer the telephone you will say 'Very well' and hang up. Then comes number four. After you hang up, you must come into the dining room, where my son and I will already have started eating, and you will say to me, to *me*, 'Your daughter-in-law has just telephoned to say she will not be home for lunch." Four steps. Now see if you can repeat them." Luisa folded her arms and turned her ears with pedagogical misgiving, but Carmela recited without error. "Perfect. I see you have understood."

"I understand one, two, three, four." Carmela squared her dust cap to settle straight across her low forehead and tapped her temples with her fingertips. "But I don't understand the other part."

"What other part? There is no other part. There is nothing else you need to understand." Luisa would suggest some day that Carmela leave her brain for scientific study. One could almost hear the grinding of its wooden wheels when it was functioning, and with customary regularity it had now slipped a cog. "Stop drumming on your head. What other part? What are you babbling about?"

"It's the part when the telephone rings and I say 'Very well.' Suppose Donna Carolina says something that 'Very well' doesn't suit? And, too, why will she tell me she isn't coming to lunch when already she has told me she isn't?"

"I didn't say *she* was going to call. I simply said the telephone would ring and you are to answer and say 'Very well.' And hang up."

"But then who is going to telephone?"

"Teti is going to telephone, if you must know. And they are going to say that it is two-fifteen o'clock and you are going to say . . ." Luisa grasped Carmela by the shoulders. "What?"

" 'Very well.' "

"Ohhh! Finally! Now hurry. And remember, no word of any of this to anyone. Ever." Luisa set Carmela on course with a spin, marveling, as the woman tacked off, at the patience of animal trainers. She lifted the receiver of her desk telephone and dialed 114, the telephone company's number for operators charged with such tasks as waking and alerting subscribers and interrupting long-winded conversations. They were unfailingly prompt, and Luisa hung up, after making her request, confident that her little playlet would run off as conceived, if only the wheels in Carmela's head revolved without faltering.

Lorenzo was gathering some errant grains of *risotto alla milanese* into a mound for a last mouthful when the telephone rang on schedule. "Wasn't that the telephone?" he asked, lifting his fork.

"I think it was," said Luisa, feigning unconcern. "So, instead of having an aperitivo at Babbington's, we went to the Via Veneto. It really is becoming quite impossible to transport Elisabetta about. When I think how she once . . . yes, Carmela, what is it?" Fortunately Lorenzo's back was toward the door, so he didn't observe Carmela in trance. Her eyes were shut tight and she was listing at such an angle Luisa fully expected her to topple over. "What is it?"

"Your daughter-in-law has telephoned to say she won't be home for lunch," Carmela intoned mystically.

"What did she say?" Lorenzo whipped around, but Carmela had already vanished from sight.

"That Caroline won't be home for lunch," Luisa repeated.

"Won't be home for lunch!" Lorenzo addressed his empty plate that Mario was removing to replace with another for the second course. "But where is she?"

Luisa averted her eyes and pressed her napkin to her lips to give the appearance of trying to conceal a certain preoccupation. "I really don't know, dear."

"Mario, send Carmela back here," Lorenzo ordered.

"No, no, Mario, that won't be necessary," Luisa countermanded and waited until Mario exited through the door that opened onto the pantry. "There's no sense in quizzing Carmela. If Carolina had given Carmela any other message, Carmela would have reported it. Whatever her shortcomings, Carmela is precise. Perhaps Caroline . . . well, perhaps she . . ."

"Perhaps she what?" Lorenzo snapped.

"Well, obviously she's been detained for some reason."

"Detained where? Where did she go this morning?"

The pantry door swung open, and Mario entered bearing a large platter.

"She went to Anna's wedding." Luisa helped herself to two slices of boiled beef garnished with green sauce and a dab of carrots and wagged a finger against the purée of potatoes. "After that I really can't say because I was out myself."

Lorenzo speared a slab of beef and plopped it onto his plate. "Mario, did my wife say anything to you about where she was going after the wedding?" He banged a spoonful of carrots and another of potatoes onto porcelain flowers.

"She said nothing to me at all." It wasn't like his master to be careless. Lorenzo had dropped a blob of green sauce on Mario's spotless white serving glove, and he hurried off to change.

Luisa chewed thoughtfully as Lorenzo slashed away at his beef. He was quite beside himself with perplexity and reacting so exactly as his father used to that she was inspired to carry on without fear of failure. "How fortunate I ordered the beef for lunch, instead of something you don't like," she said lightly. "As I was beginning to tell you, Cesco Casano passed by and he, too, is showing signs of disintegration. I think this beef wants more salt, don't you?"

"What?"

"Think the beef needs more salt."

"No, no. It's all right." Lorenzo took another bite and chewed it with as much satisfaction as if he were eating rubber, glowering meanwhile at the service across the table from him that had been set for Caroline.

"Oh, Mario," said Luisa as the servant reappeared drawing on a fresh glove, "do remove those things." She fluttered her hand at the silver and plates intended for Caroline. "Ah, that's better," she said when he had gathered them up and departed. "There's something dismal about eating with a place set for someone who isn't coming."

"It would seem to me that someone in this house should know where the people who live in it are. It is supposed to be a house, is it not? Or a hotel?"

"Oh, now come, Lorenzo. You know Caroline is all right wherever she is. She would hardly be telephoning if she had been in an accident."

"That's a ridiculous observation. Of course I know she hasn't been in an accident." Lorenzo stabbed a carrot and ground his teeth on it.

"What about the land?" Luisa asked sweetly. "Have you come to any agreement?"

"What land?"

"Why, the land for the golf club, dear."

"I've decided not to sell it. I detest golf. I don't want to see a lot of cretins walking around with sticks after a ball even from a distance."

"Perhaps it is just as well. As Cesco Casano was saying . . ."

"I'm not interested in what Cesco Casano was saying." Lorenzo banged his knife and fork down on his plate and gave it a shove.

Luisa maintained a commiserating silence while Mario collected their plates and cleared the table of odds and ends. Mario went again through the swinging door, and Luisa gave Lorenzo's sleeve a soothing pat. "Now, Lorenzo, you mustn't let yourself get all agitated over a small thing like Caroline's not showing up for lunch."

"I don't consider it a small thing." Lorenzo jerked his arm away from Luisa's hand. "It's a beautiful day and I come home with the idea of taking Caroline and the children out to the country for the afternoon, only to find she is off God only knows where."

"Oh, that is a pity," Luisa crooned sympathetically. "No, Mario. No cheese for me. But you must try the pecorino, Lorenzo. It looks lovely."

"Furthermore, I have a perfect right to be annoyed. No, no, I don't want to try the pecorino. Will you please quit pushing food I do not want under my nose, Mario!"

"Go get the fruit, Mario," said Luisa. The waters were nicely troubled, but what she had to provoke was a typhoon. "Carmela tells me Bruna found some beautiful pears."

"Or to be agitated, as you call it. For the first time since our marriage, my wife doesn't appear for lunch without some logical explanation, and . . ."

Luisa shot her eyebrows aloft. "For the first ti . . ." she murmured and then broke off with a tantalizing catch of her breath. The ensuing silence was encouragingly prolonged, and she filled it by smoothing her napkin.

"Yes?" Lorenzo inquired icily.

Ah, at last she was on her way.

"What were you about to say?" Lorenzo demanded again.

"About what?" Luisa asked with the obvious evasiveness that she remembered had maddened Raffaello.

"About Caroline. I can't think of a time she hasn't come home for lunch, that is, unless she had planned beforehand to . . ."

"You, my dear . . ." Luisa picked at the tines of her fruit fork.

"Go on."

". . . are not always at home." She held the back of her hand against her forehead as if she might be relieving her distress and peered out from under a visor of fingers for Lorenzo's reaction. A kind of mummification was in progress.

Mario emerged from the pantry carrying a still life of bananas, oranges and pears arranged in a bowl.

Luisa tossed her chin up, affected a struggle for a change of mood and then clapped her hands together. "Now, Lorenzo, you must admit these pears do look delicious," she cried, selecting one with a great show of care. "You really must have one." But Lorenzo had already bolted from his chair and was streaking across the room. As he left it, he brushed his hand across the top of his head. Quite possibly, Luisa fancied, testing for horns already sprouted.

Luisa smiled at the pear and cut into it. It was indeed beautiful, and she dispatched Mario to fetch a bit of the pecorino, which she had refused earlier, to eat along with it. While he was out she heard the telephone ring, and when he returned he announced that it was Mr. Fuller of the American Embassy.

"I told him that the apartment wasn't yet ready to be seen,

but he said he understood there was a problem of repairs and would like to see it anyway."

"Very well," said Luisa. "Tell him he may come at half-past three. And, Mario, I want you to give this letter to the American boy in the cortile apartment." Luisa withdrew the letter she had tucked under her place mat and handed it to Mario. "On second thought, tell Mr. Fuller to make it four. I plan to have a long siesta." It had been so many years since she had staged and performed a leading role in a drama of this sort that she was really quite exhausted.

Il Pomeriggio

The murals in the Trattoria allo Spiedo had been painted by the great-granduncle of Tullio, the present proprietor, and depicted various ruins and remnants of imperial Rome. The artist had taken considerable license with the city's topography. The Colosseum rose a stone's throw from the tomb of Hadrian and on the same bank of the Tiber, instead of a good crow's flight away and inland on the river's opposite side. A little boy rolled a hoop under the Arch of Constantine directly into the Appian Way, which came to a dead end in the Campo dei Fiori's open market. Despite their years, the murals were as fresh as in the days of their origin. Each spring, a brother of Tullio's who had inherited some of his ancestor's talent restored the ivy on the columns and the grass that grew between the cobblestones to vivid greens, and the sky over all to a blistering blue.

"Dino wanted me to change the place completely," Tullio confided to Beppe Bonaccorsi. Beppe had gone into the restaurant kitchen on the off-chance that he might find a last sliver of the roast spring lamb that had been accompanied by fresh spring peas and tiny new potatoes as the second course of the wedding feast. "Wanted me to cover the murals with pine wood and buy special checkerboard tablecloths and put little brass lamps on each table."

Beppe's jaw dropped in disbelief. Dino was Tullio's son-in-law, the husband of Fiorella, the oldest of Tullio's five teen-age daughters. Beppe stared through the open door and tried to imagine how the dining area would look if Tullio had conceded to Dino's proposed alterations. The room was so vibrant with color and motion that he found it impossible to envision sickly pine blotched with knotholes as a backdrop for the banquet table that ran the length of the room and around which sat some fifty relatives and close friends of the bride and groom. "Milano," said Beppe contemptuously, and Tullio bowed his tall white chef's hat in assent. Dino had spent a year working as a waiter in Milan. He was now darting in and out between the guests' elbows, removing plates, and Beppe followed his course and marveled that the crown of his head under his jet-black hair hadn't blown off, stuffed as it was with nonsense he had adopted from the Milanese and the Milanese had copied from the Americans.

Beppe cast an eye over the great roasting pans on top of the oven, but there wasn't a remaining morsel of lamb. Even as he looked, Signora Neri, Tullio's wife, whipped one of the utensils across to the kitchen sink where her twin daughters, Gemma and Gilda, washed and dried. If Dino had had his say, an automatic dishwasher would be splashing away, instead of the twins, enriching the national electric company and leaving the girls' hands idle for mischief. Beppe detoured around the massive flanks of Signora Cristina, Tullio's mother, who sat in a straight chair shelling peas for the evening trade, to stand beside Tullio, who was placing a miniature, plastic bridal couple atop the five-tiered cake. "It's a work of art," he said.

"Mimmo made it," said Tullio. Mimmo was a cousin of Tullio's wife, the proprietor of a pastry shop two doors away from the Trattoria allo Spiedo. Tullio backed off to give the masterpiece a final scrutinizing and then clapped his hands and barked out, "*Lo spumante!*"

Claudio, Dino's brother, who had been hired for the day as an extra waiter, came up through the trap door from the cellar with a load of bottles. The champagne had been furnished by Riccardo's father and was a grade superior to any of the sparkling wines he sold in his shop. It was not French champagne, as the label claimed, but it was an Italian *spumante* of reasonably respectable vintage. It was a secret of the trade, which Signor Lauria had shared with Beppe, that it was bottled and so labled especially for sale in nightclubs, where it brought twenty to thirty times its wholesale price.

Beppe was to propose the first toast. He had composed it and rehearsed it in front of his wife the evening before. He had stood up at the supper table, lifted his wine glass and said, "health, prosperity and a long and happy life together," with such feeling that Signora Bonaccorsi had broken into spontaneous applause. Several times during the morning, he had raised an imaginary glass in the tower and addressed the good wishes to his bells. Not until this instant had he felt the least bit unsure of himself. Beginning with the word *brut* on the bottles, his surroundings started to look unfamiliar and less friendly. The door from the dining room leading on the summer garden was open, and some of the guests had left the table to stand out in the sun. Others had moved from their own chairs into those that had been vacated to chat in new company. Beppi recognized an atmosphere of intermission much like that between the acts of a play. In a little bit the stage would be reset, the *champagne brut* ready to serve and the cake to be cut down tier by tier. And he would be the character opening this performance. Although most of the guests were friends of his, or acquaintances at least, he suddenly saw them as an audience, and possibly a hostile one. Supposing they laughed? The word *brut* clouded as the symptoms of stage fright set in, clammy hands, respiratory difficulty and accelerated heartbeat. He left the kitchen quickly and made his way in a daze to the toilet on the landing, midway up the stairs leading from the dining room to the second floor, where Tullio had his living quarters.

Not surprisingly, the bathroom was occupied when he turned the knob, but almost at once the door opened and a small boy toddled out, followed by his mother, who was Riccardo's sister. Beppe made a ceremonial bow and dove inside.

He was astonished to discover that his face in the mirror over the basin was the same as ever. His graying hair was still neatly combed. His wife had been right about his new glasses with the dark frames. They definitely gave him the appearance of a thinker. His confidence began to return. He straightened his tie and then raised his hand as if it were clasping a goblet. His mirrored eyes sparkled boldly as his lips silently formed the words of his toast. His mute recitation over, he quaffed down a gust of air from the imaginary glass. Although the dramatic action would have to be excluded from his actual performance, he smashed the glass to the floor, just for the fun of it. The gesture was so realistic that he even fancied he heard the fragmentizing of the goblet. But infinitely more realistic was a succeeding sound. It was that of a woman's voice, so disconcertingly near that Beppe clutched the sides of the basin and guardedly searched the tiny room for some opening through which his rehearsal had been watched. To his relief, he found that the voice was rising from the summer garden and coming within his earshot by way of the bathroom window, which wasn't quite closed.

"Did you take it?" the voice asked in a menacing sort of undertone, but there was no response.

Beppe eased the window open wider and looked down. He saw that the speaker was Ersilia, the brazen daughter of Gino's brother, and a girl he couldn't abide. She was demanding an answer from the bride, of all people.

"No. Of course you didn't. I can tell by the expression on your face," Ersilia went on.

"I couldn't," Anna protested apologetically.

"And why couldn't you? Why not?" Ersilia hissed.

Anna lowered her head, and Beppe wished that he could

give the nape of her neck, where some stray strands of her magnificent hair coiled, a pat of solidarity. Whatever this was all about, he was on her side.

"Why?" Ersilia insisted.

"Because I must ask Riccardo first," Anna said softly.

Ersilia put her hands on her hips and flipped her head impatiently. Beppe supposed she thought her hair looked good, dyed as it was a dead yellow like provolone cheese and with its black roots beginning to show near the scalp.

"And I haven't had a chance. There have always been people around," Anna added.

"Oh, certainly. You must ask Riccardo," Ersilia sneered.

Naturally she should ask her husband, like any good wife. It was all Beppe could do to restrain himself from saying it aloud. But even if he could, it would be wasted breath. What did such a girl know of the finer womanly sentiments? It was hard to believe the two could be cousins.

Anna put a finger on one of the rolls of her elaborate chignon. "It's right here that it hurts," she said, trying to change the subject.

Ersilia poked at the coiffure professionally and extracted a long hairpin. "Well, if you don't ask him soon it's going to be too late." Ersilia replaced the pin. "There. How does it feel now?"

"It's fine now. Thank you."

"They work like any medicine. You can't expect results in a few minutes." Ersilia took the wedding veil that was attached to a circlet of valley lilies from Anna's hand.

Beppe summarized everything that Ersilia had said and it added up to exactly zero. What could it be that this awful girl was wanting Anna to take that needed Riccardo's permission and worked like medicine?

"I'll ask him. I really will, Ersilia," Anna promised.

"Now. Go ask him now. They should be taken in the morning. It's almost two."

"But he's talking to people," Anna protested.

"You can call him aside. How can you be so timid and silly?"

Oh, no, thought Beppe. Much better to be like you, Ersilia. Bold and bronze-faced and cold as a piece of sculpture.

"Even if he said 'all right,' I still don't know," Anna said.

"Still don't know what?" Ersilia spread out the tulle and raised the circlet of flowers above Anna's head. "If you don't stand up straight how am I supposed to set this on evenly? What don't you know?"

"Whether it's right to do," Anna said, lifting her head.

"Oh, *Dio mio,*" Ersilia moaned.

"I can't believe it isn't a sin," Anna said.

"Even the Pope doesn't think it's a sin," Ersilia stated with authority.

Ah, well now, Beppe asked himself, how was that for the summit of impudence, professing to know the innermost thoughts of His Holiness?

"He can't come out and say so yet," continued Ersilia, "but it's only a matter of time until he'll be forced to by public opinion. And by then you could already have no telling how many babies."

Oh, it was the Pill. Beppe was annoyed with himself for not having realized it sooner. So that was what Ersilia was trying to shove down Anna's throat. And by what right, he would very much like to know. And for what reason? So she wouldn't have babies, of course. And why shouldn't she have babies?

"But I want a baby," said Anna guiltily.

"Very well. But this way you can decide exactly when. This way you can wait a few years and have a little fun out of life before you do."

"There's something more," Anna said. "It's . . ."

"It's what?" urged Ersilia.

"It's that I have prayed to the Virgin. I prayed that the day of my wedding would be beautiful." Anna saluted the heavens with a wistful smile. "Just as it is. And I promised the Virgin I would name my first child for her. Riccardo agreed that it would be called Mario. Or, if it's a girl, Maria."

"Name your first child for the Virgin. I don't see the difficulty."

"The Virgin might be offended. If *I* decide when to have a baby, instead of leaving it to God to decide, I might be punished. Perhaps it would be that I would not be allowed to have a baby at all. Don't you see?"

It was an argument that struck Beppe as being logical. Actually he hadn't given the matter much thought, although it was a subject with which he wasn't unfamiliar, having read a magazine article on it quite by accident. The words "The Pill" had been printed in outsized type on a magazine cover, and he had been moved to investigate the content, finishing it on the spot, without buying it, at the kiosk where a number of copies had been stacked beside his daily newspaper. He had assumed that the article dealt with some new cure and had hoped it was for the common cold, which plagued him in the winter. It wasn't the first time the magazine had taken him in with a sensational blurb. One had made the insinuation that the Loch Ness Monster had actually been photographed. Another had intimated that a being from another planet had arrived via a flying saucer and been taken captive by the American intelligence service. He had relegated the report on the Pill to the cellar of his mind with these other stories, never dreaming that it was to be taken any more seriously.

"I see very well that you'll be punished by losing your looks and getting old with a lot of children hanging on your skirts," snapped Ersilia. "But, if that's what you want, it's your own affair. Don't forget to give me the pills back if you're not going to use them. They cost money, you know."

Beppe dug his eyes into Ersilia's black hair roots. If Ersilia was taking this thing and advocating its use, she mustn't be the only one. Could it be possible it was a practice that was widespread? Was the country swarming with girls like Ersilia who had turned themselves into empty, sterile bags? And doing it without the consent of their husbands, no doubt. As much as men might complain about supporting a large family, and he himself had done plenty of that with six sons and four daughters, it was unthinkable that any man would accept making love with a woman who wasn't all there. Moreover, risk added zest to the game.

"But don't hand me the bottle in front of Carlo," Ersilia warned.

Ah, it was as he had suspected. Her husband did not approve. Beppe was relieved at that. On the other hand, it signified that deciding how many children Carlo would father would be left up to Ersilia.

"But I thought Carlo knew you took them," Anna said.

"Why should he? It's my affair. After all, I'm the one who has to have the babies, not Carlo."

"You do want to have children later?" Anna pressed hopefully.

"Maybe so, maybe not. I haven't made up my mind."

Her mind! What man lived who didn't know of the contrary winds that wafted through the drafty female brain? Beppe considered the consequences of a general take-over of Ersilia's attitude. What was all this preoccupation about the population explosion—another subject that he had explored gratis at his kiosk? It was far more evident that the human race was threatened with extinction. He suddenly felt the foundations of the society he knew tremble under his very feet. Supposing they gave way? He closed his eyes and they did. They thundered down to the center of the earth, carrying all the past and the present into the great chasm that opened as they crashed. The new Italy slid over the awful abyss, a land where life was cold and calculated as it would some day be on the surface of the moon. Women with dull hair and sly eyes consumed the Pill in such quantity that manufacturing it became the country's chief industry. Fewer and fewer children were born, and those that were born were so listless from lack of companionship that they looked withered and old before they could walk.

In the Via della Scimmia months passed without a blue or pink satin bow being hung in an entrance to announce a birth. In the side streets giving off the Via della Scimmia, where the poorer families lived, the clotheslines that were strung along the building's outer walls still sagged with the weight of workmen's heavy underdrawers and undershirts, but it was rare to see a baby dress dancing in the wind. The cobblestones were trod clean of all hopscotch traces chalked by giggling little girls. No more flocks of shoving, shouting, laughing schoolboys in black smocks slowed traffic as they played in the middle of the street. A few forlorn scholars still straggled past Santa Maria del Portico, but there weren't enough of them in the whole quarter, Corsco Vittorio included, to make up a decent soccer team.

Not that it mattered. The great national sport had died out. The heroes of the new Italy were all scientists, men with huge heads and legs so spindled they could break kicking a ball. They worked long hours in artificially lighted laboratories and computing centers, hastily consuming their midday meals like Americans. They ate their evening pasta in the sickening silence of their childless houses and were dragged by their wives to bed. There an act took place that had a mechanical resemblance to what had once been called "making love," but was nearer in spirit to treatments given to revive victims of asphyxiation and attempted suicide which Beppe's cousin Otello, who worked in the reanimation department of the hospital of San Giacomo, had frequently described. The men huffed and puffed and groaned and ground upon the flaccid flesh of their women. But plunge and prime as they might, their efforts were no more effective than those of a rusty pump on a waterless well. Within their women the sources of life were as dry as their straw-tinted hair; and, passion spent, their fertilizer dumped on sterile soil, the men dropped their great lolling heads upon foam rubber and slept.

Beppe shuddered and clasped himself in his arms, his eyes still shut tight. Was someone calling him? The muffled sound came again. It was his name, but his reflexes took little note of it. There was a short wait and then the flat of a hand smacked the bathroom door with such force that the key fell from the lock and clattered on the floor. Beppe's eyelids shot aloft and he whirled about.

"Are you in there, Beppe?"

Beppe stared at the key as a prisoner might a file before he swooped it up. Just how long had he been locked away? Nothing like as long as it seemed, surely. Five minutes? Ten? Maybe it had been as long as it seemed. Perhaps the cake had been cut and the toasts drunk without him. His brain suddenly whirled with such cross currents that he made several false stabs before he centered the key in its hole. The door swung inward on sagging hinges and the opening framed his wife.

"Ah, at last," she said with a sigh and a smile. "I've been looking all over for you."

"I had a . . ." he began, but the spidery fingers that had crept under his scalp had started loosening their hold at the sight of her. He took a deep breath and drew in the rich, ripe perfume of her body, her freshly-baked-bread smell, her sweet, talcumed sweat smell.

"You had a what?" his wife asked in her common-sense voice.

"Nothing. Nothing," he said. "I had to go to the toilet, that's all." Perhaps what he had had had been a seizure of some kind. People who were subject to seizures were never able to give any sort of an account of what they had experienced.

"What are you looking at?" his wife asked.

A seizure brought on by the chatter of that delinquent girl. That was it. What he was looking at were his wife's arms. They burst forth from capped sleeves of navy blue lace like salamis from the outer casing, the skin firmly packed and gleaming. In the twenty-seven years they had been married, he had seen those arms roll enough pasta to reach from Reggio Calabria to the Swiss border, sweep more floors than were laid in all of

Rome, rub and wring through sudsy waters and empty enough washtubs to flood the Tiber. They had lovingly cradled his ten children and furiously flailed his ten children. They had tended the sick and laid out the dead. They were as strong as steel and as soft to touch as silk. Even in repose, as they were now, they were charged with vitality, throbbing with life, impatient to resume their mission as extensions of the heart.

"At your arms," Beppe said. "You have nice arms, Amelia."

Amelia frowned and held her right arm up for a quick appraisal. "I have fat arms," she pronounced almost at once.

"I don't like thin arms. I don't like women with thin arms and sunken chests. Or with dyed hair. Women should be like you."

"Why, Beppe." Amelia blushed and turned her head aside. "What are you saying?" She slanted him a long look and then faced him directly again. "You're sure you feel all right?" she demanded in her common-sense voice.

"Of course I feel all right," Beppe said. He wondered how he could ever have let that girl upset him so.

"Then we'd better be getting downstairs. People were already beginning to come back to the table. That's why I came to look for you." She tucked down one of the peaks of his pocket handkerchief, smoothed the navy blue lace over her abdomen and indicated the urgency to depart with a flip of her head.

Beppe followed her down the stairs, his eyes riding the waves of her free, full buttocks, his mind amending his toast. When the time came to make it, he raised his glass with a steady hand. "Health, prosperity, a long and happy life together." He brought his glass near his lips. "And may the Virgin bless you with many, many children." He took a sip and surveyed his audience through the upper half of his bifocals. The palms of Anna's hands flew to her cheeks and Riccardo laughed and put his arm around her. Beppe hadn't noticed until now that Fiorella, Dino's wife, was pregnant. She had come to stand in the doorway to the kitchen for the toast-making. She held a glass in one hand and gently massaged her rounding belly with the other. Counting her, there were three women in the room who were visibly with child. It more than made up for one barren, bony Ersilia.

The kitchen of the Fregene house had a musty, mousy smell from being closed all winter. The water, released from long imprisonment, burst forth in a series of rapid spurts when Pippo turned on the spigot in the kitchen sink. He waited until it ran clear of rust before he bent over and filled his cupped hand. He sucked in a mouthful and spat it right out. His tongue and lips felt as if they had been coated with corroded copper. Typhus, he predicted to himself. The probability that the disease was even now initiating its fatal assault was verified by a tickling in his throat. Microbes digging toward the blood stream! He gave his throat a violent clearing, spat again and wiped out the inside of his mouth with his handkerchief. It made him thirstier than ever. He had the international whore upstairs to thank. Make love well and you are hungry enough to eat two Florentine steaks afterward. Make love badly and you were thirsty enough to drink two liters of aqua minerale. It was one of the first of the cardinal rules he had learned about sex, but it always took him by surprise. His mistake had been to open his eyes when he did, but then he had expected to find that hers were closed instead of staring at him with a steely challenge. He had just managed to meet it.

He found a bottle of Campari in the third cabinet he opened. He took a swig of that and changed the taste in his mouth from corroded copper to gall. He lit his last cigarette, inhaled deeply and went into the dining room. It was walled entirely with mirrors. He'd as happily sit down to a meal inside the house of the labyrinth at Luna Park. He preferred his left profile to his right, and he devoted several minutes to the pleasure of posing it in various attitudes and seeing it multiplied into an infinity of rewarding reflections. He was less satisfied with the view of his back. For all the fittings he had had on his jacket, there was still a slight bunching where the sleeve was set in at his right shoulder. He had given his tailor ten thousand lire on the hundred thousand he owed, and before he handed over another ten thousand lire, he would insist on perfection. When the money started pouring in from Go-Go Grow, he would go to the best tailors in Rome and order a dozen suits at a time. He would also change shirtmakers. The shirt he was wearing didn't hold up under close inspection. The collar had a tendency to curl. It wasn't obvious, but it was there. He smoothed it and went into the living room.

He crossed the floor of glittering red tile and sat down on a white lacquered chair that stood on a disc and was supported by a single rod and looked to him like something invented for the training of astronauts, took a red telephone off a white lacquered table and dialed. The maid in Donatella's house answered. Donatella was longer than usual in coming to the telephone and when she did he detected a frostiness in her voice. "*Ciao, tesoro,*" he said cheerfully, ignoring it.

Donatella had telephoned him from Maestosi because she had been undecided about choosing her dress material. Her mother had recommended a navy and white silk print, the salesman had favored a sky blue because it was more youthful. She herself had liked a modern design in pinks and reds. So, she had called him. And she had been told by their new girl from Abruzzi that he had gone out . . .

He had forgotten to instruct the Abruzzese slattern in the art of responding to telephone calls in such a way that he was never compromised.

And, Donatella went on, she had called again a half hour later. And then she had just called five minutes before and he wasn't home yet. And he had told her this morning that he would be working in his father's studio and where was he, if it wasn't asking too much?

It was asking a lot too much. Interrogations of this sort were his prerogative, not hers. "Which did you choose?" he asked, taking an indirect route toward straightening her out.

"The one I liked best," said Donatella.

"The one of pinks and reds?"

"Yes."

"You are joking, of course." Pippo affected an ironic chuckle.

"I am not joking. Why? What is wrong with pink and red?"

Pippo reserved comment and snuffed out his cigarette in a ceramic ashtray that was shaped like a fish. Her self-confidence would fade faster in silence.

"Well?" Donatella asked after a lengthy wait.

"Well, what?" said Pippo.

"Is there anything wrong with pink and red?"

"Nothing. On a blonde." He allowed time for her to become thoroughly shaken. "If I were you I would return the material for exchange."

"I can't."

"In other words, you aren't interested in dressing to please me or in caring what . . ."

"Oh, no, Pippo," Donatella broke in with a wail. "You know it isn't that. It's that it's been cut from the bolt and they don't like to . . ."

"Never mind making excuses," Pippo advised shortly.

"But they're not excuses. It's that once the material has been cut . . . I mean no one would ever think of trying to return material that had been . . ."

"Calm down, Donatella. You're saying the same thing over and over again."

"But, please, Pippo, you don't understand, and . . ."

"I understand. I understand that none of this would have happened if you had consulted me before making this ridiculous purchase."

"But I did. I did telephone you."

"Did you or did you not consult me?" Pippo lifted the lid

of a cigarette box that was shaped like a fish, a companion piece of the ashtray.

"No, Pippo, but that was because . . ."

"You have done well to admit it," Pippo imitated his father in courtroom condescension. "Now then, I am sure that if you go back and explain that you made a foolish choice and that your fiancé is displeased there will be no question about an exchange."

"Oh, what will they think of me?" Donatella moaned.

The cigarette box held some children's crayons and several rubber bands. "Are you interested in what they will think or what I will think?" Pippo took a rubber band out of the box. He adjusted the telephone receiver to rest on his shoulder and took the butt of his cigarette out of the ashtray. "Go ahead. Tell me."

"You," Donatella answered in a wee, tearful bleat.

"That's better. Next time perhaps you will wait to discuss matters with me. Next time perhaps you will realize that I have a lot on my mind and that I can't be called away in the middle of my work to answer questions that are not of immediate importance. I left orders with that girl to say I was out because I cannot be disturbed. I am busy! I told you that this morning. I am very, very, very busy, Donatella." Pippo let go the rubber band that he had twisted into the shape of a sling, and the cigarette butt shot through the air and pinged against a brass umbrella stand beside the front door. He put the rubber band back in the box and replaced the cover. "Yes, of course I forgive you." He could afford to mellow now. "Certainly I love you. Stop crying, *tesoro*. I told you I had forgiven you. I must go now. Papà is calling me. We must eat and go back to work without a siesta . . . you'll be at Bianca's. I know. I'll call you there. *Ciao, tesoro, ciao*."

Pippo stood up and stretched and went across the room to search the drawers of a desk for cigarettes. Nothing. There was a box on the mantel that held promise, but it turned out to be filled with sea shells. He stared for some time unthinkingly at the leopard coat that had been tossed on the red-and-white striped sofa, and hope stirred anew. There was a lone beige suede glove in one pocket and nothing in the other. "*Mannaggia la* . . ." he muttered. If women had to smoke, why didn't they smoke their own cigarettes? He should have thought twice before putting his package with only three left on the table beside the bed. She had reached out and taken the one he could have been smoking now after he had rolled off her, while he was getting back his wind. The initials A and W were embroidered in an elaborate script on the lining. So she really had given her right name. The least she could do if she was going around the world making love with strangers would be to pretend to be someone else. Who knew how much she had paid for a coat like that? One of his first presents to Donatella would be one equally good. Even better. Donatella would have jewels fit for a queen, too. He would exchange the engagement ring he had given her for the biggest diamond in Bulgari's window. "Who is the woman with the stupendous jewels?" would be the question on the lips of men and women at every opening of a new musical comedy, at the tables in the roof-garden restaurant of the Cavalieri Hilton on New Year's Eve, in the first-class cocktail lounge aboard the *Raffaello*. "The wife of Pippo La Rosa. The wife of Filippo La Rosa. The wife of Commendatore La Rosa. The wife of . . ." No. Without doubt there would be pressure on him to enter politics, but he would refuse. Far better to stay behind the scenes. Politicians were no more than puppets. The real power was in the hands of those who pulled the strings. He flung the coat down, sauntered to the front door and went outside.

The house was set two blocks inland from the sea in the shade of a grove of towering umbrella pines. A cobblestone walk bordered by a high, dense hedge of pittasporum wound toward an iron gate in the wall that surrounded the grounds and kept them concealed from public view. Pippo walked toward the gate. Through the foliage on his right he caught glimpses of the red-surfaced tennis court. He stopped and peered through the hedge on his left at a rectangular swimming pool. He had seen it once before, but without water it looked smaller. His own would be constructed along Olympic proportions. He went on down the walk and passed from under the sheltering pines through the gate into the street.

Walking slowly, he took less than five minutes to reach the broad avenue that ran parallel to the sea and along which the bathing establishments backed. He turned in at Toni's, his favorite. The bar and restaurant were still boarded up. No one was about. He went under the arcade, past the shuttered ticket window and out onto the sand.

The sky was fiercely blue, and the sun had risen in it to full command. The water teased away lazily at the shore and the sand was swept clean. The cabins had taken something of a beating during the rains, but he saw that a tarpaulin had been spread on the little porch of one of them and that there were cans of paint and brushes. Before long they would all be freshly coated. The double row of chairs and umbrellas would be set up to face the sea near the line of the shore. It would be summer. Summer!

Pippo stretched his arms wide and breathed in deeply. He clapped the palms of his hands against his abdomen and gave himself a gentle massage. He could feel his ribs, all right, but he had to suck his breath in hard to make the small roll of fat beneath them disappear. It was the result of over-indulgence in *pasta asciutta* during the winter, and it had to go. He took off his jacket, dropped it on the sand and raised his arm above his head. Knees rigid, he touched his toes. He repeated the exercise ten times and had the immediate gratification of pains in the back muscles of his thighs. Fifteen vigorous minutes every morning and he would be his usual trim summer self, a perfect V of firm bronzed flesh over taut muscle. He did a half-dozen slow knee bends that left him puffing. There would be some days of torture before his body became conditioned, but he would walk across this very sand six weeks from now in a bikini that fitted as if it had been painted on.

Some of his friends complained about bringing their fiancées along to the sea, but he found Donatella hardly any problem at all. She was busy from the moment they arrived setting up housekeeping on a miniature scale, arranging folding chairs and tables, inflating mattresses, adjusting the umbrella to give proper shade, and hanging up her wardrobe of bathing suits and his wardrobe of bikinis and their jackets and sweaters and beach hats. After her first swim, she had to change suits and put rollers in her hair and cover them with a scarf and lie in a secluded spot until her hair was dry. And, once dried, it had to be combed out and sprayed. By then it was time for setting the table and loading it with mountains of food she brought in a huge wicker basket. She took a long nap when lunch was finished and then had a second swim and went through the hair-setting process again. She dismantled the cabina and showered and dressed and gave her hair some final attentions, and the hour had come to go back to Rome. Her heavy schedule gave him a lot of legitimate free time, and it didn't take much ingenuity to invent excuses for more.

There had been one day last summer when he kept fixed dates with three other girls and even worked in an impromptu fourth. While Donatella prepared lunch, he had gone for a long walk to the Fishermen's Village with one of the ushers from the Cinema Capranica. He had picked her up at the Sogno del Mare, the establishment adjoining Toni's on the north, in accordance with arrangements made on a trip to the men's room when he had taken Donatella to see a film the night before. The promise the tight blue serge usher's uniform held had been magnanimously kept in a white nylon fishnet bikini behind a shield of asbestos roofing on the back porch of a deserted shack. After lunch, Donatella had slept, and he had gone to the establishment adjoining Toni's on the south to have coffee with Adrianna, the cashier from the Bar Flaminia. Adrianna had a long, pale face set in a huge mane of hair black as carbon. She twitched nervously when she made change and whinnied without altering expression when she was amused, symptoms from which Pippo had diagnosed an unnatural prolongation of a state of virginity. Not that he had ever entertained any ideas of undertaking her cure. Being the first one, even with pretty girls, was a repellent operation he gladly left to specialists in that field, but he did carry on a mild flirtation with Adrianna, throwing one of his sensual impulses her way occasionally as he leaned against the bar, catching a strand of her wiry black hair around his finger while he studied the temptations of the candy counter or complimenting her on the beauty of her eyes, which she rimmed in mascara, making herself look like a raccoon. The return on these little attentions was considerable. When she presented him with his monthly bill, it was for half the amount he had actually consumed, and if he was out of money, he winked and she whinnied and kept their hilarious secret from Pino, the owner.

He had accompanied Donatella on her second swim, and then, when her hair had been safely set once more, he had put the blame for having to leave her on a faulty carburetor and the urgent need of finding a mechanic if they hoped to get home without trouble. He had then driven into the village shopping center to keep an appointment with a girl who had been a runner-up for the title of Miss Italy three years before and had now opened a boutique. It hadn't turned into the quiet interlude in her private office he had anticipated. There was no private office. The shop consisted of a single room, so small that three customers gave the impression of a crowd and the proprietress was hot and harried because the girl who helped her hadn't come to work. He was pressed into delivering a parcel at a house he had to pass anyway on his return to Toni's and had been satisfactorily compensated for the courtesy. A tall, blond girl of heroic proportions who looked as if she had been air-conditioned had answered the door. Scandinavian, he had judged, and rightly. She had told him that she was Norwegian and had taken a summer job caring for the two small sons of the mistress of the house, and he had put on one of his best-selling, long-playing records about the cultural climate of Rome and arranged to meet her on her next day off at two-thirty and escort her through the Vatican Museums, which he knew very well closed on the dot of two. Nordic girls were suited to hot weather. Going to bed with one was more like going to bed with a mermaid than a woman. Their skin had the color of their pale sun, and he suspected that something closer to the waters of their fiords than blood ran through their veins. It was no wonder they came in droves to be warmed up in Italy.

Pippo picked up his jacket, shook the sand off and hooked it over his right shoulder with his forefinger. He cast a farewell smile across the water, remembering his father's telling him when he was a little boy that if the world were flattened out he would be able to look from this shore of the Tyrrhenian Sea directly at the coastline of Spain. Spain had seemed so far away then, a mystic land that clung to the perilous curve of the earth beyond the confines of safety marked by the line where the sea met the sky. Today everything seemed near. Yesterday, tomorrow, summer, the boy he had been, the man he was and the man he would be, Donatella, his father and his mother and his brothers, his friends at the Bar Flavia. Life radiated through him and he felt his pulse beat at its very center. He let out a long, grateful sigh and toyed a hard, dried sea ball into position with the toe of his shoe. He gave it a kick and watched it sail through the air and drop at the water's edge before he spun around and started back.

Sergio was coming down the stairs as Pippo walked through the front door. "*Ammazzete!*" Sergio said and shook both his hands from limp wrists. "She needs more than two men. She needs a regiment."

"What's she doing?" Pippo asked.

"Getting dressed." Sergio lifted the receiver of the telephone and dialed.

"That shouldn't take long, since she's not wearing anything," said Pippo, impatient to get the drive back to town over with and see the last of her.

"*Ciao,*" Sergio said into the telephone. "It's me. Sergio."

Pippo took his black book and his pen out of the inside pocket of his jacket.

"Really! When?" Sergio asked.

Pippo put a mark beside the day's date, gritted his teeth in resentment and stuffed the book and pen back in his pocket. "What is that whore doing?"

"Really!" said Sergio. "When? What time was it exactly?"

Pippo went to the foot of the stairs and made a megaphone of his hands. "*Allora,*" he bellowed. "Let's go."

Sergio pressed the receiver hard against his left ear and plugged his right ear with his finger. "Yes, yes. And then . . ."

"In another minute I'm going up there and . . ."

"Quiet, Pippo. I'm talking to the office. The boss called."

Pippo sprang to Sergio's side. "What about the tape? Did it work?"

"That's what I'm trying to find out. Go on, Carla. What then?" Sergio tilted the receiver so that Pippo could listen as well, and Pippo lent paternal attention to the report on the performance of a favorite brain child.

Sergio's boss made frequent trips to Germany and France and England to confer with the automobile manufacturers he represented, which should have liberated Sergio during these absences from the boring routine of regular office hours, except that his boss had a habit of making unexpected telephone calls. Sergio had had some misgivings about recording a response, even though Carla, the firm's secretary, was in love with him and would happily have bitten off the hand of the boss that fed her to prove it. Pippo's logic had prevailed eventually, particularly since these conversations between Sergio and his employer followed an unvarying opening pattern, mutual identification, an exchange of greetings and then a demand from the boss to know how everything was going.

At this point in the script that it had taken Pippo five minutes to write, Carla was to hold a folded handkerchief over the telephone mouthpiece, applying pressure to it gradually to make Sergio's recorded voice grow fainter and fainter, after which she was to lift the handkerchief long enough for Sergio's voice to go through clearly with a request to "please speak louder because I can't hear a word," followed shortly by Sergio's shout that "there's something wrong with the telephone and they've promised to come fix it late this afternoon, so could you please call back first thing in the morning?" A pen scraped back and forth across the grill of the mouthpiece added an authentic note to the final breakdown of communications before Carla was to hang up. On the chance that a second call might be put through, she was to take the receiver back off ten minutes so that the busy signal would be in operation. Rehearsals held with Pippo acting the part of Sergio's boss from the telephone in the Bar Flavia had gone remarkably well.

"At one point he was shouting so that he didn't even need a telephone to be heard all the way from Frankfurt," Carla was saying. "And at the end, at the end . . ."

"Are you laughing or crying?" Sergio demanded, perplexed.

Carla dropped down from high C. "Laughing. Because he was so mad. Exploding like Etna, the way he did that time when the little boy smashed the headlight of that new MG that had just come in."

"And what did he say at the very last?" Sergio asked.

"That he's going to sue."

"Me?" Sergio exclaimed in alarm.

"No. The telephone company. He's going to sue Teti."

Pippo snatched the telephone out of Sergio's hand. "*Brava*, Carla, *brava*. Take the rest of the day off. You've earned it."

Sergio reached out a remonstrating hand. "She can't do that."

Pippo waved him away. "How can an office function without a telephone anyway? It's beautiful. It's spring, Carla. Get one of your girl friends and go for a walk. Stop by the Bar Flaminia. Anything you want, and tell Adrianna to put it on my bill."

On the drive back to Rome, Sergio had a second thought about the office being closed on the first fine day, when the seeds sown by the winter's new-car advertising campaign were to begin germinating. "What if someone tells my boss it was closed after he gets back?"

"I can give you a hundred excuses to have ready by then." Pippo eased his hand over the clasp of the pocketbook that was wedged between his thigh and the thigh of the bag's owner and flipped the clasp open with his thumb. "When are you going to stop thinking like a slave anyway? A few more months and you can tell your boss to go to the devil." Pippo used two fingers like pincers to extract Lorenzo Salvini's card.

"You're sure nothing can go wrong?"

"I'm positive. Go-Go Grow," he murmured lovingly, and slipped the card inside the pocket of his jacket.

It had been a mistake to come. Caroline had realized it after it was too late to turn around and go out. She had thought of the drier as a blessed retreat, quite forgetting the preliminary operations one had to go through to get to it. It was partly because of those that she always did her own hair, and also because the magic touch of more than one highly recommended hairdresser had transformed her into a golliwog in times past.

"Would you like to try Signor Michele's special shampoo?" asked the girl in a pink uniform with the name Wanda embroidered in block letters of white on the breast pocket.

"No, thank you. Simple, ordinary shampoo, please," answered Caroline.

"It gives body and texture," Wanda went on, as Caroline had known she would. "Signor Michele advises it especially for fine hair like yours." Wanda gathered Caroline's hair in a fist and held it up, shaking the ends to cascade like palm fronds.

"All the same, I'd rather have the regular shampoo." Caroline rested the nape of her neck against the cushioned groove of the drainboard, and Wanda let the hair fall. Caroline closed her eyes and for a blissful minute thought of nothing while Wanda kneaded soap into her scalp.

"What kind of rinse do you usually use?" asked Wanda.

"A half lemon in a glass of warm water," Caroline answered in a swift breath and shut her eyes tighter.

"Lemon is drying," stated Wanda as the beginning of a discourse on rinses. "The reason people use it is to get out the soap, never considering that the natural oils . . ."

Caroline went stone deaf. She was so tired. Suddenly tired. Desperately tired. Achingly, agonizingly, physically tired. Used up to frightening, twilight depths within bone and muscle and nerve. It was a paralyzing fatigue beyond any curative power of normal sleep. She didn't want to sleep. To sleep meant waking up, returning to the present, running and running and running once more in the closed circle of now.

". . . has to be nourished the same way a plant does," Wanda said.

This must be how it was for refugees. This same limbo. This undreamed-of rejection. This abrupt expulsion into nowhere. What gave them the strength to go on? What made them believe there was any destination to reach? If there was no longer anything behind, why should there be anything ahead? What propelled them forward? How could they move under this deadening weight of weariness?

". . . loses its sheen and gets brittle." Wanda turned off the water and hung the hand spray on its hook.

There were those places in Switzerland where you were put into a kind of coma by doctors, and crisp, white, rubber-soled nurses watched over you while the days and nights slid over the silent peaks of eternal snow.

"We have lemon, if that's what you really want, but I know if you try the special rinse you'll like it."

But when the coma ended, then what? Time would have passed, but everything would be the same.

"All our customers are enthusiastic about it. It's a special formula that Signor Michele . . ."

Oh, dear God, how could she do all the things she would have to do before she could leave? How, when she felt like this?

". . . sold in the most luxurious stores in New York and London. Why don't you try it just this one time?"

If only she could go by ship. Perhaps the nine days at sea would work some miracle. A ship was the last place left on earth where there was anything like privacy. She could have all her meals sent to the cabin and lie in the dark, where there was no sound but the rhythmic heartbeat of engines and the soothing grind of stabilizers.

"All right?"

Caroline jumped. The girl had shouted into her ear. "All right, what?" Caroline asked.

"The rinse."

"Yes, yes." The more the girl did and the longer she took at it, the better. Anything so she could go on lying like this with her eyes closed. No. There were the children. Even if there were a way, the ship would be no good. She would have to spend hours with them on deck, and they would magnetize passengers who would insist she come to cocktail parties in the claustrophobic intimacy of their cubicles. Mr. and Mrs. Harold P. Wingate of Dallas, Texas, Suite 9, Sun Deck, where the sleep-creased-navy-poplin-piped-in-white pajamas of Mr. Harold P. Wingate ("Like him or not, there's one thing you've got to admit, and that's that Lyndon was the smartest goddam politician the country has ever known.") hung on the bathroom door beside the beigy-pink-nylon-lace-made-in-Paris-expressly-for-Neiman-Marcus nightgown ("We've given up buying *anything* when we go abroad because there's *nothing* you can't get at home *and* in American sizes.") of Mrs. Harold P. Wingate ("Do please call me Muriel"). How could she pretend to be an invalid in a darkened cabin when she had two small children? What excuse would she have not to watch the toy horses race when they were asleep?

"It doesn't change the color in any way. What it does is light up the true color."

They would sleep on the plane. A lot of the way, at least. She had to think about getting off the plane, too. When she and Lorenzo had gone back the year before Beatrice was born, they hadn't been able to find anything at the airport that looked like a porter and had had to push their luggage all the way through the terminal to the street on carts like those in supermarkets. Outrage mottled Lorenzo's face to this day when he remembered it. It was a springboard from which he dove into his oration on the Disproportionate Ratio of American Richness to American Comforts. All that free soap in hotels and no heated rods for the bath towels. In fact, no bath towels, for the biggest were one fourth European size. All that hot water and no bidets. He asked here how a people could be called truly civilized who gave that portion of their anatomy which logically required frequent cleansing during a day no more attention than their neck and ears. All those beds the size of soccer fields and only one pillow per person. All those vegetables and all that fruit at all seasons and all the flavor frozen out. All those shirts and suits to buy and nothing that really fitted. All the public leering and Lutheran lechery and the private prudery and frustration.

"*Allora,*" said Wanda, and took a towel from a cabinet beside the wash basin.

How long would it be until her mind could be her own once more? When, merciful heaven, would Lorenzo stop ploughing through the furrows of her brain? It was this above all that was making her so tired. Oh, God, she was so, so tired. What was she to do? Her arms seemed inert masses, long and ponderous as oak trunks. Her legs felt lifeless, detached, as if the only thing holding them on to her body was the garter belt attached to her stockings. Perhaps she was going to die of fatigue. Go into some fatal, total eclipse. Give up and give out right here with her head on the drainboard. Any second now, the garrulous Wanda would grate out the command to lift her head, but it would loll on, beyond the control of her neck, which had no more strength than a broken flower stem. Instead, and instantly, there was a metallic *bong*, and the chair on which she was sitting sprang upright. Her eyes opened automatically, like those of a doll, upon neon tubing and nylon draperies and mirrors and chrome and pink plastic upholstery.

"I think I'd better massage a bit of conditioning cream into your hair. It makes fine hair easier to comb." Wanda poked about in the bottles that littered the dressing shelf and shook her head. "I'll have to go get a new jar." She wound the towel around Caroline's wet hair turban-fashion and disappeared through the curtains.

Why, of course, it was all too simple. It wasn't hope or some mysteriously sustained courage that drove the dispossessed onward. They were prodded ahead by strangers, by unwitting, secret agents of fate. There would be other Wandas along the way, unconsciously fulfilling their ghoulish assignment to raise her from the dead and send her stumbling off again. The airline hostess: "Fasten your seat belt, Mrs. Salvini; we're coming into Kennedy." The taxi driver from Kennedy into New York: "You'll have to keep those kids quiet, lady, if you don't want me to go nuts in all this traffic." The hotel telephone operator: "It's eight o'clock, Mrs. Salvini, and you asked to be called at eight. Good morning." If she found a hotel, that was. What if they were all filled? There might be conventions, a massive assembling of Masons or Moose. How could she cable anyone to meet her when she didn't know herself what time she would arrive? And, even if she did, it would be unthinkable. It would seem a plea to be taken in. "As you know I adore Caroline and I hated myself for not asking her to stay with us especially since she knows we do have room but Jim is wildly busy and snapping with nerves and *just* Caroline would be a pleasure because Jim adores her too but Caroline *and* two small children!"

"*Eccomi,*" said Wanda, returning.

The talk behind her back. She was in for that, too. "Caroline's so evasive I haven't a clue you know says things like there was too much difference in viewpoints that she is too American and he too European but of course it has to be another woman or other women more likely since he *is* a wop my dear let's face it and they're all the same prince or peasant it doesn't matter."

"Lean against the head rest." Wanda had tilted back the chair again. "Signor Michele has found we get the best results from massaging it in thoroughly."

Caroline closed her eyes. It was leaving tonight she must concentrate on. Once she was on the plane, she'd have hours and hours to plan what she'd do when she got off it.

". . . stimulates the roots."

And also to decide on the best way to break the news to her father.

". . . luster . . ."

Oh. Oh. Oh, no! She wouldn't have the chance to break the news to her father at all, much less break it gently. Her father would be the first person Lorenzo would think of checking with. Lorenzo would assume that was where she was going and telephone. And when they had finished talking, her father would hang up and slowly take off his glasses and put them on his desk. And that heartbreaking bruised look would come into his blue eyes, which otherwise regarded the world with amused benevolence. Perhaps he would be working on the lectures he was to give in London in the fall. He would be too distressed about her to give a second thought to himself, to consider that it might mean canceling his trip to Rome following London, to wonder if it would be an end of his yearly sojourns in the pensione in the Piazza Trinità dei Monti.

". . . and split ends."

It was typical of him never to be persuaded to stay with them. Partly because of not wanting to impose. Partly because he was bound to schedules the rest of the year and loved being free. He was even allowed the luxury of skipping a meal if he became absorbed in deciphering some inscription or reading some moldering manuscript. Back home Milly, who had stayed on to keep house for him after her mother died, enforced dietary laws of her own making with fanatic zeal. Now he would feel betrayed by this city that had given him such pleasure and her such pain. She had sometimes joined him on his early-morning walks and felt like a child again as he lit up the past in a dim museum or neglected crypt of a church. She had looked forward to the time when Andrea and Beatrice would be old enough to follow him along the familiar paths he had worn on his lifelong pilgrimages through the magic maze of history. But Lorenzo had chosen to banish them all, to deprive his children of the reality of these visions, to limit her father to a Rome confined between the covers of his books. She was having trouble breathing. Her lungs felt as if they were filling up with fur. Death on the drainboard. This time it was a certainty. She tried to inhale, and the acid odors of hair bleach and dye and polish remover pricked the insides of her nostrils like needles.

"*Allora,*" Wanda sang out in duet with the *bong*ing chair.

The chair delivered a prophylactic smack along Caroline's backbone before settling into its rigid sitting position, and she gave a gasp that cleared her nasal passages. The air sighed back into her lungs and her heart resumed beating the drums. The march was to continue. Wanda swept the curtains apart and waved for her to follow. She was seated this time in a chair that swiveled, one of four in a row before a long counter attached to a mirrored wall. On her right, a woman beheaded by a dryer held a cigarette in one hand and a copy of *Elle* on her lap. The chair to Caroline's left was empty. Michele, the miracle man, flourished his comb like a wand above the head of a customer occupying the place next to it. He conjured up a forelock dyed the color of smoked salmon and turned it into grace notes across his subject's forehead. The forehead's owner tilted her chin, considered Michele's composition tentatively and smiled. "Mirror, mirror on the wall," thought Caroline. The girl was somewhere in her middle twenties, but the development of her features appeared to have been arrested around the age of eight. Her eyes weren't a color, but shot through with many colors, like pale opals, and set wide in her broad boneless face. False black lashes of an incredible length were glued to her pinkish lids, and her brows were arched in rust pencil. Michele brought the flames that licked out above her ears and neck under control with hair spray and held up a looking glass for final approval. It came in the form of diffident dimpling, as Caroline had expected. What else would be sold in beauty parlors but beauty? The mirrors in all of these places were enchanted, and the customer was served. It was no accident that the greatest fortunes in this business had been made by women homely as witches. Who would know more about creating illusion than they? Attract, arrest, allure, appeal, bloom, blaze, craze, daze, express, excite, fascinate, fulgurate, innovate and intoxicate, galvanize, hypnotize, magnetize and mesmerize, create, cultivate, radiate and operate, tranquilize, tantalize, scintillate and titillate, tempt, taunt, tease, please. Of all things to remember. She had made it up when she had first gone to work, after Smith, as a copywriter for Doyle, Dane.

"*Va bene?*" Michele asked the girl, twirling his wand on high.

The little putty nose went up and sniffed haughtily at more refined air. The girl was transfixed by the girl she saw, too far under the spell to hear. Caroline had never known such envy. Oh, to be like her.

"Ees how you like?" Michele sought to recall her in her own language.

The black lashes fluttered like injured moths. "Perfect," she answered in an ecstatic peep.

Oh, to believe the myths.

"I am so happy that madame eez pleez-ed." Michele tossed the comb onto the shelf.

That any woman can be beautiful. That every dog has his day. That life begins at forty. That you're as young as you feel.

Michele took another comb from a glass cylinder that held a bath of disinfectant.

That anyone can afford to buy soap! That money doesn't count. That honesty is the best policy. That crime doesn't pay. That the best man wins. And cheaters never do. That murder will out. That the meek will inherit the earth.

"I just hope I can remember exactly how you set it so I can tell the woman who does my hair back home."

"In New York," Michele said to the comb and flipped it dry.

"Yes. Well, New York State, that is. Rochester, New York. I imagine you've heard of it."

Michele picked at the teeth of the comb.

"It's a good-sized city," the native daughter affirmed with civic pride.

That there's no place like home. That there's room at the top. That all good things come to him who waits.

"Ah, *sì*. Rowchestair," said Michele, pretending to be suddenly oriented geographically.

"You can be sure that any of my friends from there who come here to Rome will be advised by me to come to you."

That justice will triumph. That experience teaches. That we're brothers under the skin. That love conquers all. That God is on our side. That there really is a Santa Claus, Virginia.

"*Grazie. Grazie*, signora." Michele dismissed himself with

a curt bow and an actor's smile and moved on to Caroline.

There was a fairly recent issue of *Today* among the magazines Wanda put on Caroline's lap after she went under the dryer. It had been a year or so since she had seen one. The format was the same, of course, and the girl on the cover gleamed on, month in month out, year in year out, as if she had been printed on patent leather. The magazine was too much of an easily identifiable, coffee-table status symbol to change any of that. Most of the names on the masthead were new, but there were several left from her time, and Molly Draper was still editor in chief and would never relinquish her hold this side of the grave. And thank God. The hope she had for making that fantasy future in the brownstone real lay with Molly. Molly had always liked her, and she prayed that she still did, despite their last unfortunate encounter two years ago.

Molly had swept into Rome like a tempest with her coterie of assistants and models and photographers. Flash bulbs had exploded for three days and three nights. "Fabulous, fun shots," Molly had told her while showing the contacts. A mulatto mannequin wearing a caftan and turban "inspired by those sublime Moroccan Blue Men" posed with marble workers, their faces chalky and their eyebrows and lashes fluffy-white from the flying dust of the polishers. Six girls in drifting chiffon draped themselves against six of the Temple of Vesta's Corinthian columns. "Not a virgin in the lot," Molly had laughed. Penelope Perkins de Costa had been lured out of retirement to don a great picture hat and play Lady Bountiful to an urchin selling flowers before the doorway of a Trastevere trattoria. Penelope had received an "astronomical sum" plus the gift of the hat, and the boy had been paid off with an American dollar. This inequity had been rectified in typical Trastevere style. The scene had been rehearsed several times before it was frozen on film; Penelope, hand in open pocketbook, elongated neck swan-diving toward the boy and the boy looking up at her, his left hand clutching a bouquet of anemones, his right hand Penelope's wrist. Or rather, as it turned out, Penelope's bracelet.

"Not prop jewelry, but Penelope's very own, a heaven cobra with emerald eyes, custom-made by Van Cleef." Molly had reviewed the details of the unsolved mystery on her last night in Rome at a dinner she gave for her little court to which Caroline and Lorenzo had also been asked, voicing her indignation at breath-taking speed in those special phrases that her staff admiringly called Draperisms. "That child. That beast of a Botticelli *bambino*. That monstrosity!"

"How old was the boy?" Lorenzo had asked, to Caroline's relief, for he hadn't appeared to be listening and Molly's recital had been mostly for his benefit, since the others present had been eyewitnesses.

"Newborn. Wee. Wee. Minute!" Molly had said, indicating a height far below table level with both her hands.

"Not more than seven at the most," Janice Wilson had intoned. Janice was Molly's chief acolyte, a dark, gaunt giantess who made it her duty to interpret the gospel according to Molly to those wanting in perception.

"The police will be able to trace him," Lorenzo had said. "What better evidence might they have than a photograph?"

"But, my true love, how exactly right you would be . . ." Molly had touched Lorenzo's sleeve with the tips of her long fingers. She was famous for her beautiful hands and using them for emphasizing her dramatic pauses. ". . . except that the boy's back was to the camera in every shot. And the back of one seven-year-old boy is the back of *every* seven-year-old boy."

"All little Italian boys of seven look alike," Janice Wilson had paraphrased dutifully.

"Rather like the Chinese," Lorenzo had added dryly, making a motion for a waiter to refill his empty glass with mineral water.

Molly had swept a sidelong glare at Janice, before she

banished her from her sight by closing her eyes and turned her head toward Lorenzo. Molly was famous, too, for her long, Garbo-like eyelids and speaking at length with her eyes closed, a mannerism she used effectively to bring the most distracted audiences to attention. "Janice hasn't understood at all what I said. Obviously there are hundreds of little boys with bare, bronzed torsos and ragged jeans and a mop of black curls in Trastevere who look identical from the back." Molly's eyes had sprung open, expecting to find Lorenzo under her spell. But Lorenzo was intent on some of his own mesmerizing. The waiter had filled his glass half full, and Lorenzo was making a wordless communication that half a glass was only half the amount of water he wanted. The evening was proceeding as Lorenzo had predicted it would when he at first flatly refused to attend that dinner or any dinner in a restaurant on Saturday night, when all restaurants were noisy and crowded and the service was impossible.

"Just as the police said," Jerry James, the models' make-up man, had put in.

"What did the police say?" Lorenzo had addressed the question to his brimming water glass, sparing himself, Caroline had understood, the spectacle of Jerry's bleached hair, which he had taken in like a quarantine warning when they had been introduced.

"That there wasn't a hope of identifying the boy," Ken Kraft had said. Ken was the unbleached one.

Lorenzo had smiled for the first time and only time during the evening. "The perfect crime," he had said, lifting his water glass.

"You find it amusing?" Molly had asked.

"Reassuring," Lorenzo had answered.

Molly had closed her eyes. "Reassuring!"

"That we are not in danger of losing our . . . I believe the word you Americans use is 'image.' "

Molly had opened her eyes and her mouth, but as she had been uncertain as to exactly what Lorenzo had meant, had remained speechless. Lorenzo wouldn't have heard her in any case, because Millicent Murphy, who was sitting beside him, had let out a gasp. A waiter had inadvertently knocked askew the tower in which her hair had been piled.

"Oh, damn," Millicent had wailed, supporting the edifice with both hands. "Oh, Christ, Ken, it's had it."

"All the waiters in Rome go mad on Saturday night," Lorenzo had said.

Molly had closed her eyes, stretched out her arms full length and set her fingers dancing. "Ken, do be a true love and take Millicent out to some private corner and put her together again. Ken does the girls' hair," Molly told Lorenzo, opening her eyes.

"And Jerry's." The mulatto model, whose name was Chloe, had uttered her first words of the evening.

"Bitch!" Ken had said, narrowing his cupid-bowed lips into a mirthless smile. "Come on, Millicent."

Jerry James had got up from his chair, too. "I need the little girls' room myself. I think the way the boys and the girls use the same john over here is absolute heaven."

"Makes it a lot easier for you, doesn't it?" Chloe had commented.

"Bitch!" Jerry had squealed, and given Chloe's shoulder a playful poke.

"Why are you always putting Jerry and Ken on?" the model whose name was Fifi Fenton had demanded of Chloe as the boys had gone out with Millicent.

"They love it."

"I don't believe they love it at all." Fifi had lifted her cover-girl features on high. "They're sweet. I'm mad for them both. They've been together for years. They are just as married as any woman and man."

"That's for sure," Chloe had said.

"What you don't understand is that homosexuals have the same feelings we do. They're just like everybody else."

"Oh, I agree," Chloe had said and then leaned across the

table and rolled her eyes like a minstrel man at Fifi. "But would you want one of them to marry your sister?"

Except for Lorenzo, the table had been convulsed. Caroline herself had thought it was funny until she had tried to explain to Lorenzo why it was funny and then, of course, it hadn't seemed funny at all. "It's one of those things you have to be an American to understand," she had finished helplessly.

"It's what we call an inside joke," Mr. Erwin Epstein, the brother of Mr. Morris Epstein, who owned *Today*, had said to Lorenzo. "This Chloe is a damned funny girl. A brain, too, by the way. She's a college graduate."

Lorenzo had looked from Erwin Epstein to Chloe to a plate aflame with smoked salmon that had just been put before him. "This is not what I ordered," he told the waiter.

"Oh, that's mine." Mr. Erwin, as he was called, had reached across the table and taken the fish.

"*Scusi*, Signor Marchese," the waiter had apologized, placing a clear broth before Lorenzo.

"I'm in the administration end of the magazine," Mr. Erwin continued, "so I don't usually get in on the fun. Just happened that some foreign distribution problems brought me to Rome at the same time, so I could have dinner with the swinging side of the establishment." Mr. Erwin's fingers had skipped down the bare arm of Fifi Fenton on their way to his fork.

"It's always a ball when Mr. Erwin's along," Fifi had said. "And just take a guess how old he is," she had challenged Lorenzo.

Lorenzo had supposed it was a challenge he was expected to meet and had prepared himself by a candid study of the pampered parchment that covered Mr. Erwin's nearly hairless skull. Like most Italians, Lorenzo was deadly accurate at guessing ages, and Caroline had managed to catch his eye just in time.

"Now, now, Fifi, that's another inside joke. You mustn't put Marchese Salvini on the spot. I am seventy-four years of age, Marchese."

Caroline had wished that Lorenzo might have shown some evidence of surprise, and also that Mr. Erwin could have resisted addressing Lorenzo as "Marchese" with such relish and peristency. She furthermore wished for the good sense never to repeat this sort of confrontation with herself in the role of tightrope walker between two continents.

"And two thirds of those seventy-four years I've been wearing the same harness. . . ."

Lorenzo had divided his attention between his soup and Mr. Erwin's monologue, a warp and woof of Mr. Erwin's life story and the history of *Today*, which Caroline had heard before.

". . . realize full well that an Italian edition of *Today* is pretty much of a gamble, but taking chances is how my brother and I have got most of our kicks out of this life . . ." She had come back from afar to hear Mr. Erwin saying, "One of our problems, perhaps our main problem, is going to be to find someone to run the show, an editor over here that gets the message of all that *Today* is really about, some woman who is intelligent, of course, but basically . . . basically . . ."

"Provincial," Lorenzo had offered, and quite unmindful of Mr. Erwin's astonishment had gone on, "I should think that only a woman who was essentially provincial could maintain a prolonged enthusiasm for . . ."

Mercifully, Jerry and Ken's squealing re-entrance with Millicent had cut Lorenzo short. Perhaps she had simply imagined that Molly had overheard him. Maybe Janice's eyes hadn't really raced around the table soliciting a refutation of the heresy. Looking back now, it seemed unlikely that Molly had actually tried to save face by suddenly becoming even more animated than usual.

When the interminable evening was over and they were driving home, Lorenzo had refused to believe that he had created an awkward moment, much less to regret it. "I listened to the old man with the greatest attention and gave him my opinion as he had asked."

"But it wasn't the opinion he wanted," she had said. "The

last thing he wants is a woman who is 'basically provincial.' What he wants is . . ."

"Someone who is highly veneered, of course. But he knows that any truly sophisticated woman would find the job intolerably boring. What he wants is someone who believes in all the magazine's silliness as much as the women who read it."

"You've missed the whole point. He doesn't think there is anything in the least silly about *Today.*"

"It is you who have missed the point, *tesoro*. You weren't listening. You didn't hear his note of irony when he said he wanted someone who 'got the message of the magazine.' Being a businessman, he must pretend to take it seriously, naturally, but the message is money."

"But he wasn't being ironic. He truly believes that the magazine does have a mission of sorts. He's not pretending. He's serious. And so is Molly Draper."

"What mission?" Lorenzo had asked, without much interest in an answer.

"Oh, to set standards . . . you know . . ."

"I do not know. What standards?"

"Well, not exactly standards . . . but to dictate the fashion in dress and decoration . . . and places to travel . . . resorts and hotels and restaurants . . . and a lot of other things. Even people."

"Which is precisely what I have understood the old man to have said. Do you believe that any woman who isn't basically a provincial could take such nonsense seriously?"

"That's just it. Molly was born in some little town in Georgia and may have thought you were making fun of her."

"I had no idea where she came from, although I'm not surprised. It proves my point."

"She may have thought I told you, if she heard you."

"I don't think she heard me. She was too occupied with the pederasts and the Gorgon-woman with all the hair. However, if she did, the offense was not intentional. In any case, I trust you to arrange a future in which I shall never see any of them again."

This had been simple enough so far as Mr. Erwin was concerned. Then days later, she had read in *Time* that he had "died of a heart attack on the dance floor of a supper club . . . in Manhattan." Cards had come the last two Christmases from Molly, addressed in Janice Wilson's best Bennington backhand. They wouldn't have been crossed off the list the first Christmas, for it would have been too obvious. But they most certainly would have on the second if Molly bore even the slightest resentment.

Caroline scanned the magazine's table of contents. It would be diplomatic to make a pretense of having kept up with the issues. She read the first and last paragraphs of an article entitled "Maxi-Dining on Mini-Money." In between there were photographs. Sake and sukiyaki and chopsticks on a low, black-lacquered table. On a rough-hewn refectory table, tequila and tacos and fried beans and guava. Aquavit and fish aspic and . . . oh, good God. How would she ever be able to go through with it? Where could she learn the secret formula for making the mask of hypocrisy invisible? She dropped the magazine into a rack beside her chair and clasped her shaking hands into a ball in her lap. It seemed she heard her name being called through the whir of the dryer. But who knew it here? It was the first time in her life she had ever been in the shop, and Michele, Wanda, none of them could possibly have the faintest idea who she was. Nevertheless, the call came again, distinct this time. and the metal hood was lifted. Hands felt her head.

"Your hair is dry, Marchesa Salvini."

A girl who wasn't Wanda was speaking to her. The name Ersilia was embroidered on the breast pocket of the pink uniform. She knew this girl from somewhere, the face, not the name. "Oh, oh, thank you." From where? She seized her pocketbook as she rose and made an unnecessary check of its contents, trying to remember, and remembering only a reverse occasion when she had failed to recognize her own dentist in a restaurant because he was a totally new personality outside his smock and disguised in a dark suit.

"I wasn't here when you came in," said Ersilia. "Signor Michele gave me a half day off to go to Anna's wedding."

Ah, Anna's cousin, of course. "How beautifully you did Anna's hair." Caroline smiled brightly, on her feet, on the march again. It would have been so easy to choose another hairdresser, but then she had known only that this girl worked for *a* hairdresser, not this hairdresser.

". . . toasts and they were all still there when I left," Ersilia was saying. "I am sorry I wasn't here to shampoo your hair, Marchesa, but I also do pedicures now. Would you like one?"

It would kill some more time. Too, Ersilia would report to Gino, who would report to Mario, who would report to Bruna, who would give a full account to Carmela to be passed on to Luisa. "The niece of Gino, Ersilia, has this afternoon given to your daughter-in-law a pedicure in the shop of the hairdresser, Michele," she could hear Carmela saying. The perfect alibi. A woman planning to flee would hardly be worrying about the appearance of her feet. "What a good idea," she said to Ersilia.

Randy read: "The road ran straight now, bordered by scrub, down through memories of Mashpee trails, toward the sea. Along the Cape's south shore, an arm struck out from the main body of land and thrust a fist into the surf, pointing an index finger toward Nantucket."

Randy eliminated "down through memories of Mashpee trails" with a pencil line and reread the sentence. He definitely liked it better the first way, but how would it seem to other people? He threw back his head, commanded his mind to pass the impartial judgment of an editor, and returned to his original version. A searing flame of shame shot through him. The cool wind of reason put it out. What was wrong with being poetic? His critical eye softened. He accepted the book for publication. It was printed and bound with the sentence intact.

He relaxed and read on: "Pride's Point had, until recently, been accessible only by foot, and even now that the bulldozers of the George M. Eaton Construction Company had cleared the scrub . . ." He stopped short. What about using the word "scrub" in alternate lines? That was just the kind of thing the reviewers would love to latch onto. A small thing like that was probably enough to make them bend double with hysterics. "This first novel by Alexander Palmer might better have been titled *The Scrub Book* and handed out gratis over the counters of supermarkets by a detergent manufacturer than published by the distinguished house of . . ." He substituted "bracken" for "scrub," erased it and tried "bush." Did that ever sound phony and foreign. Bush was Australian, maybe even African, but he was writing about America where scrub was scrub and nothing else. He could get around the double use by redoing one of the sentences, but anyway, why was it so bad to use the same word over again if it fitted? It wasn't, of course. Or was it? When he had first started his book there had been none of this self-doubt. It had all begun the day he had come home and found Charlie seated at his improvised desk reading the manuscript. He always kept it in the drawer under his shirts when anyone was around, and no one could get into the apartment when he was out because he always took the key, but that day he had left the key with Gino, who had needed it to get in to fix the pipes. Charlie hung around so much of the time that Gino had turned it over to him without question. Utterly absorbed, Charlie hadn't even heard him enter the open doorway. Charlie was smiling as he read, which Randy had found unnerving, since he couldn't remember ever having written a single sentence that was intentionally humorous.

"Help yourself," Randy had said, his chagrin finally giving way to anger.

"Hi," Charlie had said, without looking up. "What's Mashpee mean?"

"The Mashpee were an Indian tribe," he had answered with withering calm, advancing across the room. "Do you read other people's letters, too?"

Charlie had flipped over to the next page and looked up with a smile. "What'd you say?"

"I asked if you read other people's mail, too. Just any private stuff that you happen across?"

"What's private about this?"

"If you don't already know, it'd take too long to explain."

Charlie had dropped the sheets he held on the desk and thrown up his hands in exaggerated apology. "Well, excuse me. I figured it was a book and that writers wrote books to be read by anybody . . . the more people the better."

Randy had set about putting the pages back in order in silence, and Charlie had shuffled off to sprawl in the upholstered chair. "So what happens when What's-his-name meets this chick on Pride's Point? He finally socks it to her, right?"

"That's right," Randy had said, patronizing and controlled.

"And good and sexy, I hope. Personally, I don't see why he didn't screw her the first night he met her. Maybe you don't realize it, Ran, but there's a lot to wade through before this Pride's Point episode. If I were you, I'd shove in a couple of sexy scenes earlier. I'd cut out stuff like about those Indians. People skip all that anyway when they read. It'll give you more room to put in what people really want—sex, sex and more sex. Take my word for it, man."

"Thanks for the advice."

"And not just straight sex. That's a drag, it's been done so much. You've got to get far out if you want to sell. Like the other night I heard a thing that'd go great in your book. You remember that kooky Marsha I introduced you to?"

Randy remembered perfectly. "No," he had said.

"Sure you do. She's from New York. That blonde with the great shape. And the Mercedes. And you asked me where she got all the loot and I told you it was from making it with rich guys. You remember?"

"Vaguely."

"Well, she's got this guy that licks her all over. From head to foot. Even between the toes. She says it takes him about an hour and afterward she's like glue's been poured over her, and has to take a shower. I don't think that's been in a book yet. It was new to me. I asked her how she could stand it, but she thinks it's a gas."

"Well, thanks a lot, but there's just one small problem."

"Yeah, and what's that?"

"My book's about normal people." Randy had patted the sheets back into form to insert in a folder.

"These are normal people. Marsha hasn't got two heads. She's great-looking. She knows how to dress and has a sense of humor and everything. And the guy happens to be an international wheel with some oil company. He's got a wife and kids, and Jesus, he even wears a hat. What could be more normal than that?"

"While he's licking her?"

"What do you mean while he's licking her?"

"I mean is that when he wears the hat?"

"Very funny. Anyway, I met him with her. Once after she told me. He had on one of those square business suits. And a hat. Believe me, you couldn't dream up a more normal guy. Your trouble is that you haven't caught on that all normal people are abnormal today. Everybody. It's normal to be abnormal."

"Like your friend Duke Dawson."

Charlie had reflected several moments before commenting. "Well, Duke might possibly be an honest-to-God nut. If it's true, that is. What people do to each other is one thing, but Jesus . . . with chickens . . . I don't know. It's hard to believe."

"Not for me it isn't." He had loathed Dawson on sight.

"It's true he grew up on a farm, and maybe guys all alone in the wilds without any girls around go nutty. On the other hand, there's a good chance he's making it all up because of his career. That's what Lisa thinks. She thinks he thinks it will help his reputation. He's already crazy-looking and if he acts crazy, too, it'll get around that he's right for playing loony guys in movies. Could be he's really got a hang-up, or it could be he's playing it smart. After all, he's had a couple of bits in horror movies already, and I heard that Fellini was . . ."

"For God's sake, shut up." As usual, Charlie had persisted until Randy reached the boiling point. "I'm not interested in the career of that subnormal slob."

"Who's talking about his career? I'm talking about your career. I want you to make it big, Ran baby. And you're not going to unless you slow down on all that thinking your character does before he takes action and about how it looks on the Cape. That nature crap is for the *National Geographic.* 'I Helped a Robin Build a Nest' kind of stuff. Jesus, who needs it? Sex and violence, Ran baby. Sex and violence. Take my word for it."

Randy had risen above an urge to demolish Charlie in a literary debate by reminding himself that he would be taking an unfair advantage. He held a university degree. Charlie had been kicked out of three American prep schools and two prep schools in Switzerland before achieving his rightful status among the mentally retarded.

"I'm giving it to you straight because I'm a friend."

Randy had risen above a second urge to set him right on that score. It had been his misfortune to be assigned to a tent with Charlie and two others at summer camp when they were kids. And his bad luck had dogged him to Rome, where they had met again twelve years later at a party in the Via Margutta. And the day Charlie got lost once more, he'd sure as hell never go looking for him.

"So take it for what it's worth. Now I admit you didn't give me a chance to read much, and it's possible that once things get going down at old Pride's Point, it turns into the kind of book it's hard to put down. But, from what I did read, just those twenty pages or so, well, I read those because of you, the author, because you're someone I know. But on the level, if you weren't the author and I happened to give it a quick once-over in a bookstore, you know what it'd be? Now, no offense, Ran baby, like I said I'm only telling you because I'm your friend. It'd be no sale."

Rising above that hadn't been quite so easy, although he had managed not to show it. On further thought, he had been able to convince himself that Charlie's reaction should be taken as a compliment, as a good omen, even as a guarantee. If his writing didn't appeal to Charlie, it followed that it would appeal to those that the evolutionary process had not bypassed. Charlie's place in the animal kingdom wasn't much above chimpanzee level, and he was aiming for that small, discriminating audience of men who were capable of thought. It would have been unkind to point this out.

"You're quite an authority on writing, aren't you?" he had observed instead.

"Hell, no. I'm an authority on reading," Charlie had responded brightly.

It had been as if a poison dart had pierced his brain. The more he twisted and turned the statement, the deeper it penetrated. The fact of the matter was that Charlie *was* an authority of sorts on reading. He never set out to read a book. He just happened to read a book because he had listlessly picked one up that he had found beside a chair where he was sitting or because he chanced to come upon a bookstall and some title or dust jacket had caught his attention. He either read a few pages and tossed the book away or became so engrossed he couldn't put it down until he had finished it. He had gone through *The Fascinating Insect World of J. Henri Fabre,* which he had found on the top of a box of trash, at a single sitting, and he had spent one whole weekend engrossed in a Merck medical manual that he had filched from the office of a doctor who had treated him for a torn ligament he had got dancing at the Piper.

A message had been coming through from all this for a long time, steadily growing clearer and clearer. It was that once he got started, Charlie would read anything that offered a minimum amount of novelty or diversion, and that Charlie had found nothing in the first twenty pages of Randy's book that had given him the slightest incentive to want to read more. In short, his writing had bored the hell out of Charlie. And, no matter how he looked at it, this was some kind of indication that it might bore the hell out of everyone else, too. Might! Would, more than likely.

As long as he had finally admitted this much to himself, why not go the whole way and admit that it never had been much of a story from the very beginning? The cold truth was that Alexander Palmer and his junior-year jinx, Leslie Cavanaugh, were not Tristan and Isolde. Or Abelard and Heloise. They weren't even Bonnie and Clyde. There had been some sniping between the houses of Palmer and Cavanaugh, but it suffered sad comparison with the warfare waged by Montague and Capulet. When the head of the House of Palmer had found out that the head of the House of Cavanaugh was a child psychologist, his old man had banged away on his familiar theme that it wasn't Marx and Mao who were America's deadly enemies, but Sigmund Freud and Benjamin Spock. Randy had confessed to Dr. Cavanaugh that he and his father rarely saw eye to eye, and Dr. Cavanaugh had sorrowfully commented that "the tragedy of our century is the inability to communicate." Randy had passed this observation on to his father during a dramatic discussion following Randy's spectacular fall from the dean's list to the dunce list.

"The tragedy of our century is double-talk," his father had snapped. "Since most minds are empty or foggy, it stands to reason that they are incapable of formulating lucid messages to communicate. Anyone who knows what he has to say has no difficulty whatsoever in transmitting his thought to another, and that other has no difficulty whatsoever in understanding the message, provided, of course, that he isn't an idiot. Assuming that you are not an idiot, I'll give you an example. You are in serious danger of flunking out of college. If you pull yourself together and make passing grades next semester, I shall continue to pay for your food and clothes and entertainment and gasoline for your car during your senior year and give you a substantial sum of money as a present when you graduate. If, instead, you fritter and moon away your time for the rest of the year, you can get a job and pay for your own food and clothes and entertainment and gasoline and forget about graduating from college. The choice between being a mess and amounting to something is yours." His father had stared at him long and intently. "I gather from your sullen silence that you have understood, that I have 'communicated' with total success. Or have you any questions?"

Randy hadn't had any. He had made it through the rest of his junior year. But just. He only wished the reason had been because of sex, sex and more sex with Leslie Cavanaugh, but sex had been an incidental, almost accidental, part of their affair. Whenever anything had happened, it had been more or less like Charlie's happening to read a book. What there had been a lot of was talk. Leslie had talked and he had listened, mostly to about how, although she loved him, she "needed to be free to express herself." Who could be expected to give a damn for a story about a girl who was obsessed with herself and a jerk who hung around listening to her nerves snap like rubber bands and waiting for her to close her mouth long enough for him to kiss her? The torch he had carried all the way across the Atlantic had gone out long ago, he knew now, but he had never really understood why he had put up with Leslie in the first place until he had slammed Maria Pia this afternoon. It was because he hadn't known any better. Like his old man said, how could she have put what she wanted into words when she hadn't known what she wanted? No women knew. You had to tell them. And back it up with force.

With an enormous sense of relief, he realized that he hadn't been able to write any more than he had because there was nothing more to write. He had mistaken what was an episode in his life for an epic. And a lot of enthusiasm, in the beginning, for talent. The enthusiasm had waned as his money had dwindled. With money, writing had been a game, but without it, it was work, and work that paid off late and sometimes never. He wasn't cut out for the life of an artist. He didn't want to drudge away in dank rooms by day and sleep in musty sheets at night. He couldn't bear being hounded for unpaid bills. He had hidden the letter Mario had brought from the Marchesa Salvini under his dress shirts. It made him dizzy with humiliation to think of it. ". . . paid at once . . . ask you to vacate the premises. . . ." Nothing like it had ever happened to any member of his family. Paternal ancestors were spinning in New England graves, and maternal ancestors were churning the sod in old Virginia.

He closed the cardboard cover over the manuscript and drummed his fingers on it. The proper end for such an abortion was burning, but as there was no fireplace, that was out. He could tear it into pieces and dump them into one of the big garbage cans that Gino kept in the palazzo's service entry, but the spazzini were anything but thorough, and he could envision scraps of paper with senseless phrases from sentences he had agonized over littering the Via della Scimmia or being carried by the spring breeze to the seven hills. Somehow he didn't like the idea of strange eyes falling on these bits and pieces of himself. Perhaps a final rite was premature. He got up and carried the manuscript to the hulking armadio and put it into an empty canvas suitcase. When he went, it would go with him. He'd put it in the foot locker back home with his diplomas. It represented a kind of graduation, too.

His old man was going to be wild no matter what hour he telephoned, but he decided the blow might fall softest at seven P.M. Connecticut time, which would be one A.M. Rome time. Being a weekday, his parents wouldn't be having guests, and around seven, his father would have had or be having or be about to have the two martinis he drank before dinner. If he had already had them, his mood would be reasonably mellow, and if he hadn't had them, they'd help him recover from the shock. It wouldn't be the money, but "the principle of the thing." Long distance, fortunately, there wouldn't be too much time wasted in emphasizing that. To his father long-distance calls were excusable only in case of death or disaster. Well, in a way, this was a disaster, or at least as near to one as he ever hoped to come.

He went back to his desk and checked the list of debts and added the column of corresponding figures once again. There was no getting around it. He had to have five hundred bucks to clear himself and to pay for his flight home. He'd give anything not to have to make the call, but where else was he going to get that kind of money? His last hope had been Charlie, but now Charlie was having some kind of row with his mother, and it might be days before she came across, as she always did in the end. He had allowed just fifty dollars for the busted refrigerator, having reasoned that there must be some way to repair it, but it might not be enough. Since it was an antique, spare parts could be hard to come by. It was the sort of thing Gino knew about. He'd made several trips out to the sentry box to see if Gino had come back from the wedding dinner. At least an hour had passed since the last one, so there was a good chance he had returned.

He found Carmela enthroned in Gino's place. "Gino has not yet come back from the Trattoria allo Spiedo," Carmela told him. "Donna Luisa is expecting a visit from a personage of great importance from the Embassy of the United States."

"Oh," Randy said. Maybe it had something to do with him. Maybe the Marchesa had found out about Lisa. Or the busted refrigerator. She might have some mad plan to have him deported.

"With Gino away, this personage might be unable to find his way to Donna Luisa's apartment, so she wished me to receive him," Carmela continued.

"Sure. Naturally," Randy mumbled. Wouldn't that be great? They probably sent marine guards who conducted you to some U. S. ship in Naples.

"It is about the vacant apartment," said Carmela. "He is interested in renting it."

Randy passed his hand over his forehead. Jesus, how psycho could you get? The worst he had done was to get drunk and sleep with a colored girl and be behind in the rent, and here he was jumping out of his skin with guilt every five minutes. About nine tenths of the people in the world must be behind in the rent, and he hadn't even known he was asleep with Lisa, so what was all this? "Well, when Gino does come, would you mind telling him to knock on my door? There's something I want to ask him."

"Oh, but certainly, signorino. It is now well past the three and the wedding dinner began at midday, so I should think . . ." Carmela threw up her hands and directed a frown toward the street.

The sound of a motor screeching up the Via della Scimmia was drowning out her voice. As it came nearer, she gave up competition entirely and folded her arms to wait for it to pass. But, instead of passing, the roaring engine propelled a gigantic glittering black-and-chrome motorcycle through the *portone*. The monstrous machine shot past them, pierced the heart of the cortile like an arrow, and stopped just short of the fountain, where it quivered and sputtered and coughed and choked and expelled air from its exhaust.

The motorcycle was, without question, the most obscene vehicle ever invented, Randy decided.

"Silenzio," Carmela called out. "Donna Luisa is having her siesta."

The helmeted driver was too busy calming his metallic beast to hear. And, if he had, Randy knew it wouldn't have made any difference.

"Oh," cried Carmela, wringing her hands and looking up toward Luisa Salvini's bathroom window, the only window of Luisa's suite that was visible from the cortile.

"Leave him to me." Randy crossed the courtyard quickly and stepped in front of the motorcycle. "Cut out the noise, will you? It may be news to you, but in Italy people take a nap after lunch."

"Hi, Ran." Duke Dawson righted the front wheel with an elaborate theatrical maneuver of the handlebars, switched off the motor and swung off the seat. He held his right hand out to Randy and took off his helmet with his left.

"Hi," Randy said and suffered his hand to be shaken. He would wash it the instant he got back into his apartment. He noticed that Duke's fingers were blunt on the ends and that the nails were bitten. It was the first time he had ever seen Duke close up and in the light of day. They were about the same height. Duke would have the edge on him if he stood straight, but his shoulders, although broad, were quite rounded. Probably from affecting that half-assed, tough-guy kind of walk. Duke's head was quite a lot too small for his body, and his eyes were a nothing color, like the eyes of a goat. Randy pretended an interest in the gleaming headlight so as not to have to look at him.

"I bumped into old Charlie and he invited me over to your place," said Duke. "He's not here yet?"

"No," said Randy and started toward his door. He was anxious to wash his hand.

"Well, he should be here any minute," said Duke, following. "It was about a half an hour ago when I saw him. Up on the Via Archimede. He was going into that building where that Marsha lives to borrow a projector from her. What is all this about a dirty movie, anyway? He told me he'd invited quite a few others over to see it, too."

"Not so loud," warned Randy. He had caught sight of Pippo La Rosa getting out of a Jaguar in front of the main gate.

"Hell," said Duke, "these guineas don't speak English."

"Don't ever bet on it," Randy advised. "It so happens that that guy getting out of the car speaks English as well as you do." This was no exaggeration, considering Duke's grammar.

The driver of the Jaguar kept the motor running and waited while Pippo ran through the gate and up to Gino's enclosure. Randy saw Carmela look about the cubicle and hold out empty hands.

"The cretin didn't deliver the film," Pippo called out to the waiting driver.

"Why don't we go over to his shop?" the man in the car called back.

"It's closed now," Pippo said as Randy and Duke came alongside to make the turn that led to Randy's apartment.

"*Allora!* What do we do, then?" the friend in the car wanted to know.

"He'll be open again at four. I'll go in and get something to eat, and you come back for me in about forty minutes. We can pick the film up and go on from there. "All right, Sergio?"

Randy saw the man Pippo had called Sergio give a signal in accord, and he heard the Jaguar's motor gun off as he closed the door behind Duke and himself. Randy went immediately to wash his hands. As if life weren't already complicated enough, he was now an accomplice to the theft of a film.

"Not a bad little pad you got here," Duke said.

Randy searched his bath towel for the cleanest corner and dried his hands, wondering what kind of dump Duke must live in if this place looked good to him.

Duke hooked his thumbs into the wide belt he was wearing and strode around, clicking his boots like an SS agent.

"If you like it so much, maybe you can get the woman who owns it to rent it to you. I'm leaving soon."

"No kidding. Fed up with Rome, huh?"

"No, Rome's great. I'm just anxious to get back home, that's all."

He hadn't realized it was true until he had put it in words, and he suddenly found himself wishing fervently that today were tomorrow. The telephone call to his dad would be a thing of the past. And so would the busted refrigerator. And Lisa's wig. And this impossible interlude with Goat Eyes. And whatever was coming up with the film and whoever was about to descend on him, thanks to Charlie. And his final sene with Maria Pia. He hoped to hell she hadn't been on the level about loving him, but he had a feeling that she had fallen in love with him the instant he belted her. And how was he going to get out of that? Or wasn't he? Murders of passion headed the crime list in Italy, and God only knew she was passionate. What if she took it into her head to shoot him? Or herself? Well, he'd know all the answers tomorrow.

Coiffured, manicured, pedicured, and there was still a half hour to kill before the bank opened at three-thirty and she could withdraw her money and go to the American Express for reservations and traveler's checks. As the Consulate was almost opposite the bank, she would dash in there between the bank and the American Express. She hesitated beneath the pink-and-white striped awning that shaded Michele's entrance, looked right and left, and chose to walk left up the Via Frattina toward the Piazza di Spagna. The city drowsed to the lullaby of the siesta. The roar of the traffic had calmed down to a purr, and she could hear the click of her heels as she slowly made her way along the nearly deserted street. The wares in the shop windows were safe behind iron lattices, and the paternal eye of the sun kept vigil outside the shuttered windows of the apartments above. The multiple midday courses had been washed down with just enough wine to prime the digestive juices and weight the eye. The great Italian family slept.

She crossed the piazza, climbed the Spanish Steps, and went along the broad, shaded avenue to the terrace of the Pincio in the Villa Borghese. There were fewer persons than she had ever seen in the square, but then she had never been in the park at that time of day. A young man, obviously a tourist, stood at the balustrade, binoculars trained toward St. Peter's. A student priest in a black soutane and sky-blue sash sat on a bench reading his breviary. There were no customers at the counters of the small pavilion where *caffé espresso* and drinks were sold, and the barman had dragged a chair out into the sun to sleep with a towel over his face.

Caroline went to the balustrade and looked directly down onto the Piazza del Popolo. The great central obelisk and the sculptured lions that crouched at its base spewing water were reduced to the dimensions of toys. An automobile, a miniature Citroën from Caroline's elevation, emerged from a side street, rounded the obelisk and climbed out of sight in the direction of the Tiber. A diminutive man came out of a diminutive Bar Rosati and entered a diminutive taxi. A silent, satin breeze carried a scrap of paper the size of her hand down, down to where it was no bigger than her thumbnail, and then she could see it no more. The breeze died away and, for a motionless interval, the city seemed a city painted on a theatrical screen. Sections of the screen fell away to reveal the interiors of dwellings. The children slept in cribs, on cots. Their parents slept in matrimonial beds with modern headboards. The parents' parents slept in matrimonial beds with headboards of golden oak and carved walnut. The plague of singleness found hosts in other cultures, other climes. Here there were only a few like herself. Outcast, Isolated. Forgotten.

She leaned heavily against the balustrade, and sun-struck domes and crosses drowned in the waves of her tears. This was only the beginning. This was the first day. And she had a whole, desolate life to get through. Day after plodding day. And the long passages down the dark tunnels of night. The sickening silence of solitude. The aching hours of longing before sleep came. The waking up to hopelessness.

She didn't want any of the sad substitutes. She didn't want to join the army of itinerant divorcées and rally to the battle cry of "Independence while we're young and money for the menopause." She didn't want to belong to clubs and circles and parties and societies and sets and associations and organizations and committees and movements and leagues and missions. She wanted to belong to a family. She didn't want to be the first female jet pilot or chairman of the board of Bethlehem Steel or four-star general or president of the New York Stock Exchange or Harvard or the United States. She wanted to be a wife. She didn't want a lot of lovers. She wanted one love. One husband. And the husband she wanted was Lorenzo. She didn't want time to pass, even if someday it would be easier. She wanted time to go back. She wanted it to be last year, even last month when Lorenzo had loved her. Before he loved someone else. Then Lorenzo had wanted to be with her. Now he wanted to be with this other woman. The woman he was with right now. At this very moment. She blinked the tears from her lashes and stared at Lorenzo and this other woman, locked in an embrace and projected against the sky. More tears washed them away. She blinked again and Lorenzo smiled and put his arm around this woman, and they floated off into the horizon.

A volcanic eruption of visceral origin set her shoulders shaking and her chest heaving. It was coming at last. She was going to pieces. She was slipping out of control, going over the brink, and there was no stopping herself. All the nerves and muscles she had held in check were coming loose. She was going to scream and scream and scream and tear her hair out by the roots. She was going to fall on the ground and roll and writhe and froth at the mouth. When one reached the limit of sanity, there was no place to go but beyond it, out into the wilds of madness. It was bound to happen sooner or later. What an immense relief to let go, not to try, not to care. Her breath was like fire. She felt herself growing taller and taller. Her hands were gathering strength, doubling, tripling, quadrupling in size. She could demolish the earth, tear down the sky, put out the sun. She threw back her head and opened her eyes wide as a first step toward executing these projects, but a disarming shadow moved into her line of vision, cutting her threads of action short.

The shadow belonged to the tourist. He had left his position at the far end of the balustrade, had come up almost to her side and was watching her with stupefaction. She turned her head with a jerk and narrowed her eyes on his. What was the meaning of this invasion of her privacy? With what permission was this stranger taking part in this intimate and most painful experience of her life? Couldn't he understand that he was robbing her of her chance to escape by the mere fact of his presence, blocking her way to that world where the walls were softly padded and the doors barred? Going crazy was a trip to be set out on in secret.

When she was some distance away from the park, she took a cautious look behind, to see if the man might be following, and slowed down when she saw that he wasn't. Thank God he was a German, a deduction she had made because he had been wearing his country's traditional sandal and sock. The Germans, children of mist and moods, respected the right to the pursuit of unhappiness. An Italian would have concerned himself instantly with her deliverance. He would be prancing along at her side now, gesticulating grandly, as he remarked on the imperishable beauty of Rome, the glory of this day, the recurrent miracle of spring, the promise of summer, the luster of her hair, the admirable length and shape of her legs, the simple elegance of her dress and, of course, his own suitability as her private cruise director on a voyage he would propose to the moon.

He would be right about her appearance. She had caught sight of herself reflected full length in the windows of the Hotel De la Ville, which she was passing. The disparity between how she looked and how she felt was confounding. It was as if she had suddenly come upon a photograph of a woman now dead taken long ago, and been amazed to realize that this woman had ever been so golden and glowing. This woman she saw had nothing to do with the woman she was. But she must remember that the woman she saw was the woman the world saw. If she had anything to be grateful for, it was that the wounds that had killed her were invisible. The sole witness to the death of her inner self was a wispy-haired, sallow-skinned German tourist who didn't know her name. And that was how she intended to keep it. Emotional *rigor mortis* had commenced with the awareness that he was watching her. There would be no more mourning. She was through crying for herself. The funeral was over, and her tears were dry.

It was Lorenzo's turn. How happy could a man be who had

lost his children? How long before he came to hate the woman he had got in exchange? How long before he tired of having a mistress? Even a succession of mistresses. Perhaps he had forgotten that he was a citizen of a country where there was no divorce. Even if the proposed divorce bill passed, as threatened, he would have five long years to get through before he could sue for one. Oh, there would be a great many things for him to remember. After she'd gone.

She sailed into the Banca Commerciale Italiana on a new wind of self-assurance, quite prepared to cope with the irrational conviction of tellers and cashiers that the depositors' money was their own and with their consequent reluctance to part with it. She was the first customer of the afternoon, and twenty minutes later she was back on the street with her total assets, part in cash, part in a certified check, in her pocketbook, advancing on the American Consulate in swift strides. The siesta was ending. A stream of office and sales help, still drugged by sleep and slightly feverish with the spring sun, was flowing into the espresso bars to down strong coffee and wake up for the second time that day. She brushed past three girls sauntering arm in arm, and zigzagged through a crowd of passengers descending from a bus. She gained momentum with each step. She had the ball this time and was running with it. There was no stopping her now. There was no interference or obstacle that could slow her down. She tore across the Via Veneto on the yellow light and dove through the Consulate gate. She had the money and she would have her passport. After that, the checks and tickets—and she would have all she needed to make her goal. Sometime during the next twelve hours she was going to get herself and her children out of this country. She'd face what was in store for her after that when she came to it. Bad as life might be for her alone with the children, it was going to be a lot worse for Lorenzo alone without them. It was a thought to hold onto.

"I assume my passport is ready." The young man at the reception desk seemed taken aback momentarily. Because of her crisp delivery, her crisper smile, no doubt. He had probably never thought of her as a woman who knew exactly where she was going and had no time to waste getting there. "You're not going to tell me that it isn't, that I've made a useless trip."

"Oh, it's ready," he said quickly.

"Well, then." She held out her hand.

"But I am afraid you have made a useless trip, Marchesa. You see, your passport had to be signed by Mr. Fuller. It was ready early and, by a coincidence, Mr. Fuller had an appointment with your mother-in-law to look at a vacant apartment, so he thought . . ."

It was instantly, monstrously evident. "That he would do me a favor and deliver the passport directly to me." What could be more logical?

"Exactly," said the receptionist.

"And not finding me at home. he will undoubtedly leave it with my mother-in-law." She marveled at the steadiness of her voice.

"Oh, undoubtedly," the receptionist reassured her with warm solicitude.

She glanced down at the lines of her still-extended palm, half expecting to find a record of when and how the controls she had held on the future had slipped from her own hands into the hands of fate. "So it will be at home when I get there."

The receptionist nodded, smiling.

"Do thank Mr. Fuller for me," she said, drawing on her glove.

"It is a pity you came all the way unnecessarily."

"These things happen." It was the sort of statement she had never made in her life, one of those phrases she had heard drop with no meaning from the lips of other people. She had borrowed it because there was nothing she had ever experienced or imagined to prepare her to comment on an inexorable destiny. She returned the receptionist's smile and turned quickly away.

She didn't take the elevator this time, but went down the

stairs. There was less chance of meeting anyone she might know. The stairway was deserted and she descended slowly, clinging to the banister, completing a step at a time the way the very young and the very old do. "Oh, my God," she whispered to herself again and again as she inched along. "Oh, no. No," she prayed.

When she stepped back onto the Via Veneto, the traffic was at flood tide and still swelling. Rome flowed up hill and down hill, afoot and in automobile, rolling under the triumphant sun in great easy waves. She viewed the opposite side of the street as a distant shore. She might or might not be able to make it. She was beyond predicting when the little strength she had left would give out. There was a weakness in her ankles and knees such as she had never known. A semiparalysis had fastened onto her brain, so that she could only begin a thought. Halfway to any conclusion, her mind blacked out, stopped dead as if impregnable partitions had been set up within her head to block any process of reasoning. She was just barely able to chart a course which would take her across to the kiosk and on for another fifty yards beyond that to the taxi stand. She set out on it when the light changed, treading uncertainly in the midst and borne forward by a group of other pedestrians. As she stepped onto the curb, a florist's boy, navigating blindly behind branches of white lilac encased in cellophane, caught her broadside, so that she fell back against the part of the kiosk counter where the books were stacked. She clutched the wooden table and clung on.

A dagger, dripping blood, stabbed at her from a paperback cover. The fangs of a creature half man, half beast snapped out from the one at its side. Female breast and buttock protruded and pointed and poked and pushed and promised obscenely. Musclemen sucked in umbilici with draughts so profound their torsos seemed on the verge of splitting in two. Color in shocking shades and antipathetical combinations fought and bled over asymmetrical print which seemed to have been typeset by drunkards.

Her gaze wavered right of the books and on over the rows of quarterlies and monthlies and weeklies in Italian and English and French and German. Read, shrieked the blurbs, read what the experts have to say. Buy their last word on every subject under the heavens. Take their advice. Heed their warnings. Rely on their predictions. Trust their judgment. Fall in line. Get in step. Follow the leaders. The Suburbs That Spell Status. Prayer Is Power. The Case Against Miracle Drugs That Cure You Now and Kill You Later. Your Destiny Is in the Stars. The Mysteries of Making a Million Revealed. What Are Your Chances of Surviving a Nuclear War? Sex and the Six-Year-Old. Ten Theologians Give Their Views on the Moral Issues Involved in Transplants of the Human Brain. The Climate of Crime Grows Hotter. The Beautiful Houses of the Beautiful People. LSD. Mao and Maoism. The Living Dead—Hibernation in the Cemeteries of Tomorrow. The Box Office Stars of the Fifties—Where Are They Now? Safaris Are for Sadists. A Plastic Surgeon Trading a New Face for an Old One—Photographed in Color. Beware of Barbiturates. Hate Is a Four-Letter Word. Is There a Microbe Menace in Outer Space? ESP and What It Can Mean to You. So What's So New About Nudity? Learn Karate at Home. Your Great-Grandchild May Be Born in a Test Tube.

The sort of test tube she had used in college chemistry or something larger and of a different shape? Plastic, no doubt, she thought dimly, and clung onto the counter harder. The coastlines were eroding. The forests were being leveled. Natural resources were dwindling steadily. The fields were exhausted. They were polluting the rivers and lakes and oceans. They were poisoning the atmosphere. Fish had been dynamited from the depths, and great areas were now depleted. Floras were perishing beneath mammoth oil slicks. Sea-living mammals faced almost certain extinction. They were closing in on the beasts of the land species which still survived, and guns were trained at wings in the skies. Whole segments of the human race were being systematically exterminated by starvation and bombed into oblivion. The knuckles of her hands whitened with strain. The ground was moving under her feet. The whole kiosk was rocking. Copy was running from one magazine to another, making senseless anagrams, blood-curdling declarations. She was going to slide off it. There was nothing left to hold onto. Nothing. No one at all. First Lorenzo. And now the children. She drew in a breath sharp as a knife and pushed herself free of the counter. She had only a few yards to go to reach a taxi and she stumbled toward it.

One minute she had been on the Via Veneto and the next minute, or so it seemed to her, the taxi was nearing the palazzo's portone. A few minutes more and she'd be going through the gate, crossing the cortile and then . . . She'd never be able to make it without help. Her hand was shaking so that the coins the driver gave her in change slipped through her fingers. She retrieved the two which had fallen at her feet and made no attempt to pick up the third, which had rolled into the gutter. Of what use was a hundred lire? Any amount of money now? An old woman wearing a long black skirt and a black shawl came out of the church across the street. A serene smile softened her rugged face. Please, God, help me, too, Caroline prayed, entering the deserted cortile. Her eyes darted from one window to another and came to rest on Randy's door. Perhaps he could help in some way. She couldn't begin to think how, but she had to talk to someone before she saw Lorenzo.

The projector went into a fit for the third time and hurled colored blobs and blurs at the screen. Randy had expected it would. Amateur films and amateur theatricals ranked high on the list of things he detested. He was next to certain that Charlie was crazy for concluding the film was dirty anyway. It was probably some boring record of a Sunday excursion to Ostia, featuring Pippo's fat mother and Pippo's sausagy girl friend upholstering straight-backed chairs in some fish joint. The tinny din of battle between metal and celluloid rattled to a finish within the projector and it blacked out.

"God damn it," Charlie's voice came across the darkened room. "Can't you make this thing work, Marsha?"

"Whose thing, sweetie?" asked Marsha in a voice husky with innuendo, which evoked a general tittering and an explosive guffaw from Duke Dawson. "Your thing?"

Randy tried to picture Marsha and the guy who licked her all over in action without much success. It was hard to imagine anyone who looked as clean as Marsha being such a pig.

"It's your projector, for Christ's sake," Charlie said, switching on the overhead light, "I'd think you'd know something about it."

"It was a present from a fellow I know who manufactures them. This is the first time it's ever been out of the box." Marsha picked up one of Duke's black leather gauntlets from the bedside table.

"Ah, is here I have make my mistake," Fausto said. Fausto was a friend of Charlie's who operated the projector in a small theater in Trastevere which specialized in American underground and Italian experimental films. So little of him was visible that it was hard for Randy to tell what he really looked like. His hair was in full shock, as was his beard, and he was wearing a belted tunic and billowing trousers stuffed into boots. He had brought along a girl named Dacia he had presented as his "cheek," and her appearance was concealed, too, under a flowing cape and a snarl of chains and rusty jewelry. Her tiny features peeked out from behind hair that was draped around them like tattered curtains. She had quietly made a heap of herself on the floor against the wall, and there she stayed looking like a pile of unsorted clothes waiting to be picked up by a dry cleaner. There was nothing to indicate she was alive except her eyes, which burned on high. She was turned on good, all right, but on what Randy didn't know. Or care. Up until now, he had drawn a line on who Charlie could drag in. It no longer mattered. Like most people who have decided to make a break, he could afford to be charitable to those he would leave behind. Once he left Rome, there was small likelihood he would ever see any of them again. If he had anything to do with it.

"This better be good, Charlie baby, after all this trouble," said Lisa.

Lisa had given Randy back the thousand lire the minute she had come into the apartment. He had refused it at first and then taken it, having realized that it was important to her regaining her self-possession. She was stretched out beside Marsha on the India print now, unaware or uncaring how much darker she looked in contrast with Marsha's pinkness.

"I've got an appointment with my agent at six," Duke said.

"Like this it go," said Fausto, threading the film around a coil.

"Ask him if he has something for me. I'm thinking of resuming my acting career," Marsha said to Duke.

Duke balanced himself stork-fashion against the wall, folded his arms and narrowed his eyes on her. "Oh, yeah?"

"Yeah," Marsha said. She thrust her hands into Duke's black gloves and made them creep over her torso.

"Maybe the thing's busted," Charlie said. "*Rotto*. Kaput."

"No, no. Was me I made mistake," Fausto said.

"Very sexy," Duke told Marsha.

Marsha changed her expression from sensual ecstasy to wide-eyed terror. "Oh. Oh, no!" she shrieked. She brought her gloved hands above her head and lowered them slowly until they circled her neck in a strangle hold.

"Ah, is feexed," Fausto said.

Marsha emitted a series of gasps and gurgles as she pretended to be choking to death.

"Okay, everybody. Fausto's got it fixed," Charlie announced.

Marsha struggled free of her own hands. "Help! Help! Help!" she shouted. "Somebody save me."

"Knock it off, Marsha," Charlie commanded. "Fausto's ready to go."

"Man, but she breaks me up." Lisa slapped herself on her hips as she laughed.

"No. No, no!" Marsha slithered about the bed as her own hands chased her.

"Oh, Christ," Charlie groaned with exasperation.

Randy saw an exchange of a kind take place between Fausto and his Rag Bag. They gazed at each other dully and briefly, nothing more than that.

Marsha gave up the fight. The black gloves closed on her throat again. Her eyes bugged wildly. She sputtered and gulped and sputtered. The leather fingers eased away from her throat. Her arms went limp and fell at her sides. She stared at the ceiling, her mouth open, her tongue thrust between her teeth. Lisa leaned over her. "She's dead, all right."

"Thank God for that," said Charlie.

Lisa covered Marsha's face with a corner of the India print. Duke made the sign of the cross and flopped down on the bed. There ensued quite a lot of grabbing and giggling and guffawing. "So who says I can't act?" asked Marsha, emerging from the cover.

"You've got a nice pair of money-makers there, too." Duke twisted first one and then the other of Marsha's breasts as if they were dials.

"You just better believe it." Marsha smiled slyly and swatted his hand away. "*Via*, baby. It's cash or no carry . . . ings on."

"Do you want to see this or not?" Charlie thundered.

"But sure, sweetie. I didn't know your 'thing' was fixed. Why didn't you say something?"

"I've been yelling my lungs out for ten minutes." Charlie flicked off the overhead lights. "Okay, Fausto. *Dai.*"

The projector resumed its weary, worried breathing, and its tiny light reached feebly for the corners of the room. Mercifully, the figures on the bed were shrouded in gray, their features indiscernible. Randy had had about as much of them as he could stand. If he had had to decide which of the three he would be forced to see again, it would be Lisa. Lisa hadn't had much of a chance to be different from what she was, but Goat

Eyes and Marsha had chosen to be loathsome. The hand of one of the girls was caressing Goat Eyes' hair, which Randy had noted earlier was a nothing color like his eyes, and crinkly. It was Marsha, because he saw Lisa get up and go to stand beside Charlie. Jesus, how could she do it? What it was like was pubic hair. Maybe they'd do the world a favor and shack up together and cancel each other out.

The colored snowflakes the projector was casting at the screen were taking form, but it certainly wasn't human. There were some objects of uniform size lined up in a row. They looked like boulders. It was undoubtedly, as he had thought all along, a documentary of some kind. The things seemed to have ears now. Animals. Squat animals with wide-set, perky ears. Toy animals. Stuffed things. The photography, though in color, was pretty lousy and it was hard to tell. Who cared, anyway?

"It starts slow, like they say," observed Lisa.

The camera moved in closer. Ah, said Randy to himself, it was even worse than he had imagined. A commercial.

"They're bags of something," Marsha said.

"They've got something written on them," Duke said.

" 'Go-Go Grow,' " Lisa read.

"It must be some kind of plant food," Marsha said.

"Maybe some wop got smart and put that bullshit they're always slinging in sacks to sell as fertilizer." Duke said.

"You're a real diplomat, aren't you, baby?" Marsha stabbed a finger into the dark toward Fausto.

"Oh, hell, he didn't get it," said Duke in a lowered voice.

Randy tuned them out. He was also able to look at the screen without seeing it. There were more important things to occupy his mind. With a little luck, it would be his mother who would answer the telephone, and he'd be able to give her a fast summary of his situation. She'd break it down in that quick way of hers for his father, so it'd be easier for him to digest. He could count on her to work wonders with the Old Man's mood in just the few seconds it would take him to walk from the chair where he had his drink to the desk, where the telephone was. Once in a while, his Old Man did answer the telephone. He only prayed this wouldn't be one of the times.

"Ah, the action begins," said Duke. A pair of trousered legs were walking slowly past the row of Go-Go Grow bags.

"Who dat?" asked Lisa.

The camera panned up from the legs, past a plaid vest and a superbly fitted white shirt to the flashing smile of Pippo La Rosa.

"*Mamma mia,* is he ever *bello,*" sighed Marsha.

"*Bello!*" hooted Duke. "Don't tell me you go for that type."

"He's a jerk," Charlie said.

Pippo La Rosa walked off from the bags to a window and opened it. There was a flower pot on the ledge with one puny daisy in it. Pippo looked at it, shook his head, spread out the palms of his hands to indicate hopelessness and sat down in a straight chair that was nearby. He scooped up a newspaper from the floor, crossed his legs, and started reading. A very pretty girl wearing a ruffled apron came from off-camera to stand behind Pippo. She put her arms around his neck and kissed the top of his head. Pippo read on, paying no attention to her. Her gaze wandered off to the flower pot in the window and she fell back and threw up her hands in dismay. She strode briskly to the bags of Go-Go Grow, unknotted the ear of one of them and took out a handful of whatever was inside. She went to the window and sprinkled a substance that resembled talcum powder over the puny daisy. She closed the window, walked over to Pippo and snatched the newspaper away. She caught him by the hands, pulled him to his feet and dragged him to the window. He covered his eyes as instructed. The pretty girl opened the window and Pippo opened his eyes. Instead of the puny daisy, there was a daisy the size of a sunflower in the pot. Pippo and the pretty girl fell into each other's arms. The pretty girl was Maria Pia.

"That Go-Go Grow is groovy," Lisa said. "Real groovy, man."

"Cool it, Lisa," Charlie growled. The camera swung away to close up on one of the Go-Go Grow bags. "I guess everybody's had about enough."

"I haven't," Randy said.

"If I had known, Ran, but, no kidding, I didn't have the slightest idea . . ."

"Relax," Randy said. "Let's see what happens next."

"You really on the level?" Charlie said.

"Of course," Randy said.

"What's all this about?" Marsha asked.

"Charlie can explain it to you later," Randy said. The camera was swinging away from the bags.

"That's more like it," said Duke.

The camera held quite a long time on a shot of Pippo's hands clutching Maria Pia's buttocks before sneaking up Maria Pia's spine. She was holding her head aside and Pippo was giving her neck a going over with his lips, rather like a vacuum cleaner nozzle. Maria Pia wore an expression of wanton abandon, and Randy was convinced she was in earnest when she suddenly wriggled herself free and burst into laughter. Pippo laughed, too. There was some joke between them that Randy couldn't get. Pippo opened his arms and Maria Pia fell into them again. This time she was the aggressor. Her tongue plunged into the shell of Pippo's left ear, shot out and made a centrifugal excursion around and down to the lobe, which she bit.

"Is *she* ever *bella!*" Duke said.

"But she bites," Marsha said.

"Nice and easy," Duke said.

Pippo bared his teeth and made a pass at Maria Pia's ear, but she broke away and fled to another part of the room where many more bags of Go-Go Grow were arranged in orderly rows. The area where the film had been shot was large, a warehouse perhaps or a garage. The light that had fallen on the puny daisy had been the dim light of late afternoon, a late rainy afternoon. Yesterday afternoon. There was no doubt of it in his mind. It must have been just about an hour later that she had telephoned to break their date. Years seemed to have passed since then.

"Here we go," Duke announced.

Pippo seized Maria Pia by the shoulders and forced her down onto the Go-Go Grow bags. Pippo fell on top of her. Maria Pia put up a struggle, or at least pretended to, turning her head rapidly from side to side so Pippo couldn't kiss her. Pippo caught a fistful of her hair and twisted it until she was subdued. There was a prolonged, writhing embrace and then, still clinging to each other, they rolled over and over, Maria Pia on top of Pippo, Pippo above Maria Pia, on and on over the great bed of Go-Go Grow. And now they laughed.

"What's this with the laughing always, just when they get going?" Duke asked.

Randy had caught on at last. They were burlesquing love scenes of films, but Randy felt under no obligation to enlighten Duke. Maria Pia, thumb in mouth, watched Pippo take off his shirt. He draped the shirt over his head and knotted the sleeves behind his neck. An Arab sheik, Randy decided.

"*Ciao, bello.*" Marsha made kissing sounds at the screen.

Pippo's eyes pierced hypnotically from under lowered lids, and Maria Pia, feigning terror, inched back. Pippo's hand shot out and caught her by the wrist. He spun her around so she faced away from him and his free hand ripped off the apron she was wearing and slashed open the back of her dress by the zipper. He whirled her around to face him. Eyes still piercing, he pushed her dress down off her shoulders and it fell around her feet.

How about that, Randy asked himself. She's wearing those godawful turquoise bikini things I bought her.

Maria Pia's eyes darted up and down and right and left in imitation of the manner of film stars of the twenties. Pippo had a short outburst of laughter and then composed himself and took her in his arms. Slow stuff. Long, sexy stares like in the twenties films, too. With expert swiftness Pippo's hand went around Maria Pia's back, unhooked her brassiere and snatched it off. Maria Pia ducked and covered herself instantly, so the camera caught nothing but shoulder and arm.

"That's it, man, that's it." Duke smacked his hands in applause.

"You're sure you want to see any more of this, Ran?" Charlie asked.

"Why not?" said Marsha. "What is he, a saint or something?"

"Sure I want to see it," Randy said.

Maria Pia was herself now, stalking after the retreating Pippo, menacing him with fiery eyes and thinned lips, but amused. Pippo dangled the brassiere tantalizingly near to her and then snatched it back. She advanced again and he repeated the motion. She made a sudden grab, but Pippo was too fast for her. He flipped the brassiere behind him and pointed his finger at her exposed breast. Maria Pia made a move to recover herself but reconsidered the action midway. She had lost the game, she seemed to be thinking . . . and Pippo had won . . . so what the hell. Her lips stretched in a great, good-natured smile, and she flung her arms high, wide and free.

A star is born, Randy told himself.

"Christ, what a pair of . . . of . . ." Duke was struck stuttering dumb.

"Boobs, boob," said Marsha. "When they're that big you look lousy in clothes."

"Sure, Miss Sour Grapes," Duke sneered. "Who needs clothes?"

"Wait'll she's had a coupla kids—she'll be able to throw them over her shoulder."

Randy swept a quick, withering glance at Marsha's profile. Profile in pornography. Portraits in perversion. By what right did this tawdry, two-bit tart dare criticize Maria Pia? What excuse did this snickering, sly slut and all her sex-is-sin sisters have for living? Working over the mined-out bodies of senile slobs or long-suffering husbands and panning what ore there was in their pockets.

"Maybe she won't have any kids," Duke said.

"What? Are you kidding? That kind always has kids."

Sure, she'll have lots of kids, Randy continued silently. She loves kids. She knows what she's made for. But not you, you pilled-up fake of a woman. You'll still be sitting on the Via Veneto. With some fag you've adopted.

"They don't age well," Marsha said. "They get fat."

Not you, though. You won't weigh an ounce more than you weigh this minute. Less, in fact, dried out and trussed up like an old chicken. Still with the make-up and phony eyelashes, dressed by some new Pucci, waving your fly-specked old hands and rings at your fag. Randy winced.

The ghost of Cora Study had strolled into his mind, and he exorcised it by concentrating on the screen. Just look at her up there. Just look at her! All rounded and smooth and firm. No sharp edges. No jutting collarbone. No cutting pelvic bones.

"For my money she's already too fat," Marsha amplified.

What you mean is that she looks alive, that her bones are all covered with flesh, unlike those scary tubercular models you probably admire who are so near death that you can already see their skulls and skeletons lying just under the skin. Look at her lips. Look how soft and moist they are.

"Get her, would you, with that look-at-me expression," said Marsha.

And you've got a mouth like a shark under that pencil outline you fill in with some kind of Max Factor or Elizabeth Arden colored axle grease. She isn't saying, "Look at me." She isn't saying anything. For her, sex isn't something you talk about. It's something you do. She's never read one of those how-to books. She was born knowing how to.

"Okay, come on, do something. Don't just stand there," directed Marsha.

Sure, slither around, snake it up, give the big come-on through slitty eyes. That's your style, isn't it? The big invitation for a wallow in the slime. Two slugs oozing over each other in some dark hole.

"Like take your panties off, too," suggested Duke.

In the dark. Dirty stuff. Like Leslie Cavanaugh saying, "Tell me what we're doing . . . say the word . . . say it." What kind of an idiot had he been, whispering a dirty word over and over again in the back seat of a car, as if it were some kind of password to get through the barrier of her inhibitions? And he had had some screwed-up idea that he had been making love, instead of working over a limp body like an orderly in a hospital reanimation department. Maria Pia made love as easily as she drank a Coke when she was thirsty. She made love the way she'd eaten the bread on that first day after the night they had met. He'd never forget it. They'd been on their way to lunch at a trattoria, and she'd suddenly jerked him to a standstill before the doorway of a shop where a baker was pulling a huge tray of fresh bread out of the oven with a long, wooden pole. She had run in and run out with two big buns and shoved one of them into his hand and started eating hers on the spot. "Not now, not right before lunch," he had told her, and she had answered with her mouth full "Why not? I have much hungry and ees so goood!" He had tried to clue her in on the hazards of eating between meals with all the zeal of a damned missionary persuading a naked savage to cover up in a Mother Hubbard, but she had eaten all the bun and all her lunch, too. Leslie Cavanaugh had emitted a series of high-pitched squeaks when she had finally had, or at least pretended to have, an orgasm. It had interfered with his own enjoyment because he couldn't keep the memory of the sounds of a pig-sticking he had heard once on a farm in Maine out of his mind. Maria Pia moaned distantly and briefly and then was silent while she drew him down, down through long magic timeless tunnels. And when they came back to the light she always said "*Va bene?*" *She* asked *him*. Smiling. He and Leslie had made their trips in separate compartments of a kind of jerking, halting milk train, and when they'd finally met at the end, she'd been like some inert piece of luggage he'd had to haul home. Big-mouth, best-seller Sane Sex Doc Cavanaugh and Maria Pia's father, who couldn't even read. Boy, there was a confrontation he'd like to see take place, there was a . . .

"Ahhhh. *Aaaahhhhh* . . ."

At first Randy thought it was Lisa, but he heard Lisa gasp "Jesus," so that left her out. The groan came again on a higher pitch. It was like nothing he had ever heard produced by human vocal cords, and he heard Marsha murmur "Mary and Joseph."

"Dacia!" Fausto's voice quivered with apprehension.

Randy had forgotten about the Rag Bag. By squinting, he made out her formless heap, still piled up on the floor against the wall and quite motionless. Even as he peered, a piercing shriek soared up from her animal depths and clung to the air by a shrill, sustained note. Randy found himself mummified, mute, mystified in the midst of sudden action. The shadow of Charlie's head momentarily obliterated the image of Pippo, who was taking the outsized daisy in its pot from the ledge. Fausto started from the projector toward his agonizing heap and stopped short, for some reason. Lisa shouted for someone to turn on the lights, and Charlie, between oaths, explained that he couldn't find the goddam switch. He found it seconds later but, illuminated, the scene didn't make much more sense to Randy than it had in the dark. Fausto had disengaged himself from a snare of light cords and rushed to kneel before Dacia. She was quiet now. Fausto took her hand, and her hollow, hopeless eyes fixed on his with a noncommittal stare.

"*Dimmi,* Dacia, *dimmi, cos' hai?*" Fausto urged.

Dacia's eyelids lowered in answer, and her head sagged onto her chest. She toppled over slowly, so gradually that her audience was hardly aware what was happening until her head hit the floor.

Dead. The announcement was made in newspaper print, headlines a foot high, directly in front of Randy's eyes. He could read every word distinctly. GIRL HIPPIE DIES MYSTERIOUSLY IN AMERICAN'S ROME APARTMENT.

"Brother, how freaked-out can you get?" Duke asked Marsha softly.

"Can it," Marsha hissed.

ALEXANDER PALMER HELD FOR QUESTIONING IN ROME'S REGINI COELI PRISON.

"Dacia, Dacia!" implored Fausto.

"I'll get some water," Charlie said.

That was typical. It was a wonder he hadn't said beer. Randy opened his mouth with the intention of issuing a command to restrain Charlie from dousing the dead or dying girl with water, but his tongue was rough and dry as tweed and he couldn't get it to work. ALEXANDER PALMER CASE PROVOKES NEW INVESTIGATIONS ON THE REASONS FOR DELINQUENCY AMONG SONS OF THE PRIVILEGED CLASSES.

"She's white as a sheet," Lisa said.

FATHER OF ALEXANDER PALMER SMASHES CAMERA OF PRESS PHOTOGRAPHER BEFORE BOARDING PLANE FOR ROME.

"Or maybe a shot of whiskey, Got any whiskey, Ran?" Charlie asked.

Randy's tweed tongue ached with the effort of speech, but he got out the words, "No . . . no . . . I haven't." Somehow he managed to get to his feet, too. Maybe she wasn't dead. He couldn't ask from clear across the room. He'd have to go near to her and see for himself.

"Whiskey might be the wrong thing, anyway," Lisa said. "Depends on what she's on. What was it, Fausto?"

Fausto sprang to his feet. "She thinks maybe she expect *bambino*. Last week she had demonstrate at the university. A Revisionist have kick her in the stomach."

"What's a Revisionist?" Duke asked Marsha.

"Shut up!" Marsha whispered.

It was almost worse than if she were dead. What if she were about to have a miscarriage right here on the floor? GIRL MEMBER OF ROME'S MAOIST FACTION ABORTS

AND DIES IN APARTMENT OF AMERICAN. RIVAL RUSSIAN REVISIONIST DEMONSTRATOR BLAMED. Pippo was making a sweeping bow and presenting the gigantic daisy to Maria Pia.

"We gotta get her to a doctor," Lisa said.

"Right away," Marsha agreed.

PALMER'S FATHER DENIES SON HAS OR EVER HAS HAD COMMUNIST AFFILIATIONS.

Charlie came back into the room holding a glass up to the light. "Gee, I don't know about this water. It looks kinda rusty."

Lisa shoved him away. "What she needs is a doctor, not water, stupid. We've got to get her to one fast."

The iron grip on Randy's brain eased somewhat. "Absolutely," he said. He tried to feel some sense of guilt for thinking of himself instead of the girl, but somehow he couldn't imagine her possessing any sort of normal human emotions, much less having conceived a creature that would ever take human form. Even so, it wasn't decent for Maria Pia to be bounding around the screen so nearly naked, with that crazy daisy in her teeth, while God only knew what was going on with the girl. He walked the few feet to where the cord of the projector was attached, but the wires were so tangled he was afraid the room might explode if he fooled around with them.

"Go get your car turned around and we'll carry her out to it," Lisa ordered Charlie.

Charlie flung the door open and rushed through it, and the light of early evening entered and mingled eerily with the artificial light within the room. Fausto bent down, worked his arm under Dacia's shoulder, slowly raised her to a sitting position and tried to lift her, but the dead weight of her limp body was too much for him. Here I go, Randy told himself, horrified at the prospect of touching her. He took a step forward, but Duke flashed past him.

"Here, kid, let me," Duke said to Fausto. Fausto let go as

Duke's arm circled the girl's shoulder, and Duke scooped her up as easily as if she were weightless. "Come on, let's go," Duke said.

It wasn't until Duke reached the door that Randy saw Caroline Salvini standing in it, her lips parted by incredulity. He had no idea how long she had been there. She stood aside to let Duke pass. And Fausto. And Lisa. And Marsha. And then she looked at Randy. "Who is that girl?" she asked sharply.

"I know what you must think," Randy crossed the room and came up to her, "but I swear I never laid eyes on her in my life until about an hour ago. She's the girl, or the wife or . . . anyway, she came with the guy with the beard. And I never saw him before either. She was just sitting here and all of a sudden she slumped over, and they're taking her to a doctor. I know it must look awful to you, but you've got to believe . . ."

"I don't mean that girl. I mean *that* girl." Caroline pointed to the screen, to a girl wearing only a turquoise bikini trimmed in black lace, pretending to flick castanets while engaged in a Spanish-type dance.

"Oh. Her. Well, she's . . . she's . . ." Before he started trying to explain who Maria Pia was, he wanted to get who Lisa was squared away with Caroline. One thing at a time, for God's sake, if she'd only give him a chance. He wanted to start at the beginning, but there wasn't time. All at once there wasn't time to explain anything at all. Because the real-life Maria Pia was standing behind Caroline. Just like that. Out of nowhere. Christ, it was all too goddam much. Maria Pia was on the screen and Maria Pia was looking at herself on the screen and Caroline was glaring at Maria Pia in the flesh and identifying her with the girl on the screen.

"I keel heem," Maria Pia shrieked and ran toward the courtyard.

"Who does she mean?" Caroline demanded.

"I don't know exactly, but she's capable of it." Randy longed to escape, pass out, drop dead. He could hear Charlie gunning the motor of his car in the courtyard to the accompaniment of shouts and rabid cries. Caroline ran out the door and he followed her.

Pippo was standing in front of Charlie's car, brandishing his arms and blocking Charlie's exit. He was yelling that Charlie was a thief, that his father was one of the most influential lawyers in Italy and would see the lot of them in prison, and Charlie was inching the Porsche toward Pippo and the gate, threatening to run him down if he didn't get out of the way.

"*Via, via,*" Lisa bellowed. It was one of the few Italian words she knew. "There's a girl in here who may be dying," she added in English, looking down anxiously. Lisa was in the shallow back seat of the Porsche, and they must have thrown the Rag Bag in on top of her. Fausto was seated beside Charlie.

Maria Pia was directing a torrent of oaths toward Pippo, her face a wild storm of fury. She took a swing at his head with her pocketbook, but he ducked, gave her a push that sent her reeling back and stood his ground in front of Charlie's car.

"Okay, you asked for it." Charlie's lips set in a thin, grim line.

"Oh, he wouldn't," Caroline cried out.

Randy thought she said something else, but a thunderous roar from the far end of the courtyard drowned out all other sound. Duke was bent toward the handlebars of his gleaming motorcycle, Marsha on the seat behind him, her arms gripping his waist. The vehicle seemed to rise into the air before it bulleted across the cobblestones, passed the Porsche and swerved in so near to Pippo that Randy couldn't believe it hadn't got him. Charlie's hand slammed down on the horn as Pippo jumped aside and flattened himself against the wall. The Porsche bolted through the gate after the motorcycle, and the dual din of Porsche and motorcycle engines split the canyon walls of the Via della Seimmia.

"*Stronzo,*" gasped Pippo, breathless from fright.

"These belong to you," a voice intoned. It was Carmela's, but Randy was by now too inured to incongruous confrontations to be surprised that she had come silently and irrationally onto the scene, that she was addressing Pippo and that she was holding a pair of turquoise panties edged with black lace out to him. "Donna Luisa said to tell you . . . she said to say that . . . that . . ." Carmela's chin jutted forth and set, as if she had felt a sudden stab of excruciating pain, and her eyes rolled up under their lids. "Donna Luisa said to say she saw you from her window putting them into our car last night. Donna Luisa said to tell you it was a reasonable mistake, since your car and our car are of the same model." Carmela brought her eyes down to meet Pippo's and hold them stonily. "There," she said and thrust the panties into his hand.

Pippo frowned down at the turquoise nylon, slithered a glance toward the twin Fiats parked side by side across the courtyard and then toward Maria Pia.

"*Brutto zozzone*," Maria Pia spat the word through clenched teeth and cut in between Pippo and Carmela like a lance. "*FIJO DE NA MIGNOTTA!*"

Maybe at the Met, thought Randy, or La Scala or among mountain callers high in the Alps there had been a few to equal her. His head went up involuntarily, following the route her cry had taken to pierce the sky. Windows had opened around the cortile. The red-cheeked maid of the La Rosa family was holding a dish towel and a plate and her head and shoulders out of their kitchen window. Vespa Virgin Vaughn was peeking around the nursery curtains. He saw the Marchesa Salvini briefly. Perhaps she had caught sight of him looking up, because she quickly disappeared. He would have expected her to go right out of her mind witnessing the succession of insane events that were taking place in her courtyard. The astonishing thing was that she had been smiling, a crafty, secret smile as if what she had seen had pleased her.

Maria Pia was silent now. Ominously silent. Randy knew it was the kind of stillness between two thunderclaps. She was holding her arms rigidly at her sides, but rage rippled through every muscle of her body, so that she was literally vibrating from head to foot. Randy couldn't begin to predict what was coming when she let go. Nor, he saw, could Pippo, who was transfixed, rooted to the stones, his back to the wall, with the crazy panties still in his hand. He stayed rooted as she rammed her knee into his stomach. Randy could almost see the same stars Pippo saw as he doubled over. Randy was certain Pippo would have passed out if Maria Pia hadn't straightened him up with a crack on the shin like a rifle shot with the square toe of her loafer.

"Oh, that girl," Randy heard Caroline murmur hoarsely.

Maria Pia was taking aim at the other shin, but Pippo was prepared this time. He flung the panties into her face, whirled about and took off across the cortile with Maria Pia in pursuit. Midway, she stopped short and removed her left shoe. To bash him over the head, Randy presumed. The pause cost her the battle. Pippo reached the doorway leading up to the La Rosa apartment a good three yards ahead of her. "Mamma!" he bellowed. "MAMMA." The great bulk of the Signora La Rosa had appeared as if by magic. When Maria Pia gained the entrance, she found it totally blocked by one hundred and eighty pounds of Italian motherhood just over five feet tall.

Randy turned to Caroline. "I guess we don't need to wait for the end, since we know how it's going to come out." Why the hell was he giving her a sheepish smile? Like he was guilty or something. Luckily she hadn't seen it. Her bewildered attention was on the La Rosa entrance.

"My trouble is that I don't know how it all began," she said finally.

"That's what I'd like to tell you. It won't take long. But not out here in the open like this." Carmela was still firmly planted nearby, spellbound by the rumblings of wrath and the wild gesticulations of the Signora La Rosa and Maria Pia, which continued in the doorway. "My apartment's a mess, but you've already seen it and we could sit down there for the short time it would take."

"Yes. Yes, we could talk there," Caroline said absently and started toward it.

"First of all there's that colored girl you saw leaving this morning," he began as he walked along beside her.

After a bit, Caroline set her features in a mold of sympathetic attention and only half listened to what Randy was saying. He had two problems, if they could even be called that. He had fallen out of love and he was broke. A return to solvency seemed to be a matter of a telephone call to his father. And some new girl would come along before long. He was the age for imagining he was in love. What he had was no more than a temporary indisposition, while she was suffering from an acute and fatal sickness. Her finger traced a flower on the cover of the armchair he had insisted on enthroning her in as she thought what would be the best way of explaining that to him.

"The money!" Randy was saying. "Thrown to the four winds is how my father will put it. And he'll be pretty much right. As long as I'm confessing all, you might be interested to know that those crazy panties that have been flying around were bought by me. That's a comic note, at least."

How about that for an opening, Caroline asked herself. I could say, "Oh, incidentally, that's why I'm losing my husband and my children . . . you see, I thought Lorenzo was having an affair with someone, and then when I saw those panties in our car this morning I was certain he was, and I tore off to the Consulate, and now, when he finds out about the passport—with the *children* on it . . ."

"Another comic note is that of all the things I ever gave her the one she seemed to appreciate the most was the smack in the face." Randy got up off the foot of the bed and walked over to the snarl of cords attached to the projector. "You've lived over here a long time now. Maybe you can tell me. What is it that makes these women take being bossed around?"

It was the wrong way about. How could she make him understand that she was the one who needed to be asking questions?

"Is it because they have to take it? Or because they like it?" Randy asked.

"A combination of both, I guess. The laws are all on the side of the man, although that's slowly changing. A man can't have an unfaithful wife arrested any longer, for example. But women like to be dominated by men. No matter what they say. Law or no law."

"Even when she's sitting at home and he's out with some chick?"

Caroline felt a scalding blush. It had sounded so pointed, but after analyzing his expression, she saw it wasn't intended to be. "Of course not," she said, composing herself. "No woman enjoys that. But . . ."

Randy nudged a length of wire into a coil with the toe of his shoe. "But what?"

"An Italian woman is brought up to have only one profession—to be a wife. They are conditioned to be tolerant of their fiancés and husbands. To put up with their weaknesses. To forgive them."

"I'd call cheating on your wife a little more than a weakness." Randy sat down on the foot of the bed again. "It's hardly in the same category as betting on the horses or spending half your life on the golf course."

"Maybe cheating doesn't come as so much of a shock if one is prepared for it. I don't even know if it could really be termed cheating. Here it's a *scappatella* . . . a little escapade . . . an adventure."

"Boys will be boys. Just shrug your shoulders and forget it, honey. Is that it?"

"Not quite so simple, but something like that."

"It's great for the guys, but I still don't see what's in it for the women."

"They keep their jobs," Caroline said and hesitated. "They

go on being wives. The marriage lasts," she finished, answering herself, not him.

"I don't see how it can. With something like that between them, what can bring them together again?"

"The past. The future. If it was only an episode, they were never really apart."

"You are not, by any chance, suggesting I adopt this attitude toward Maria Pia in some way?" Randy glanced at the empty screen as if expecting he might still see her dancing there.

"Of course not. You're a man," Caroline said.

Randy leaned forward, clasped his hands between his knees and studied Caroline with a grin. "Look," he said, after a while, "you don't really mean you go for this different-rules-for-the-boys-and-girls stuff . . . this double double standard thing they have over here."

"Yes," she said softly, shy of her own voice as all the newly converted. "Yes, I do."

"Oh, come on," Randy said, "come on. I don't believe it. In theory, maybe. It's easy enough for you to say because you know it won't ever happen to you. Lorenzo's too nuts about you. But just try to imagine if it did happen."

Here was her opening. "I don't have to imagine" was how she could begin. Here was the place to start her dreary, terrible story. And when it ended, then what? What was this boy expected to do about it?

"I'm not saying that they aren't right, that their way isn't better, but you've got to be born to it, to grow up with it," Randy continued.

Whatever had made her imagine he could help her in some way? No one could help her. No one.

"Do you honestly think you could take it lying down the way these women do?" Randy asked.

"Honestly, no, Randy," she answered and lowered her eyes. "I'd probably come all over independent and militant feminist. Right out the window with everything that had gone before

. . . with all we had shared. If I thought Lorenzo wanted some woman instead of me, even for a little while, I'd see that he got her. I'd make him pay for it . . . never mind that the price I had to pay was even higher."

"Naturally. You don't have it in you to be kicked around by some man any more than I have it in me to kick some woman around." Randy got to his feet. "The thing is not to settle for a relationship that isn't fair on both sides." He plunged his hands into his pockets and glowered at the corridor leading to the kitchen. "You wouldn't have any idea what a new refrigerator would cost, would you?"

"Refrigerator?" Caroline faltered, her brain clouded by the sudden change of subject.

"To replace the busted one, since you said it was beyond repair."

"Oh. Oh, the refrigerator. I should say about ten dollars toward a new one should put you straight on that. It wasn't any good anyway. A new one like it costs around one hundred dollars."

"No kidding." Randy laughed. "That's terrific. Would you believe me if I told you I thought they cost about five hundred bucks new? It softens the blow I'm going to have to give my father a little. But, even so, I dread talking to him. Man, I don't think I've ever dreaded anything so much in my life."

Caroline suddenly remembered that she had never got as far as the American Express. "I think it can be arranged so you won't have to," she said, and picked up her pocketbook from the floor beside the chair.

La Notte

"Naturally I want my hot-water bottle tonight as usual." Luisa Salvini left off perusing the letter in her hand, shifted her position on the mauve velvet settee and considered bestowing her forgiveness on Carmela for not securing the bottle top the night before. If she hadn't been awakened by the leakage she would never have had call to go into the bathroom in the middle of the night, and if she had not gone into the bathroom at the precise time she did, she would never have heard the La Rosa Fiat come in, never have looked out the window to see the two cars which were so alike parked side by side with Pippo standing between them . . . would never, in short, have been able to piece together the puzzle of the disgusting turquoise underdrawers. It vexed her that it had taken so long to reach the conclusion, but she had been half awake and half asleep, and it wasn't until that shocking group had assembled in her courtyard that reality had separated from the dream and she had realized Pippo had been poking something through the window of Lorenzo's car and not his own.

"I thought perhaps because the day had been mild that . . ." began Carmela.

"The night would be mild as well," finished Luisa. "One robin does not make a spring." Now, of course, Carmela would begin searching the ceiling for a robin. She did, and Luisa decided against pardoning her. She was too obtuse to comprehend forgiveness. It would only tend to make her lax in the future. Furthermore, her contribution had been unintentional, so she deserved no reward. "And I hope to sleep the night in a dry bed."

"Oh, I will take care. I don't know how it happened that last night . . ."

Luisa fluttered the letter for silence and went back to reading it. Its author was Beppe Bonaccorsi, and it stated quite simply that he, Beppe, was prepared to testify that the Contessa de Costa always slept with her window open, so that it was in no way the fault of anyone but herself that her rug had been damaged by the rain. Well! So much for the case of Penelope de Costa. Beppe was a man of unquestioned integrity. She would summon her lawyer first thing in the morning and turn the letter over to him.

Carmela ran her hand over the angle of the bedcovers she had just turned down and stood up straight. "You will be wanting your camomile, too."

"Yes, I shall be wanting my camomile, too." Luisa sighed, crossed her legs and arms and absently watched Carmela's billowing form take leave. Of all nights, this was one when camomile was indicated. She felt tired enough to sleep for a month, and wide awake at the same time. Mr. Fuller had appeared with characteristic American punctuality fifteen minutes before the appointed hour. However, her irritation at having her siesta cut short had been mitigated by reflecting that his obsession with time would insure prompt payment of his rent. He was such a neat man, too, by all appearances. And considerate! More so than he could ever possibly dream. "I thought I could save your daughter-in-law a trip into the center," he had said, and before he could have any reservations about leaving the passport behind, she had answered, "But how terribly *thoughtful* of you," and taken the unsealed manila envelope out of his hand.

Of the numerous debates that had taken place within her head that day, the one following his departure had been the longest and most difficult to resolve. Even though she had been certain Caroline was up to something, she was taken completely by surprise to discover a plan that was diabolical beyond all imagining. Taking the children with her! Even now, just thinking about it was enough to ignite the banked fires around her liver. Kidnaping Lorenzo's son and daughter!

Her first impulse had been to let Caroline try and go through with it. What a joy it would have been to have Lorenzo catch her at the last minute, exiting with her suitcases in the wee hours, or brought to a halt by the carabinieri as she sped to the airport. Her most vengeful vision had been the one in which the children were removed from the plane seconds before take-off and Caroline was shot into the air alone. It was the fate she deserved. But it was not the fate Lorenzo deserved. Or the children. Or the family name.

The operation had been too delicate to delegate to Carmela, so she had had to carry it out herself, one hour of lurking about the windows looking out onto the cortile so that she wouldn't miss Caroline's return. And after the incredible scene staged around the dreadful hippie girl, Caroline had disappeared with her American protégé for another half hour, spent no doubt in enlisting his aid, having realized that her satanic scheme had got out of hand. Since her passport had been delivered at home, Caroline could only reason that it must have been delivered to *someone*. Luisa's design was for her to become uncertain about that, uncertain as to whether or not that *someone* was herself. But absolutely certain that the someone was *not* Lorenzo. The uncertainty about herself would make flight too risky. No woman could be fool enough to insist on carrying out a secret plan that might no longer be secret. The certainty that Lorenzo was ignorant of the treacherous depths of her nature would leave the door open for her to return to him without loss of face.

Her brief encounter with Caroline had gone off almost exactly as she had rehearsed it in her mind. She had stood beside the hall table with her back to the front door when Caroline had come through it, pretending to sort out the evening mail, a task usually left to Mario, who to avoid any complications had been set to cleaning the veranda of the apartment now let to Mr. Fuller. "Ah, good evening, Caroline," she had said and then added casually, "For you."

With a "thank you" thin as a thread, Caroline had accepted the little stack that had been prepared for her, the weekly American publication to which she subscribed on the bottom, an invitation to an opening of an exhibition at the Galleria 88, an airmail letter from Evanston in Illinois and, on top, the unsealed manila envelope containing the passport. Caroline had stood looking down, holding the mail with both hands while her thumbs beat against the manila envelope as if it were hot to the touch. Luisa had picked up her own correspondence and shuffled through it as if seeing it for the first time. There was nothing for Lorenzo except a bulletin from the automobile club. "For Lorenzo," she had said. And she had slipped the bulletin under the spastic thumbs and walked away.

Afterwards, Caroline had gone snooping stealthily about the house. This Luisa had determined by quizzing Carmela. Caroline had found out from Bruna that Lorenzo had been in to lunch, and from Mario that he had gone out right after lunch, and from Carmela that the reason he had come home unexpectedly was because the day had been fine and he had wanted to take Caroline and the children to the country. So Caroline had deduced, of course, that Lorenzo knew nothing about the passport. She had subsequently pulled herself together enough to take a shower and change, and had spent the following hour in the nursery with the children. Lorenzo had lunged through the front door and banged it behind him just minutes before dinner was called, and Caroline had taken her place opposite him at the table with a twitching, uncertain smile which Lorenzo had failed to return.

As the meal had progressed, so had Caroline's perplexity. For once Luisa had been able to read her mind as easily as if it were Carmela's. Caroline had been hopelessly mystified, quite incapable of fathoming why it was that Lorenzo, who couldn't know about the passport, was so surly, and her mother-in-law, who more than likely had examined the contents of the manila envelope, was so pleasant. At a point between the soup and the fish, she had obviously concluded that her absence at lunch accounted for Lorenzo's mood, and she had forthwith rather overdone a story about yielding to a sudden urge to go to the hairdresser's. It was not an excuse to inspire forgiveness. Lorenzo's scowl had deepened, and he had speared his unfortunate trout so savagely that it leapt about the plate as if it were alive. Hairdressers were notorious accomplices of wives in betraying their husbands. All of Italy had recently been treated to an uproarious newspaper story of the weekly course a faithless wife had taken through the front door of her Milan hairdresser, out the back door, into a waiting taxi, onto the Rome plane, into her Roman lover's arms and, reversing the route, been back home and waiting for her husband at dinnertime. Any Italian girl over fourteen would have recognized the symptoms of jealousy instantly, but Caroline had retreated into a baffled silence, worrying away at her salad as if she had expected to find help under a lettuce leaf.

Lorenzo had gone directly from the table to the television in the library and set off the hysterical cadence of a boxing match at top volume, and Caroline had murmured something about looking in on the children and disappeared down the corridor. Luisa had waited until the bout had finished, sitting behind her desk and making a show of sorting papers with her door wide open. Lorenzo had grunted a good night as he stalked past without so much as a glance aside. And now he and Caroline were closed away together.

Oh, to have a daughter-in-law with predictable behavior instead of this furtive foreigner. Well, she was on her own. The course of a wise woman was elementary. Caroline need do nothing but keep her mouth shut. Luisa had tried to tell her in every way but in words that she planned to do the same.

She folded the lined paper on which Beppe had written his declaration, to insert it into its envelope. There was an addition on the back that she hadn't noticed before, and she put her glasses on again. It was in English. And printed. It was absolute gibberish as far as she could make out, even though the meanings of all the words save one were familiar to her. Just below the sentence a tiny figure had been drawn. She leaned toward the light and peered closely. It was a black hand. A miniature black hand! She stiffened and sucked in her breath to staunch a sudden flow of adrenaline. She was being threatened. She was being threatened either by Penelope herself, or some confederate of Penelope's. "Where was this letter delivered?" she demanded of Carmela, who was coming through the door, screwing the top of the water bottle down with more than usual infuriating absorption. Luisa smacked the arm of the settee for attention. "I asked where this letter was delivered."

"Excuse me. I did not hear. It was delivered to Gino's office." Carmela held the water bottle upside down and gave it a vigorous shaking.

"By whom?" asked Luisa.

"By Beppe himself." Carmela slid the bottle between the sheets. "At least that is what the boy said."

"What boy?"

"The American boy. The one of the handsome automobile."

"How would he know? Now listen, Carmela, I wish to be told precisely what this is all about. This letter has been tampered with. Tampering with the mails is a criminal offense," she added darkly and evenly.

"The American boy was sitting in Gino's office for a time this afternoon."

"I thought I told you to watch Gino's office."

"But this was before. You told me to go there . . ."

"Never mind. Go on."

"Bruna went out to post a letter just before lunch was called because she has received word that her sister who lives in Bari has given birth to a son, and coming back the American boy handed her the letter from Beppe through Gino's window. The boy told Bruna that Beppe had left it and hurried off because he was late to the reception for Anna at the Trattoria allo Spiedo. So Bruna . . ."

"Get to the point," Luisa shouted.

"Bruna put the letter in her apron pocket, and because she was in a hurry, too, because of lunch she forgot about the letter until tonight when she put her apron on to prepare dinner, so that is why . . ."

"That is why I have received this letter now instead of this afternoon," snapped Luisa. "It may interest you to know that this letter contains an ominous threat."

"Oh, *santo cielo*," cried Carmela, listing far to one side and lacing her trembling fingers together. "A threat from Beppe! Who is to be trusted in this wicked world? Madonna. Oh, Madonna *mia!* From Beppe. Who would ever have thought . . ."

"Not from Beppe. I said the letter had been tampered with."

Carmela adjusted her cap by way of adjusting her head. "But I don't understand."

"As usual." Luisa got up, walked swiftly into her bathroom and looked down from the window. There were three cars in the cortile, their own Fiats and the Mini Morris of Penelope de Costa. However, the delinquent might have parked his Porsche in the street, out of sight. He might be plotting with Penelope at this very moment. The whole of the barbarous American colony was of a piece, linked by the terrible chains of democracy they dragged around the world. Luisa leaned forward. There was a shuffling of feet just below, accompanied by a strange scraping and pummeling. Mario backed into the feeble spotlight thrown from the street lamp in the Via della

Scimmia, pulling a cardboard carton behind him. Rubbish from the terrace for the spazzini. She watched until he disappeared through the gate and then closed the window.

She had found the sight of Mario's pate glowing in the lamplight reassuring. The sentence was probably nothing but foolishness. The tiny black hand as much as said that it wasn't to be taken seriously. She opened a jar on the ledge beside the wash basin, dug out a gob of cream and worked it into her face. What now annoyed her most of all was having to explain to Beppe why he must write the letter over again, since it was valueless with the scribbling on the back. That would take up the entire morning. Another thing she would do tomorrow would be to instruct Gino to forbid any vehicles not belonging to tenants to enter the cortile. She put her toothbrush back in the holder and returned to the bedroom.

"Your camomile," Carmela put the cup and saucer on the bedside table. Once her hands were free, she started wringing them. "Oh, Donna Luisa, a threat, a threat."

Luisa profoundly regretted having told her. "I've decided it's nothing to worry about. Good night, Carmela."

"A threat is a threat," mused Carmela glumly. "Good night, Donna Luisa."

Luisa sat on the side of the bed, kicked off her shoes and pulled off her stockings. She extended her legs, and her newly lacquered nails twinkled as she wiggled her toes. A threat is a threat. Nonsense. If she listened to every dire prediction Carmela made, life wouldn't hold a second's peace. She lowered her legs, suddenly remembering Carmela's tale of a hunchbacked woman who had come to the service door selling eggs. That same evening the electrical circuit had broken down. A few days later it had been the elevator. Finally the furnace. Carmela had prophesied that the curse wouldn't be dispelled until someone in the family tapped the back of a hunchbacked man. It was all peasant superstition, but what if this threat really was a threat? Had she the right to ignore it? This contemptible boy took drugs, more than likely, and the most appalling things occurred when they went berserk. Caroline would know what the sentence meant, if it meant anything, but this was hardly the moment to ask her.

Luisa shoved her feet into her slippers and pulled on her robe. Perhaps she would figure it out for herself. There was an English dictionary in the library. She swept the letter off her desk and hurried out and down the darkened corridor.

It wasn't different from hundreds of other nights since they had been married. Lorenzo was in their sitting room with the evening paper and she was in bed with a magazine. The door between them was partly closed, but she could see the far end of the tufted black-leather sofa and a wedge of the white parchment shade on the table beside it and the fuzzy heads of the bouquet of mimosa and the lower half of the *Giornale d'Italia* and Lorenzo's crossed legs from the knee down, the corduroys and the buckled, heavy boots he wore to the country.

Before long, he'd toss the paper aside and go into the bathroom, and there'd be the sound of running water in the shower, and the whir of the electric toothbrush her father had sent him for Christmas, and he'd come through the door in his pajamas and get into bed and turn off the light on his side and she'd turn off the light on her side and there would be the blessed, healing darkness. She had only to hang on a little longer, pretending to read, turning a page occasionally so he wouldn't suspect she was pretending.

It wasn't the first time they had been on opposite shores of an Arctic sea of silence with all communications broken down. If it was more prolonged than usual, she must take it as a good sign. When Lorenzo was truly enraged, he exploded instantly. He had never been able to comprehend pent-up anger and smoldering resentment. Bottling up emotion, he had frequently remarked, was an Anglo-Saxon and Teutonic pastime. He didn't know about the passport. And his mother wasn't going to tell him. She was almost certain about that now. Not out of any affection for her, but for love of him—or for the family name—or the children. Or all three. It was madness to lie here in such a state of tension.

She stole a glance over the magazine's upper edge, flipped a leaf over noisily and forced herself to concentrate on a colored advertisement. A woman of her own age, wearing a gray satin evening dress and dragging a chinchilla cape, was being handed into an apricot-colored limousine by a man in a dinner jacket and a frilled shirt front. Behind them loomed a great bastard child of the Parthenon under whose portico other formally attired couples were frozen in attitudes of sedate sociability.

Lorenzo cleared his throat, and her own constricted. The black letters of the words "living" and "luxurious" were haloed in the same apricot of the car. One of the couples under the portico was older than the rest. The woman had blue-white hair and the man had white-white hair. Lorenzo was sitting bent over with his hands clasped between his knees, staring at the floor. She could see all of him now. The man with the white-white hair was wearing a white-white tuxedo jacket. Lorenzo had turned his head. He was looking directly at her. The words "truly discriminating" were haloed in apricot, too.

He *did* know about the passport. He had found out. He had met Mr. Fuller quite by accident and, never suspecting the tragedy he was provoking, Mr. Fuller had . . . no, it hadn't been Mr. Fuller . . . Lorenzo had chanced to be on the Via Veneto at precisely the time she had gone to the Consulate to pick up the passport and he had followed her . . . he had overheard her conversation with the receptionist and. . . . He was still looking at her. Steel arrows were penetrating her forehead. He was reading her mind, rifling through her most secret records, discovering every move she had made all day, every plan. She turned to the next page. A girl was standing beside a life-sized gold cigarette package. Lorenzo was standing up. The girl held a duplicate but miniature gold cigarette package in her hand. He was coming into the bedroom. He was going to speak. He had prepared some final, irrevocable utterance that would end the world. The words "good taste" were printed in black and had halos of gold. He was coming nearer. Nearer. She forced her dry tongue over parched lips and shrieked silently. Lorenzo was at the foot of the bed. The girl was wearing gold boots. He was passing alongside the bed. He was going into the dressing room. He was going into the bathroom. He was closing the bathroom door. When she heard the sound of running water in the shower, she let the magazine drop and sank back against the pillow.

He would be out again in a few minutes. She must make the most of the little time, like a boxer between rounds. The life had gone out of legs, and she moved them about until the feeling returned. She was desperately thirsty, but the bottle of mineral water was on Lorenzo's side of the bed, out of reach, and she couldn't trust herself to get it. She was safest staying as she was. It was best to go on pretending to be absorbed in the magazine. Of course he knew nothing about the passport. Her fears and fantasies were products of a conscience deranged by guilt. She pressed her fingers to her temples and ordered herself to be reasonable. Lorenzo was taking a shower. Lorenzo was getting ready to go to bed. It was inconceivable that he would be preparing to spend the night beside a wife he had discovered plotting to abandon him and take his children along with her. Few men could bear such treachery in silence, let alone an Italian husband, above all an Italian husband of Lorenzo's temperament. No, no, he didn't know. He didn't know she was a monster of selfishness. She hadn't even known herself until that terrible moment in the Consulate when the fate she had planned for him had suddenly reversed and promised to become her own. The children mattered, she had told herself in the early morning, but later on the children hadn't mattered at all. Nothing had mattered but the immediate, devouring passions of jealousy and vengeance.

The electric brush was in operation now. She had only a minute or two. When he came out it was up to her to speak. On this first glorious day since spring began, he had wanted to take her and the children to the country, where everything was warm and welcoming and familiar to them. And she had wanted to drag them halfway around the world to an unknown destination, forbidding and alien.

The bathroom door opened and she heard the soft tread of his slippers on the carpeted dressing-room floor. He didn't look at her, which was disconcerting since she had prepared a wan smile. He sat on the side of the bed, wound his wristwatch, kicked off his slippers, lay on his side facing away from her, turned off the light and pulled up the covers. He hadn't left open a reasonable pause during which she might have spoken, even if she had been able to think of the right thing to say. She waited long enough for it to seem plausible to have finished reading and turned out the light.

The darkness brought none of the anticipated comfort. Instead, it created that sort of paralyzing atmosphere of intimacy she had experienced in crowded elevators and buses. The slightest movement might be interpreted as a solicitation. The very act of breathing became forced. She tried to accommodate her rhythm to his in order to seem less obtrusive, and sensed that he was aware she was doing it She held her breath briefly and then established a tempo of her own. She distinguished the smells of toothpaste and sandalwood soap and the special, warm, incensy odor that was Lorenzo himself. The walls closed in around the bed. The thousand beady eyes of night watched and waited while her nerves exploded like rockets. She couldn't bear it another second.

"Lorenzo," she said softly, but her voice seemed to boom and echo on and on. He shifted position but didn't speak. "Lorenzo, are you asleep?"

"No," he answered, finally and curtly.

"I'm sorry about today. If I'd thought . . . if I'd known you wanted to go to the country, I would have come home for lunch." Having ruined his day, she was now determined to ruin his night, he must be thinking. Or was he comparing her to some other woman who was light and gay as she was leaden and dreary? She mustn't think about that. For the moment, it no longer mattered. "I am especially sorry about the children. It would have been so nice for them." Lorenzo grunted. "I wouldn't have gone to the hairdresser's," she continued, grateful for any response at all. "It's just that I . . ."

"Wanted to look beautiful for your friends," Lorenzo suggested acidly.

"My friends?" Her wide-open eyes roamed the black ceiling for a ray of illumination. "What friends?" Beautiful! She had a fleeting but gratifying memory of her reflected glow that afternoon in the De la Ville windows.

"Your American friends. Or should I perhaps say friend?"

He *had* followed her. The friends were the Americans at the Consulate—or Embassy. *The* friend was Mr. Fuller. He knew. Everything. It was now that the sky was going to fall. He had been waiting for the right moment. If only she hadn't spoken, he might have gone to sleep. She might even have fallen asleep herself sometime in the night's small hours. Another day could have been a beginning.

"I don't know what you mean." Her wild effort to command her speech failed, and the words limped out and hung on a trembling, wispy thread.

"You don't?" Lorenzo asked. "You don't know what I mean?"

A glacier of apprehension rolled over her. "No," she said, barely above a whisper.

"You don't know what I mean."

She pressed her fist against her lips and shut her eyes. He was throwing back the covers. He was getting out of bed. A faint, golden glow seeped through her closed eyelids. The glow dissolved in sequined flames. He had turned on the light. She opened her eyes slowly to find him standing at the foot of the bed glowering at her steadfastly. His table lamp was angled so that its glare fell full on her face, like the light on a criminal being given the third degree, and she lifted her hand for shade.

Arms outstretched, his palms came down on the mattress

so suddenly that she instinctively raised herself on her elbows and shrank back. "*Allora,*" he snarled, head thrust toward her and neck muscles bulging.

The lava of accusation spewed forth without interruption, hitting the ceiling, shaking the walls, rattling the doors and windows. In his case against her there were only high points and, from time to time, he emphasized them by bearing down on the bedsprings, nearly toppling her over, and then releasing them and righting her so abruptly that her neck snapped. It was such an altogether formidable performance that he was well into the second act, stalking and storming about the room, waving his arms and shaking his fists, before she realized she couldn't follow it. It was as if she had paid a terrible price for a ticket and blundered into the wrong theater. He was alternating English with Italian, as he always did when he had anything serious to tell her, driving home the facts in both languages with such incredible speed that she lost all substance in translation. Long paragraphs were reduced to single tantalizingly obscure sentences like the subtitles in foreign films. She struggled vainly to give coherence to the isolated fragments. She recognized herself as the sort of frivolous, irresponsible mother who spends hours on end at the hairdresser's, even though this was the first time in months she hadn't done her own hair. She was an admirer of the frenzied feminists whose deserted houses were as cold and lifeless as showrooms in furniture stores. But who were these hippies he was talking about? What had she to do with *questi maledetti capelloni?*

"Why does he not go home to the Stati Uniti where he belongs?" Lorenzo wheeled about and barked at her.

Could he be suggesting that Mr. Fuller desert his post?

"All of them!"

Close the Embassy. Sever diplomatic relations.

"Tomorrow I shall attend to just that. We shall see what the police can do about this situation. *Vediamo. Vediamo,*" he promised, squinting and nodding his head up and down rapidly.

Every one of her hair roots was electrified and short-circuiting.

How could she offer a defense if he didn't make the charge intelligible? He hadn't mentioned the word passport once. How could she ask for clemency until he passed sentence? The police would be requested to take action but of what sort. "The police," she repeated dazedly.

"*Sì, la polizia. La polizia!*" Lorenzo grabbed the bottle of mineral water, filled the glass and drank it down in a gulp. He poured a second glass, but his hands froze on glass and bottle in mid-air. He was listening intently. To what, she couldn't begin to fathom. The bubbles were rising festively in the bottle, and she thought it might even be to the scarcely audible sound of their popping. "You have heard? You are hearing it? *Hai sentito?*" he insisted shrilly.

A car was driving into the courtyard and the clock on her table was ticking and her heart was pounding, but aside from that what was there to hear? "I don't know. What is it?"

"I don't know. I don't know," he mimicked and slammed the glass and bottle down on the marble top of the bureau and dove at the window. He gave the cord a jerk, and the curtains separated with an indignant swish. The windows flew in and the shutters banged out and he leaned over the sill. "As I thought. Ah, *sì, sì*. Your friend is receiving again tonight," he shouted over his shoulder.

His announcement sped back to her on a brisk gust of spring that had come from the *ponente*, carrying the smell of the soil and the woods over which it had traveled. It struck her smartly across the face. There was something like a snap inside her head as the current was restored and the light came on. Randy! Lorenzo had been talking about Randy. Randy, she repeated to herself with disbelief.

"Your very dear friend, Randy, is entertaining his very dear friend. That monster of the Porsche," added Lorenzo with loathing.

How could she have been so dense? Randy of all people.

"It's the last night." Lorenzo brought the shutters in with a crash.

It was ludicrous.

The windows rattled shut and the curtains rejoined each other primly. "My ancestors did not build this house to have it ultimately become a haven for hippies and drunkards and drug addicts."

It was so typically Italian.

"You know what is a *foglio di via?*"

It was so typically Lorenzo. The captain in Athens when they were first married.

"Sì o no?"

"*Sì*. It's an order for an undesirable foreigner to leave the country." The time he had come to pick her and the children up in the park of the Gianicolo and found her sharing a bench with an English journalist who was minding his three-year-old son while his wife was in the hospital recuperating from the birth of a daughter.

"If your country can send us back our delinquents, it's only just that we return theirs to them."

That dreadful New Year's Eve when she hadn't been able to find him in all that great throng and the lights had gone off at midnight, and that fool of a Dino Del Campo had grabbed her and planted his wet mouth full on hers in the dark. When the lights had come back on, she had been engaged in a wrestling match before a small audience in which Lorenzo had a ringside seat.

Lorenzo kicked the chair beside the door en route to the sitting room. He switched on the lamp there, lighted a cigarette and kicked the coffee table. Andrea's silver porringer and several cigarette butts sailed up and came down on the crumpled newspaper. That New Year's Eve he had kicked the fender of the car hard enough to dent it and then slammed the car door so ferociously he had broken the window, because it had crossed his mind that she might have unwittingly encouraged Dino, "given him God only knew what impression with all that damned American openness." But Randy was little more than a child. Could it be possible?

"Randy isn't a hippie," she experimented cautiously and was rewarded by seeing Lorenzo's spine stiffen.

"I should expect that you would defend him," he called back without turning around. "He is the son of your friend. It is your duty to defend him." He eased his head aside and drew in on the cigarette. "And to spend a great deal of time with him," he caustically informed a spiral of smoke.

Carmela must have told him, but only because he had questioned her. Caroline could picture his drawing Carmela out, trying to appear offhand. He would have gone to Mario and Gino, too, inventing some legitimate pretense to conceal his embarrassment. He was so ill-suited to sleuthing. It must have been an altogether humiliating pilgrimage. But would he have made it if he hadn't been jealous? And was a man ever jealous of a woman he didn't love?

"Randy isn't irresponsible," she said.

Lorenzo stalked back into the bedroom. "Go on," he urged.

"He's sweet and sensitive."

"Indeed." Lorenzo's right eyebrow went up.

She was almost beginning to enjoy herself. "And idealistic."

"Ah, *sì?*"

"He's . . ." There was a flickering change in Lorenzo's expression. She had gone far enough.

"He is what, Caroline?" he asked with cauterizing calm.

"He's been having rather a bad time lately," she answered meekly.

Lorenzo stabbed his cigarette out in the glass of mineral water and went back into the sitting room. He picked up the porringer, turned it over to the bottom side where the date of Andrea's birth was inscribed and looked at it for quite a long time before putting it back in place on the table. A man's infidelity can be purely physical, he had once told her, but a woman's infidelity involves the spirit. She hadn't believed it was true until this instant. He had spent some hours as miserable as her own this day, but the satisfaction it gave her washed away almost at once in a wave of tenderness. The polluted atmosphere and poisoned waters were no less a threat to him than to her. The foundations were shaking under his feet, too. The prospect of being a grandparent to babies born from plastic wombs wasn't hers alone. The missiles were aimed at both of them. Together they could make a try at some defense, but without each other they hadn't a hope.

Lorenzo was stooping down to pick up the scattered cigarette butts, and she sprang out of bed, caught up her robe and ran barefoot to help him. "You won't have to worry about sending Randy away," she started, bending over, and straightened up short at a pounding on the door.

"What is it?" Lorenzo demanded, admitting Carmela.

"*Quello della* Porsche," gasped Carmela, holding her forehead with her left hand a letter with her right. "*Quello della* Porsche."

"What about the boy with the car?" Lorenzo's eyes narrowed.

"*Il ragazzo americano . . . quello biondo . . .*"

Lorenzo gripped Carmela's arm. "*Calmati!*" He held her fast until she went rigid as a robot. "Now then," he ordered and listened with mounting perplexity to the incoherent chop-chop of her wooden recitation.

Caroline pieced together what she could from random details. It concerned the de Costas' damaged rug. The hippies and Penelope de Costa were in league against the House of Salvini. And the black hand of the Mafia was raised to strike for them. It was all there in a postscript, added, Carmela happened to know, by *quello della* Porsche, to an incriminating letter from Beppe. A particular victim had been chosen, but his, or her, identity was unknown because of a mysterious word that was not to be found in Donna Luisa's English dictionary. "*Santo cielo. Dio mio. Dio mio.*" Carmela chanted and swayed backward. Lorenzo straightened her up with a jerk and snatched the letter.

"What mysterious word?" Caroline asked anxiously. It seemed preposterous, but then perhaps threatening letters always did at first. "Where?" She hooked her head over Lorenzo's arm so that she could see the writing.

"It must be this." Lorenzo pointed.

" 'Bigelow,' " she read aloud. "Bigelow! 'A title on the door rates a Bigelow on the floor.' " The tiny black sketch beneath the slogan was fuzzy, chubby, more like the paw of an animal than a human hand.

"What is a bigelow?" asked Lorenzo.

"A rug," Caroline said.

"A rug!" Lorenzo repeated in surprise. "Not a person?"

"Both," Caroline told him.

"How can it be both?" Lorenzo bellowed.

Caroline stepped back and looked from Lorenzo to Carmela and back to Lorenzo and then at them both, prince and peasant, starched stiff as characters in a fable, waiting for some magic word from her that would bring them back to life. It had been so long since anything had seemed even remotely funny that her bedridden brain warmed warily to a return to health. Her lips parted in a convalescent smile and Lorenzo glanced down uncertainly at the paper he held. "My wife is amused," said the master to his maidservant.

At last Caroline laughed outright.

"*Ma insomma*," growled Lorenzo, but more in bewilderment than anger.

Caroline caught sight of the tiny, fuzzy hand and laughed harder. The grim, gray world of reality covered itself in its crazy quilt of promise once more. Bells rang. Birds sang. It was spring. She was young. She was beautiful. She was happy. She was in love.

"She finds it entertaining that we have been threatened, that my mother has been terrorized."

"*Amore*, it isn't a threat." Caroline laid her hand lightly on his arm. "It's a joke. An American kind of joke that I'll try to explain later. Go tell your mother that there won't be any more of them because Randy's going away. There was a girl, the one of the turquoise panties she was talking about at dinner, but of course that's all over now. He told me about it this afternoon." Lorenzo's expression remained impassive, as she had expected it would. "Or, if you like, I'll go tell her."

"Barefoot?" he asked. Going barefoot was of all the American habits he despised the one he despised the most. "Get in bed before you catch cold."

He was concerned about her catching cold. He didn't want her to catch a cold! She lowered her head demurely. He had resumed command. The floor swam in a mist of gratitude as she padded obediently across it.

There was something spooky about airports at night. Everyone seemed to be sleepwalking or risen from the dead. They even spoke in hushed tones, as if they felt guilty about going and coming at an hour when most people were at home in bed. The guy who was making out his ticket was asking questions in such a low, confidential voice that Randy had trouble catching what he was saying. "Palmer," Randy gave his last name.

"I got you a little *buon viaggio* present, Ran," said Charlie, coming up at his side and waving a copy of a horoscope publication called *Astro*. "The choice is pretty limited at the news stand. I asked for *Playboy*, but I forgot they don't let it into Italy. Anyway, you can pass the time figuring out your future in the New World with this."

"Thanks," Randy said, although he hadn't the slightest interest or faith in astrology. Or in *Playboy* for that matter. "Alexander Palmer."

The clerk's pencil approached the ticket hesitantly, and Charlie took charge. "Palmer. Palermo-Ancona-Livorno-Milano-Empoli-Roma. *Pal-mare*. Alessandro Palmare." He craned his neck across the counter, satisfied himself that the clerk had written as instructed and said "Bravo."

"These three bags, sir?" the clerk asked Randy.

"Yes. These three."

"Yessir, yessir, three bags full," Charlie recited and gave the clerk a broad grin that was returned with a scowl.

"I'm carrying these." Randy held up his tennis racket with his left hand and, with considerably more effort, a Pan American flight bag with his right. It was so stuffed it couldn't have been much heavier if he had had one of those black dwarfs from outer space in it. His raincoat was bulging, too. It had been Charlie's idea to tie the laces of his ski boots around the inner lining of the pockets. He had left a pile of clothes on top of his bed for Gino, but even so he was going to be a lot overweight.

"No hard feelings about carrying a Pan Am bag on an Alitalia flight?" Charlie cocked his head on the side and gave the clerk a wink.

"Thirteen thousand, five hundred lire excess," the clerk announced archly, ignoring Charlie.

"Nearly twenty-two bucks," Randy sighed.

"That's no record. The Bitch's overweight always costs more than her fare."

The clerk fixed tags to the suitcases, and they were whisked off to the conveyer. Charlie sat down in the niche for receiving baggage. To Randy's relief, he started leafing through the horoscope magazine. There was a chance he might be quiet until the ticket business was over. The clerk was already teed off but good.

"*Sei, cinque, undici,*" the clerk added.

Charlie was absorbed in his reading and didn't notice a prosperously and conservatively dressed middle-aged man who arrived carrying a briefcase. The man was followed by a porter pushing a cart which held a suitcase and a large dress box.

"Excuse me," the man said, leaning in toward the clerk. "Is Flight One Thirty-two to New York leaving on schedule?"

"*Due, otto, nove,*" the clerk nodded without looking up, "*dieci, quindici . . .*"

"Jesus," Charlie said, not looking up either, "along about the end of summer it looks like I'm in for a lot of dough. Maybe someone is going to cool The Bitch."

The man with the briefcase was taken aback, to say the least.

"*Posso?*" asked the porter, who had taken the suitcase and box from the carrier.

"Get up, Charlie. The man has to put the suitcases there."

"Oh, *scusi.*" Charlie stood up. "I may lose a close relative . . . a loved one. It doesn't add. I guess you couldn't get a relative much nearer than your mother, but this says a loved one. That leaves The Bitch out, and I haven't got any other relatives with a lot of dough. Well, good luck with yours." Charlie rammed the magazine into Randy's jacket pocket and leaned against the counter.

"Is dollars, three hundred and ten and ninety-six cents," the clerk said.

Randy drew out a roll of bills and dealt out three hundred and fifteen dollars, but Charlie's hand came down on the money before the clerk had time to pick it up. "It's your last chance, Ran baby. Think it over good. Are you really sure you want to go to a country where everybody is either a square or a kook?"

The eyes of the passenger with the briefcase traveled a dotted line from the clerk's face to Charlie's.

"Or else both, like that jerk who wears the hat and screws Marsha," added Charlie, blithely unaware of a hatted member in his audience. Briefcase swept a swift glance behind and then around the terminal, as if seeking some authority to whom he might appeal if the need came.

"I'm sure." Randy lifted Charlie's hand off the money. Charlie made a despairing grimace and shrugged, and the clerk checked the sums and pushed the change and the ticket across the counter. "Thank you," Randy said. He had left with Gino forty of the five hundred dollars Caroline had given him to cover the light and telephone bills, plus a five-dollar tip. Caroline had offered to see about the busted refrigerator and let him know. He'd get into New York about one hundred and fifty to the good. Not really, of course. Just as soon as his parents recovered from their prodigal's return, he'd have to give them the good news that it wasn't paid for.

"I don't think I could take it," Charlie said, walking beside Randy and carrying the tennis racket. "When I was seventeen, The Bitch made me spend a whole winter with my grandparents, her folks, in Waco. Those Sundays!"

"When I get a job, I plan to get my own apartment in New York," Randy said, somewhat to his own surprise.

"Even so," Charlie smacked an imaginary tennis ball with a backhand.

"Oh, hell, my passport. I should have got it out before." Randy put his Pan Am bag down in front of the police officer's little booth and dropped his raincoat on top of the bag. The ski boots landed with a muted and ominous thud, but Randy supposed that what went out of the country was the least of the man's worries.

"What about Maria Pia?" Charlie asked.

"What about her?" Randy fished into the inner pocket of his jacket.

"I hope I don't read in the papers that she's knocked herself off."

"I'll be surprised if you don't read about her, but it won't be that. Maria Pia's going to make it."

"How?"

"First it'll be small parts and then she'll meet some producer who's old enough to be her father, the way all these Italian stars do, and he'll push her to the top and marry her."

"And that's good?"

"It'll be great for her."

"To be tied to some old guy. Are you nuts?"

Randy handed his passport through the opening in the booth's little glass window. "Do you ever hear of any of these Italian actresses knocking themselves off?"

Charlie twisted the tennis racket thoughtfully. "Well, no, now that you mention it."

"Or becoming alcoholics or taking to dope?"

"No, that's true."

"At home the big stars are washed up by the time they're forty, if they get that far without taking an overdose of sleeping pills. They've married six or seven stupid actors they imagined they were in love with and, if they've got any kids, which usually they don't, the kids are as screwed up as they are . . .

Thanks," Randy said to the policeman and took back his passport. "Here they've got a whole other career going for them when they fade out. Being Mamma, just like any ordinary wop mamma. Plus the dough these guys have stashed for them."

"You've made quite a study. I'd never have thought of it."

"Maybe Maria Pia will scream and tear her hair for a couple of days, but after that she'll be okay." He'd never have seen it that way himself if it hadn't been for his talk with Caroline. "Well, I guess I better get going." The flight was being called over the speaker, and Briefcase was approaching the booth somewhat cautiously.

Charlie shook Randy's hand. "So, long, David," he said in a somber, hollow voice.

Randy laughed. "So long, Chet."

"I guess you know what you're doing." Charlie waited until Randy had the raincoat over his arm and a grip on the Pan Am bag before fitting the tennis racket under Randy's arm. "Is it bigger than a bread box? Christ! Well, good luck anyway."

"Thanks," Randy said. "And for the lift out here."

"*Prego*. Drop me a line if you get time."

"Oh, sure." Randy flipped his head in a final farewell and went through the gate.

The plane shot above Fregene and straight out over the sea. If they arrived in New York on schedule, Randy figured he ought to make it to Greenwich by five in the morning. He could see his house as plainly as if the taxi were already turning into the driveway. The garage doors would gleam white in the headlights. He'd put his suitcases down at the foot of the big elm while he paid the driver and then go along the brick walk around the bay window of the dining room and on to the front door. His father would be the one who finally opened it, wearing his robe and that squinty, suspicious look he had without his glasses. He'd be sure to tell him that he'd picked a helluvan hour to get in, but he'd be glad to see him all the same, and his mother would come running down the stairs like she was sixteen. He knew exactly how it was going to be in Greenwich, but he couldn't imagine life going on in Rome without him. He couldn't make it seem real that, about the time he was up to his chin in a tub of all the hot water he'd dreamed about, Cora Study would be getting into some crazy outfit to go to the horse show with Two-ton Colombo.

He thanked the hostess for the pillow and shoved it behind his head and looked out the window. There was no moon, and the challenging stars winked impudently at the earth from the safety of their awesome distances. He was glad they were flying away from the dawn back into the night. He was really beat, and he could sleep all the way home.

Luisa finished off the last of her camomile and set the cup back on its saucer. The cup and saucer were of a translucent porcelain, decorated with hand-painted violets, and the scalloped edges were trimmed with a fine line of gold. There had been a tea service for twelve when she had come to the palazzo as a bride; it had originally belonged to Raffaello's grandmother. Two cups and three saucers were all that had survived a spring-cleaning accident several years before, and Carmela was charged with their custody, with keeping them in a safe corner of the pantry and always serving Luisa's camomile in one of them. Strangely, Luisa set more store upon the two than she had upon the twelve, although they had always been her favorites among the china. Perhaps, she thought, it was because the more one loses, the more one values what remains.

She pushed the cup and saucer well in from the edge of her bedside table and lay back. So much had been lost forever, but she rarely permitted herself to think about it. Her last fit of nostalgic weeping was a good twenty years behind her, when she had revisited her grandmother's house, which her grandmother had left to her, on Lake Como. It had been part of her dowry when she had married Raffaello, and after the war, when Raffaello had been forced to start selling property, it had been the first to go. The buyers had converted it to an inn, and some years later, motoring back from Switzerland where she had gone to fetch Lorenzo from school for Easter vacation, they had decided to lunch there.

They had sat at a table in the loggia overlooking the lake. The service had been extraordinarily good, the food mediocre and the bill exorbitant, but then she had expected that, having been told that their policy was set to cater exclusively to rich Americans. She had felt surprisingly little emotion during the meal. Gallons of white paint covered her memories. The summerhouse was gone, and the wonderland of tall grass and woods behind had been cleared for car parking. The old boat landing had been so enlarged, she had told Lorenzo, that they must be expecting transatlantic ships. The gardeners in her grandmother's day had left nature to her wild ways as much as they could, but the gardens of the inn were trimmed and clipped and edged and rolled and weeded until they seemed quite unreal, like the colored advertisements for fertilizers in magazines.

She hadn't had a true sense of being any place familiar until she had gone upstairs after lunch and stopped before the open door of the bedroom which had been hers as a girl. The long double windows that gave onto a balcony were flung back and framed a sight that stopped her breath. Her magnolia tree was in full bloom, splendid in the sun, and the white blossoms on the distant branches seemed to float on the lake. She had taken a step into the room and then stepped quickly back. "Yes?" the voice of a woman had asked. She never saw the person to whom the voice belonged, nor the hand which pushed the door to and turned the lock. She had gone on looking at the magnolia tree right through the wood of the door until the tree withered away and the door of her room became the door of a room in an inn. Then she had gone down the corridor and into the old linen closet which had been transformed into a bathroom and cried.

Raffaello's land in Tuscany had been the next to go after the Como house. He had held out too long for his price and had practically given it away in the end. Then, fearful of repeating his Tuscan mistake, he had compounded it just the same by selling three quarters of the acreage belonging to the Tiberina villa for the first offer made him.

She had peddled the jewels about on her own initiative, pitting one jeweler against another until she had the best possible advantage. The star sapphire had paid for the elevator. She hadn't minded that. She hated star sapphires. She hated the elevator, too, for that matter. The nasty thing was forever getting out of order, but the tenants couldn't be expected to pay a high rent to walk up to their apartments. Her mother's bar pin had sent Lorenzo to Cambridge for a year, and her mother's collection of jade had paid for a new automobile and Raffaello's doctors and clinics.

Never had a thought of parting with her gray pearls crossed her mind. They were in the bank vault with the outmoded dinner ring her father-in-law had given her as a wedding present and the emerald bracelet her father had given her as a wedding present and Raffaello's great-grandmother's tiara and a miscellaneous assortment of antique gold brooches and lockets and chains and old coins.

It was still much too soon to be thinking of giving the pearls to Caroline, even though she had come through her first real trial astonishingly well. According to Carmela, she had actually been laughing, which meant, of course, that Lorenzo had not found out about the passport. And which meant that Caroline had had the good sense to keep her mouth shut. As much as Lorenzo loved her, he would never have forgiven her. For leaving him to punish him, possibly, but using the children to punish him, never. And Caroline knew this. There would be times ahead when she'd feel like escaping, but Luisa doubted she'd ever be carried so far away again. The transition from sweetheart to wife didn't take place during a wedding ceremony, as most brides thought. It was a slow process, and in Caroline's case, particularly painful, given that she had been raised in the absurd belief that one married to live happily ever after and divorced and married again and again in pursuit of this ridiculous illusion. In any case, she had hope for Caroline, although it didn't do to peer too far down the corridors of the future any more than it did to review the past.

One must live in the present and carry on. A few weeks ago she had come home from a short afternoon walk to find a small group of tourists standing in front of the house. "And who owns the building now?" a middle-aged man had asked the guide. "Oh, the family. The family own the palazzo," the guide had said. "They still live there."

Luisa reached under the lavender scarf and switched off the lamp. There was no sound to be heard, not the faintest light to be seen. The great walls held the world away while her family slept. "Yes, the family. They still live there," she whispered to herself and smiled into the dark and closed her eyes.

Printed in the United States
3468

9 780971 092952